PRAISE FOR *THE AFTER PARTY*

"A sexy thrill."

—POPSUGAR

"This is *Homicide: Life on the Street* meets *9 to 5* meets *Bridgerton* in a story that screams to become a TV series. Part thriller and part mystery, this delightful story of friendship also celebrates sex, love, and family."

—*Kirkus Reviews* (starred review)

"*The After Party* by A. C. Arthur is a thrilling head trip! This seamless blend of beautiful women's fiction and exciting murder mystery gives the reader everything—homicide, twists, laughs, sisterhood, growth, triumphs, WTH moments, and even some romance. *The After Party* is simply unexpected and fantastic. It's also your next must read!"

—*USA Today* bestselling author Naima Simone

HAPPY
IS ON
HIATUS

OTHER TITLES BY A. C. ARTHUR

HAPPY IS ON HIATUS

A. C. ARTHUR

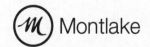
Montlake

Text copyright © 2022 by Artist C. Arthur
All rights reserved.

Published by Montlake, Seattle

www.apub.com

Amazon, the Amazon logo, and Montlake are trademarks of Amazon.com, Inc., or its affiliates.

ISBN-13: 9781542037839
ISBN-10: 1542037832

Cover design by Faceout Studio, Spencer Fuller

Cover illustrated by Gallt and Zacker Literary Agency LLC, Rachelle Baker

Printed in the United States of America

To Bishop Douglas I. Miles (1949–2021).
Thank you for everything.
To my aunt, Patricia Ann Fleet (1944–2021).
Thank you for teaching me to be myself.

When life gives you lemons,
make orange juice, and leave the world
wondering how the hell you did it.

Chapter 1

BURN, BABY, BURN.

Margarita "Rita" McCall sat up in her bed, eyes half-closed, head still throbbing from the two cups of Bern's spiked fruit punch she'd had last night. "What did you just say?" she said into the house phone because she couldn't have heard what she thought she'd just heard.

It had to be a hangover. A nightmare she was stuck in and needed to scream her way out of.

"I'm pregnant with Nate's baby."

That's exactly what she thought she'd heard this thot say. "Who is this, and how'd you get my number?"

"Is that really what you wanna know?"

"That's what I asked." Now Rita was pushing the sheet off her legs. Her feet hit the carpeted floor in her bedroom as her fingers kept a death grip on the cordless phone. Like her mother and a few other old-school folks in the family, she still had a landline, and one of Nate's side chicks had just called at what . . . ? Wait a minute, what time was it anyway?

Turning to glance at her nightstand, Rita stood as she read the large white numbers from the alarm clock—5:18 a.m. In the freakin' mornin'!

"Look, little girl, I don't have time for games. If you're sleeping with Nate, congratulations and welcome to the trick-of-the-month club. Now hang up, and call his phone with this foolishness." At forty-two years old, after two daughters and being a member of the Brighton School District's PTA for fourteen years, there were times when *patience* wasn't in Rita's vocabulary.

"I'm calling you 'cause I thought you should know."

"Well, I'm not the one having another one of his kids, so your problems aren't my concern." Then, as it dawned on her that she was giving this woman way too much of her time and attention, Rita slammed the phone down on its base. The motion was made with such force that the base and the phone fell off the nightstand with a banging sound that echoed throughout the otherwise silent bedroom.

Silent because she was the only one in it. Nate was out of town on business. Or laying his sleazy behind in the bed right next to that slut, who had no clue who she was messin' with. Rita balled her fingers into fists and closed her eyes. Expletives burned her tongue, and her lips thinned, ready to let them fly free. But she refrained. Cursing in a rage wasn't her thing. That was more like Sharae or Jemel. Her cousins, who were as close to her as if they were sisters, both had potty mouths they'd inherited from their other relatives and owned up to it without remorse.

No, she wasn't going to curse. Nor was she going to call Nate's cell phone to tell him what his little girlfriend just had the balls to do.

Rolling her neck on her shoulders, Rita recalled the deep-breathing exercises her primary care doctor had told her to employ for quick stress release. She slapped her hands to her stomach and inhaled a deep breath through her nose. Seconds later she released the breath slowly, knowing she was forgetting a step but unable to worry about it at the moment. She opened her eyes, and her fingers unclenched. Start at the beginning and repeat. This time she tried to think of what she was missing. On the exhale, her belly pushed her hand out, but her chest heaved with the pounding of her heart as well.

Dammit. She tried again, this time visualizing the stress moving from the top of her head, down past her shoulders and torso, to her hips and knees, until finally blowing away past her toes. Her head throbbed.

This crap wasn't working.

With a groan, she stopped. Unable to move or contemplate what to do next, she simply stood on the right side of the bed, where she always slept. A double set of windows with partially open blinds were a few feet away. No light poured through, not just yet anyway. It was still too early for sunrise, but the sky was that somber grayish blue, dawn just a whisper away.

A baby. Nate was forty-six years old. Taryn, their oldest daughter, was twenty-one, and Necole, their youngest, was nineteen. What was he gonna do with a baby now?

Never mind that it wasn't his wife carrying the child.

Damn him! Her voice was loud in her mind. But it wasn't enough. Those two words didn't begin to express how it felt to have a hot ball of fury now forming in the center of her chest.

Her heart continued to thump wildly, as if trying to push back against the searing anger but failing dismally. She felt like she'd just run a marathon or had the crap scared out of her. No, she wasn't scared, nor was she exhausted from exertion. She was tired of the bullshit. Also, she had no problem thinking curse words, she just tried not to speak them as much, lest she anger her father, Reverend Haley "Hale" Henderson. And yeah, she was a grown woman and all that, but old habits died hard.

Rita wasn't heartbroken, because that ship had sailed a long time ago. This wasn't Nate's first affair, and she was smart enough to know it wouldn't be his last. That little trick on the phone didn't have a clue. Nate McCall didn't know how to be loyal, and he didn't want to learn. He had one focus in life—to rake in the cash from McCall Motors, the auto dealership he'd started three years after they married. There were seventeen dealerships now up and down the eastern region, enough to keep Nate on the road seven to ten days out of the month. At least he liked to use that as his excuse.

Rita didn't care. Not anymore. It'd been too long, she'd shed enough tears, and life was too damn short.

Sighing, she turned away from the window and walked across the room. The first thing she'd fallen in love with about this house on Windsway Lane was the large master bedroom. In addition to the space to fit her California king–size bed, two dressers, and a bench at the foot of the bed, and still more room to perform her exercise routine, there was a sitting room that she'd been considering turning into a home office. The master suite also contained a massive walk-in closet and spa bathroom. For twenty of the twenty-three years she'd been married, this had been her oasis.

This morning, the walls felt as if they were closing in, and she gasped for breath. Rubbing her hand along the inside wall of the closet, she braced her eyes for the burst of light as she hit the switch. After blinking a couple of times, she stepped farther into the space and spread her arms as wide as she could, grabbing a bunch of clothes from Nate's side of the closet.

With purposeful steps she walked out of the room, down the hallway and the stairs. The house was still in mild disarray after last night's cookout. Jemel, Sharae, and some of her other family members had helped her clean up after the Johnson family's annual Memorial Day cookout. But folding chairs were still stacked against one wall in her entryway, along with a rolling cart that belonged in her garage. She dropped the pile of clothes onto the bottom of the cart and went back up the stairs.

When she was in her bedroom again, Rita went around to her side of the bed and slid her feet into her favorite microterry Isotoner slippers. She headed back to the closet and grabbed more clothes, being sure to snatch all the NFL and NBA jerseys Nate had collected over the years. All of it went downstairs to be piled on the top shelf of the cart. Then she went back again, this time grabbing boxes of the tennis shoes and designer loafers Nate coveted.

The cart was overflowing with his stuff now, and she stepped back to stare at it for a few moments. Her heart was still beating fast, but at least now she could attribute it to the mini–cardio workout going up and down those steps had been. Dragging her hands down her face, she turned and walked back to the kitchen. Switching on that light, she glimpsed unused leftover aluminum trays—long and short ones—on the table. She'd pack those away in the garage for the next cookout, which would be the Fourth of July. Another trip to Sam's Club would still be in order to get more paper items, but at least she knew she had some leftovers. Without hesitation she walked over to the sink, bent down, and opened the cabinets beneath it. The two large bottles of hand sanitizer she'd bought from Sam's to replenish the smaller containers in the bathrooms throughout the house were right where she'd stored them. Rita pulled them out. Then she went to the drawer closest to the refrigerator, where she kept all her odds and ends. One of the many multipurpose lighters she owned was inside, and she picked it up.

Her thoughts circled back to her children. Necole would be starting her sophomore year at Coppin State this fall. Taryn would begin her nursing master's program. Neither of them lived at home anymore. They were grown, as her mother would say. Grown and able to get out and take care of themselves. But, with the free car, free car insurance because they were on the family policy, and a monthly allowance, courtesy of Rita and Nate, those girls weren't hardly taking care of themselves.

How were they going to take this news? Who was going to tell them?

Rita sat the two containers of hand sanitizer on top of the heap of clothes and went to open the door. She tucked the lighter under her arm, pushed the cart through the open door, and moments later huffed as she had to maneuver it down the three front steps. Once it was on the level pathway, she knelt down to pick up the pieces that had fallen, tossing them back on top. Then she wheeled the cart down to the end of the driveway.

Her black Volvo XC90 was parked inside the double-car garage. Nate had driven his gold Lexus GX to the airport or wherever he was.

Nathaniel Geoffrey McCall, the finest dark chocolate–complected brotha her seventeen-year-old eyes had ever seen in person. Her parents had been a little wary about her dating a college student four years her senior. But Rita had fallen in love the moment Nate brushed that first soft kiss across her forehead.

With a quick motion, Rita pushed the rolling cart to the side until it tipped over and all the clothes and shoeboxes fell onto the driveway. She righted the cart and wheeled it behind her. Turning back to the pile of clothes, she had to pick through them to find the jugs of hand sanitizer, but when she did, she opened them both and poured the contents all over the clothes. Grabbing the lighter from under her arm, she flicked the switch and touched the glowing flame to the red Michael Jordan jersey first. Then she moved over a little to the box of Air Jordan tennis shoes and let the flame touch that now-damp-with-sanitizer box. Another flick, and the flame was set to a black pinstriped Tom Ford suit and then to a Walter Payton jersey.

Golden flames caught on quick, licking at the pile of clothes with savage glory. Rita took a few steps back until she bumped into the rolling cart; then she folded her arms across her chest and watched Nate's shit burn.

Chapter 2

911 ... WHAT'S THE EMERGENCY?

It had finally happened. Rita had lost her damn mind.

Sharae turned off the engine and jumped out of her car. She'd been in full panic mode the moment she heard Rita's address over the police scanner. The fire department and paramedics had also been summoned. Without a second thought, she'd switched on her police siren and driven the Howard County Police Department–issued sedan through every red light in the twelve miles between her house and Rita's.

She sprinted across the lawn in her navy-blue Crocs, heat from the flames in the driveway greeting her before she was within six feet of her cousin, who was standing as still as a statue. With her arms folded across her chest, Rita's gaze remained focused on the bonfire at the end of her driveway.

"What the hell are you doing?" Sharae asked, grabbing her cousin by the shoulders. "You tryin' to burn down the entire neighborhood? And what the hell is that smell?"

Rita jerked out of Sharae's grasp. "Lemon-fizz hand sanitizer," she said, her expression deadpan. "Some of it got on my hands and my nightshirt."

Sharae followed Rita's gaze to the big wet spot on the front of Rita's pale-pink nightshirt. "You're outside without your robe and wearing your bonnet."

When Rita only blinked her amber-colored eyes with naturally long lashes at her, Sharae continued. "You're the first to talk about anybody coming outside in their pajamas and/or hair bonnet." Rita was always dressed to impress, no matter what the occasion. She believed appearance was the first thing others judged, and she always wanted to start off on the right foot. Sharae was more of the don't-give-a-fuck-what-anybody-thought-about-her mentality, but love had her allowing Rita her idiosyncrasies.

"It's inappropriate," Rita replied with a shrug. "Except for today."

Sharae didn't have time to ask other questions—a fire truck had turned into the Willow Grove housing development. Rita and Nate had bought the model home when the development was first built, so they were close to the entrance of the forty-five-house area. Sharae looked up to see two police cruisers and the fire truck coming to a stop in front of Rita's driveway.

"Let me talk," she told Rita. Even though she had no idea what she was going to say. She was still trying to figure out what was going on. The one thing she knew for certain was that something wasn't right here.

The six-foot flames and nauseating lemon scent should've been a dead giveaway.

"Detective Sharae Gibson," she identified herself, stepping forward and tapping the badge clipped to her belt. She never kept it in her jacket pocket like her partner, Malik, did. Mainly because she had a habit of leaving the jacket to her favored pantsuits on the back seat of her car. At present a smoke-gray jacket matching the pants she now wore and a pair of black Louboutin pumps occupied that space.

Sharae recognized the first officer to approach. She'd seen him around the Northern District Headquarters where she worked but didn't know his name. Three other officers had gotten out of the cruisers as well. Two were hanging back and looking around to survey the scene, while the other watched the firefighters, who'd immediately gotten to work putting out the fire. Muted gold streaks had just begun to peek through the thick gray clouds, and in the distance birds chirped. The front doors of the three houses closest to Rita's had also opened, neighbors stepping outside to see what was going on.

"Cranston. You homicide?" the first officer with the cap of sun-kissed gold hair asked.

"Yeah. This is just a little mishap. My cousin was taking out some things for the consignment shop to pick up, and it caught fire." Sharae lied as easily as she blinked.

"That's a hell of a fire," Cranston said, pulling out his notebook.

"No shit!" the officer who'd come to stand at Cranston's right added. "Is that the homeowner over there? I'll go question her."

Sharae blocked his path. "No need, uh . . . ?" She stared at the second cop, glancing at the badge on his right uniform shirt pocket, then back up at him.

"Phillips," he said, his lips thinning into a straight line.

She nodded. "Okay, Phillips. I've already talked to her, and she's not hurt. Nobody's hurt. Just a little mishap. Sorry you guys had to be called out so early in the morning."

Phillips's brow wrinkled, his pale-blue eyes fixing on Sharae. "You live here with your cousin?"

"No."

"But you arrived before us? She call you?" Phillips asked the questions, but Cranston was writing every word of her response.

"She's my cousin. I heard the address on the scanner when I was leaving for work. I came here first," she replied tightly.

"Ma'am, you need medical assistance?" one of the paramedics who'd climbed down off the fire truck asked Rita.

"No. She's not hurt," Sharae yelled back at him.

"My gracious! My word! What's going on over here? I woke up to the smell of fire and hurried to call the fire department. Rita, what happened?" Ethel Canvers—the biggest of busybodies in Willow Grove—pushed her red-framed glasses up on her nose, her almond-brown eyes peering over Sharae's shoulder to where Rita stood behind her.

"Hey, Ethel. All is well," Sharae said and then turned to grab Rita by the elbow. "Come on. Let's get you inside."

"So, she's all right? No injuries?" the paramedic called to them. He looked concerned with his blue medic bag draped over his shoulder, his bushy eyebrows furrowed.

"No. No injuries," Sharae told him. By now there were more neighbors outside, a few standing across the street, while the bolder ones stood on the sidewalk about thirty feet from Rita's driveway. The other two officers had spread out a bit, intending to keep any bystanders from getting closer to the house. A barking dog joined the birds, and the flashing of combined red, white, and blue lights lit up the area like it was the Fourth of July.

"We're gonna need a statement from her," Phillips said.

"Yeah, us too!" That was the fire chief, who made his way around the men using fire extinguishers to tamp down the flames. When he tilted his hat back on his head, Sharae could see his discerning brown eyes.

It'd always been her practice to look at the eyes first. She could decipher so much more about a person in the first moments she stared into their eyes than she could sometimes after hours of interrogation. It was often hard to turn the practice off when she wasn't working a murder case. This morning she felt like she was working another type of case, and it was the worst kind—one that involved her family.

"Rita? Dear, what happened?" Ethel asked as she kept pace beside Sharae. How she'd gotten past the cops at the end of the front yard, Sharae had no idea. As for the other two, they were more focused on her and Rita than the nosy neighbor pressing them with questions right now.

"I'm here! Hey, Ethel. It's fine, I'm here." Jemel talked while easing her petite body between Ethel and Sharae. The officers had obviously let her through as well. Even though Jemel was her cousin, and exactly the person Sharae had planned to call the moment she got Rita into the house, the careless way in which the responding officers were managing the scene left a lot to be desired.

"My statement!" the fire chief yelled.

"I'll get the damn statement. You put out the fire!" Sharae yelled back.

"You gonna type up your cousin's statement too?" Phillips asked, sarcasm lacing his tone.

Sharae whipped her head around to face him, her gaze questioning.

He shrugged. "I'm just sayin', Sarge."

That last word was full of disrespect, and Sharae didn't plan to forget it. Sexism ran rampant in the police department, so a woman sergeant on the scene outranking the responding officers wasn't an easy pill to swallow. Add that it was a Black woman with nineteen years on the force, and there were bound to be some noses twisted out of joint. If this incident didn't involve her family—a reason for which she knew she should've recused herself—she would've verbally acknowledged the officer's misstep and made a note to report it to the captain.

Instead, she kept her gaze level with his and replied, "Fine. I'll type the report and send a copy to the fire chief when I get back to the precinct. Just get off the lawn and put the fire out!" It was too early in the morning to be yelling at people, but now, certain her captain was going to hear about this incident whether she was the one who told him or not, she didn't give a damn. Rita was her cousin. No way was she letting anybody else hear her story first.

Rita was the oldest of their threesome—Rita, Sharae, and Jemel. They'd been thick as thieves all their lives, growing up on the same Baltimore city block since their mothers were sisters. And normally, Rita was the stable one, the calm and collected one who'd walked the path their mothers wanted for each of them. She was the backbone to their trio, the moderator, and Sharae was afraid she might be starting to unravel.

"It's about damn time. I was drowning out there," Sharae snapped at Jemel as soon as they walked into Rita's house.

"Well, excuse me. I'm not nosy Ethel, peeping out my front window at every waking moment. And I had to push past Mrs. Barksdale, who'd pulled out a chair in the middle of the sidewalk to watch the activities. I try to ignore these folk around here as much as possible." Jemel closed the door behind them. "As soon as I heard the sirens and saw the fire truck pull up down here, I threw on something and came down."

Jemel had bought a house in the Willow Grove development about five years ago, while Sharae preferred the apartment she leased in a building close to the mall. She'd had to wait until she was eighteen to move out of her aunt's house, and when she did, she'd sworn she'd never live within walking distance of family again. Even of the two closest friends she'd ever had.

"Well, I'm glad somebody decided to put something on before coming out," Sharae said.

For the second time this morning, Rita jerked out of Sharae's grasp. "I'm a grown woman," she said before walking toward the kitchen.

"A grown woman who was just outside in her short-ass nightshirt standing in front of a blazing fire," Sharae whispered to Jemel.

"Yeah, what's up with that?"

Sharae shook her head. "I don't know."

"She's still wearing her bonnet."

Sharae nodded. "I know."

Jemel frowned. She was six inches shorter than Sharae's five feet seven, but wore heels all the time to hide that fact. Today her heels were in the form of a pair of pink-and-white platform Converses. "Did she set the fire?" Jemel asked in a hushed tone. Rita liked to say her motherhood status gave her the power to hear through walls. If Sharae and Jemel hadn't seen it actually happen, they might not have taken it so literally.

"Yup," Sharae replied.

They were both still standing in the foyer staring after Rita, who'd already disappeared into the kitchen.

"Why?" Jemel asked.

"Don't know."

"You gonna ask her?"

Sharae looked over to Jemel. "*We're* gonna ask her."

Jemel huffed and rolled her eyes. "Yeah, I guess we are."

They walked into the kitchen together, but Sharae continued until she was standing close to Rita.

"Why don't you sit down, honey. I can make the coffee," she said to Rita, who'd just taken the bag of the Dunkin' harvest-roast coffee she loved out of the cabinet.

"I want to be able to drink the coffee," Rita replied and moved around Sharae to get closer to the coffee maker on the counter.

Jemel snickered, and Sharae looked back to see she'd stopped at the end of the gray-and-white quartz-top island. Keeping a protective distance, no doubt. That probably wasn't necessary since Rita never lost it. While on the other hand, Jemel was the queen of drama, and at the ripe old age of thirty-six could still throw a tantrum that would put a three-year-old to shame.

"Okay, I don't claim to be a coffee maker. That wasn't my calling." Neither was being a therapist, but somebody had to maneuver around this land mine that was her normally levelheaded cousin. Sharae cleared her throat. "You wanna tell us what happened this morning?"

There'd never been a time that the three of them didn't share every detail of their lives—not ever—so the question wasn't out of line.

Rita scooped coffee into the liner and closed the lid on top of the coffee maker with a loud clap. "I was taking out the trash."

"We normally don't burn our garbage around here," Jemel added.

That remark earned her a cool glare from Rita, who seconds later pressed the "Start" button on the machine and rolled the top of the coffee bag down so tightly that Sharae expected the ground beans to burst through the seams at any moment.

"I can get the mugs," Sharae said. "That doesn't take any skill." But stopping violence did, and while Rita wasn't a criminal, Sharae knew the signs of a violent act about to be committed.

She eased the bag out of Rita's hands and put it back in the cabinet. "You have a seat."

The corners of Rita's mouth lifted, her eyes narrowing as she reluctantly stepped back to allow Sharae space to get in and out of the cabinets. Rita's big kitchen was light and airy, from the crisp white cabinets that reached to the ceiling to the gray tiled floor and all the coordinating appliances and decorations in between. There was more than enough room between the island and the cabinets, but this was Rita's domain, and she didn't allow anyone in here to assume otherwise.

On a huff, Rita took a step back, pulled one of the metal-backed stools out from the island, and eased onto it. Releasing a slow breath, Sharae grabbed three mugs, spoons, and the canister of sugar before moving to the island. With a look, she signaled for Jemel to get the creamer out of the Sub-Zero refrigerator. When they were all seated at the island, Sharae cleared her throat.

"What happened this morning, Rita?" Sharae stared into her cousin's eyes when she asked the question—not that there was anything about this woman that she didn't already know, but she would've liked to know just how bad this situation was. Because before this day was over, she would have to write an official report of this incident and explain to her superiors why she left a crime scene with a suspect who was also her cousin.

Rita rested her arms on the top of the island's smooth surface. Last night her sandy-brown hair had fallen in perfect waves to her shoulders. Dressed in designer jean capri pants and a lavender T-shirt, Rita had managed to look casual and chic, just like always. After all the guests had left, Rita would've no doubt gone upstairs and brushed her hair, wrapping it and covering her head with the bonnet. She would've washed the light layer of makeup she'd worn for the cookout from her honey-complected face, undressed, and climbed into bed. Unbothered by the fact that her husband was out of town. Again.

Sharae watched as Rita clasped her long piano-playing fingers together and stared down at them. With a tilt of her head, she eased her fingers apart, flattening her left hand on the counter to stare down at it. For extended moments the only sounds in the kitchen were the percolating coffee and Jemel's huffs every few seconds—patience wasn't her thing at all.

"Nate's having an affair," Rita said solemnly.

Jemel sucked her teeth, and Sharae barely resisted the urge to say, "So what's new?" Instead, they both waited for Rita to continue.

"I did everything I was supposed to do. I didn't sit with my legs open in church. I was respectful to my elders." Rita used her fingers to tick things off one by one. "Stayed a virgin until I was married. Cooked, cleaned." She sucked in a deep breath and released it slowly.

"The girl called me to announce that she's pregnant." Rita eased the four-carat princess-cut engagement ring surrounded by two white-gold bands of layered diamonds from her finger.

She never took those rings off, not even when she was cooking, which always sparked a robust conversation between the Aunts. Rita set the three rings on the counter and then pulled her hands back as if the rings were a poisonous snake about to attack. That set was a twentieth wedding-anniversary present. Rita always said Nate bought the best gifts. Sharae noted that he had to buy the best gifts so often because he was a lying, cheating bastard using his money and good looks to manipulate every woman stupid enough to fall for his bullshit.

Sharae had never thought Rita was stupid. Not until she'd married Nate when the ink on her high school diploma was barely dry.

"I don't think the fool was gloating." Rita shrugged. "Guess she just figured I should know."

The sound that came next was a cross between a muted scream and a painful moan as Rita let her head fall back and closed her eyes. Sharae glanced at Jemel, who quickly stood and began pouring caramel-macchiato-flavored creamer into the three gray-and-white patterned mugs.

Sharae was sitting closer to Rita, so she reached out a hand and lightly rubbed her shoulder. Rita shook her head, signaling she didn't need comfort. Sharae let her hand slip slowly from Rita's shoulder but didn't pull back completely.

"It was time," Rita said evenly. She sat up straighter, rolled her neck, and opened her eyes. "If he doesn't need the person that made this house a home for him, then I don't need him or his crap in here anymore."

Again, it took a Herculean amount of strength for Sharae not to do a fist pump and scream, "Hallelujah!" Jemel scooped sugar out of the canister and put overflowing dollops into each mug.

Rita's brow furrowed, and she reached out to put a hand over the mug closest to her.

Jemel huffed and put more sugar into her own mug. "So you burned his clothes in the driveway at dawn?"

"I did," Rita answered and then got up to get the coffeepot. "Now I'm in the mood for an omelet. Y'all want one? I need to refuel before I call my lawyer."

Sharae and Jemel shared another glance before taking deep breaths and releasing them in a collective shrug.

"You know I do," Jemel said and held her mug up when Rita returned and began pouring the coffee. "None of that low-fat cheese, though. You see how that shit wasn't even melting on the burgers last night? Tariq and Ivan were about to revolt in the backyard."

Rita's thin lips eased into a smile as she shook her head and grabbed a pot holder from the drawer to set the coffeepot on. "Can't try to give y'all nothin' healthy." She chuckled. "But really, I just grabbed the wrong package. I don't actually like it, either, but I'm trying to cut back in small ways."

Jemel sipped her coffee and then waved a hand in front of her face like she hadn't expected it to be piping hot. Sharae frowned and shook her head. "Aunt Rose got a whole lotta nerve telling somebody they've picked up a few pounds."

"I won't use the low-fat cheese. I'm gonna need all the caloric assistance I can get to have the conversation I need to have with the lawyer."

She might also require a criminal lawyer or at the very least her checkbook if the fire chief decided she'd violated any county ordinances by having a bonfire in her driveway. Sharae was fairly certain there wouldn't be any criminal charges, since she was on her own property and nobody was injured, but there was no doubt the fire could've spread, and then there was the Willow Grove Homeowners Association. Rita was the vice president this year, so she'd know better than anybody if she'd violated one of their ridiculous rules, but right now she didn't seem to be bothered by that.

In fact, Rita didn't seem overly bothered by any of this, if the burning driveway was subtracted from the equation. Sharae watched carefully while Rita moved around the kitchen doing what was as familiar to her as breathing—cooking for her family. Jemel chattered on about conversations they'd had last night with other family members. The Spades contest that had been issued by their cousin Tariq to anyone who dared challenge him, and the card night that was subsequently scheduled for this Friday. One of the Johnson cousins in Charlotte was pregnant again, and how somebody should replace Uncle Jimmy as the bartender because he was already pissy drunk and about to fall over the table that'd been set up as a makeshift bar.

Sharae joined the conversation, chuckling here and there, adding her comments, but all the while keeping her eye on Rita. In her early years on the force, Sharae had decided which unit she wanted to target. Narcotics had seemed the natural choice considering all the drug activity they'd grown up around, the dealers and users in their families and the consequences that showed up on the nightly news, but for a brief period she'd wondered about going to the bomb squad. The deciding factor had been that Sharae knew she lacked the patience and mastery to watch a ticking time bomb and dismantle it without wanting to pick it up and throw it as far away as possible from the innocent and those she cared about.

That's how it felt watching Rita. Like she desperately wanted to do something before the explosion affected everything they all knew and loved. And she was helpless to prevent it. She should've shoved her gun inside Nate McCall's mouth years ago, the dirty, no-class piece of shit.

Chapter 3

It's never a bad time for food.

"So you're divorcing him," Jemel said half an hour later when the three of them sat around the island finishing off the breakfast Rita had cooked. "When are you tellin' the Aunts? I wanna know so I can be there."

Rita hadn't thought that far. She'd known there would be obstacles to finally deciding to end her marriage. Just like this hadn't been Nate's first time cheating and getting caught, this wasn't Rita's first time considering divorce. It *was* the first time she'd felt there was no other choice.

"How many times I gotta tell y'all I'm grown?" She shook her head after speaking the question and glanced down at her plate. Her appetite hadn't been disturbed, as she'd eaten the entire western omelet she'd cooked and was now on her second cup of coffee.

Then again, she'd never had any problems eating. It seemed that food—the ease of cooking and enjoying it—was her comfort zone. The kitchen, which she'd personally designed from the large-tiled floors to the wide gray-and-white marble-top island, had served as her happy place even on days when worry and despair crept in to haunt her.

But at Jemel's question, her mind now circled around the Aunts and their reaction to what she'd decided to do. It was always interesting to see her mother, Violet "Vi" Henderson, with her two sisters, Cecelia "Ceil" Johnson Coleridge and Rosette "Rose" Johnson, go in on other family members—namely Jemel, who the Aunts had all dubbed reckless and irresponsible since she was a teenager. Not that whatever they said mattered to Jemel; she'd long ago stopped being affected by their pile-on judgment and discipline regimen. As for Rita, she wished she'd been so lucky.

"I'll tell the Aunts when I tell everybody else, I guess," she continued when neither Sharae nor Jemel had responded to her question.

"And the girls?" Sharae asked. "When are you tellin' them?"

"No," Jemel said with a shake of her head. "When are you pullin' that bitch ass Nate up?"

Rita didn't miss the warning glare Sharae sent to Jemel seconds before her cousin looked Rita's way. "What she meant was, did you call Nate? Have you told him this was the last straw?"

They'd never liked Nate. Or rather, they'd been up front with her early on that they'd disagreed with her marrying a man four years older than she was at only nineteen years old. Obviously, she'd disagreed. Age hadn't mattered because she'd believed she was on the right track—at least the track that her mother had made perfectly clear was meant for her.

Hale Henderson, Rita's father, was the pastor of New Visionary Baptist Church, one of the biggest churches in Baltimore City. That made her mother the first lady, and Benny and Rita PKs (preacher's kids). An insurmountable layer of pressure went with all those titles, but Rita had done her best to carry it gracefully every day of her life. Vi wouldn't have had it any other way. And in her mother's eyes, Rita's only goals after high school were to marry a nice man, become a good wife, have children, and live happily ever after. Well, two out of four wasn't that bad.

Rita sat back, coffee mug in one hand, and shook her head. "I don't think there's anything left to say to that man." She wasn't ready to admit—not even to the two people closest to her—that she was afraid to talk to him. Conversations about his infidelity had always left her drained yet cautiously optimistic in the past. This time, she didn't want to buckle under the pressure of saving a loveless marriage for the sake of keeping up appearances. She couldn't do it, not again.

"Oh, I beg to differ on that point," Sharae replied quickly. "I've got a lot of choice words for that muthafuck—"

"Uh-uh." Rita shook her head and frowned. "Not this early in the morning, Sharae."

Sharae wiped her hands on a napkin and tossed it onto her empty plate. "I'm grown, too, Rita, and I can call a muthafucka a muthafucka when he's acting like a muthafucka."

Rita's eyes narrowed, and Jemel grinned before replying, "And y'all say I'm the one always pushin' the envelope."

"She's just being smart as usual," Rita said and set her mug on the island. "Look, I know what needs to be done, and I'm going to take care of it."

Just like she always took care of everything.

None of them said that part. But they didn't have to. Rita knew she was the fixer of their crew. She'd inherited that from her mother. Whenever they'd gotten into trouble as kids, Rita was the one to come up with a plan to try and get them out of it. Or to at least campaign to lessen the punishment that would come as a result. Where Jemel was concerned, that took a lot of work and a lot of praying on Rita's part. The thought left a warm feeling in her chest. These two women meant the world to her. They'd always been there for her—even in the early years when Nate had first cheated, they'd been her shoulder to cry on. Then they'd both insisted she tell Tariq to beat Nate's ass and then clean him out in the divorce. But Rita hadn't done that, and in the years that followed, Sharae and Jemel had stopped saying much about Nate and Rita's marriage. Rita knew it was purposeful on their part, and she loved that they cared so much about her that they'd hold their tongues just to keep her happy. And she *had* been happy, for a while.

"You know we're here. Just tell us what you want us to do," Jemel said when Rita figured she'd been quiet for too long.

"Nothing," Rita replied. "I mean, there's nothing you can do at the moment."

"Besides keep your ass from getting a citation or, worse, going to jail," Sharae countered.

Rita frowned. "For taking out the trash?"

"Uh, no, let's try destruction of property, arson, criminal mischief." Sharae stuck out a finger to tick off each charge. "I don't have all the Howard County ordinances committed to memory because I prefer to stop killers for a living, but the fire chief wasn't happy about me whisking you into the house before he could talk to you. And my captain's probably waiting to tear me a new one the minute I walk through the doors of the precinct."

"Oh." Rita's lips formed an O before she reached out a hand to touch Sharae's. "I'm sorry. I didn't think about that." She knew how much Sharae's job meant to her, and the last thing she wanted to do was jeopardize that in any way. The decision to burn Nate's clothes had come so naturally, but at the same time had been as unexpected as the phone call from that woman. Still, it wasn't like her to act irrationally, and she prayed that Sharae wouldn't pay the price for her actions.

"There's gotta be some kinda loophole for wives who need to release some tension brought on by their cheating husbands," Jemel said.

Sharae leveled her gaze at her, twisting her lips up at the corners. It was the look reserved especially for Jemel, who had zero filter on whatever came out of her mouth. It almost made Rita grin. "That's not how it works," Sharae said.

"Sure it is," Jemel replied with a shrug. "I bet this isn't the first case they've seen of a woman burning her husband's clothes. And since the majority of men are determined to live up to the ain't-shit mantra, this won't be the last."

Sharae pointed a finger and nodded in Jemel's direction. "That last part," she said with a knowing look.

One of the top points Jemel and Sharae agreed on was that when dealing with men, they should always use long-handled spoons. Grandma Patty had taught them the concept of the long-handled-spoon approach when they'd been little girls visiting her spooky old house by the park. In essence, it meant that once a person wronged you, it was okay to still deal with them—from a distance—but to never trust or let them get close to you again. Now, that didn't mean Jemel didn't love herself some men, 'cause sex was like air to her, and she never planned to go without. While Sharae, on the other hand, could function on self-pleasure without blinking an eye. Between that and going to the shooting range every weekend, it was a wonder she didn't have carpal tunnel or some other wrist-and-hand malfunction. It had always been a wonder to Rita how very differently each of them had viewed relationships. Now she wondered if they'd had the right idea all along.

She stood then. "I'm getting a divorce." She picked up her empty plate and mug and carried them both to the sink. The words were spoken with solemn finality followed by the quick rush of water when she turned on the faucet and began rinsing her dishes.

There was a hush in the room, and for those few seconds Rita was grateful for the silence. It gave her a chance to get used to saying that word as it pertained to the marriage she'd thought would last forever.

"Well, we can have a freedom party when you sign the final papers," Jemel said. "You know a party heals all wounds. At least in my book it does. It's like I always say: 'That which does not break you leaves cause for celebration.'"

Rita couldn't help but chuckle. She'd always admired Jemel's unwavering spirit.

When Rita turned back to face them, it was to see Sharae standing to bring her plate and mug over to the sink. "We'll rent a hall and hire a decorator," Sharae added.

"And I'll cook all the food," Rita replied dryly. She cooked for every family function they had, and in the last few years had been cooking for church events as well.

"Oh, hell no." Jemel grabbed her dishes and walked to meet them. "You will not cook for your own party."

Rita took the plate, fork, and mug from Jemel and moved them under the running water. "I always cook. It's what brings me joy." And she was gonna need a lot of that in her future.

"Yeah, but that doesn't mean you have to keep that trend going. Especially not for this event. I can cook," Jemel said.

Sharae laughed and Rita smiled, shaking her head while she added Jemel's dishes to the rack and closed the dishwasher. Sharae touched a hand to her irritatingly flat stomach, and her head fell back while she laughed like they were at the Baltimore Comedy Factory. Rita might've chastised Sharae for mocking Jemel if Sharae didn't manage to look gorgeous while doing it.

The tallest of their trio at five seven, Sharae had a slim, willowy figure. Second to the shooting range, running was her favorite thing to do, so her size 8 butt stayed tight, and her C-cup breasts were still perky at forty. She kept her hair cut short and natural, opting to leave the chemicals to Jemel and Rita. Today's style was curly with a side part, with a few sassy tendrils dropping over her right eye. Her smile was brilliant thanks to two years of braces when she was sixteen, her deep, throaty laughter infectious even now, when Rita was dancing on the outskirts of misery.

"I can cook," Jemel said, lifting her chin in what Rita and Sharae knew as her defiant stance.

"Girl, you burn canned biscuits," Sharae managed between guffaws.

Jemel didn't pout—which she was also known for—but blinked at those words. "Well, those Hawaiian rolls in the pack taste better anyway," she insisted.

Rita set the dishwasher to run and touched a hand to Jemel's shoulder. "Not better than my yeast rolls," she said in a consolatory tone. "But you don't slack on bringing the top-shelf liquor. Plus, you're always the cutest one at the party."

Twisting her lips, Jemel turned away from Sharae's almost-tempered chuckles. "Well, I do dress better than you two." It was her one crowning glory.

Being the youngest of their crew and the shortest had often made Jemel feel like an outcast. There'd even been times when Jemel had mentioned that her biracial heritage made her feel different from the rest of them. But Sharae and Rita had never treated her differently or acted like she was a bother in any way. Not even when they were old enough to get into clubs and Jemel was just fourteen, too young to even get a work permit. Her breasts had hit puberty before any other part of her body, and until the rest of her caught up, she'd looked like she might tip over with how fast she'd shot to a full B cup in her teens. So it hadn't been that difficult for Rita to lie to her friend who DJ'd at the club and convince him to let Jemel in.

"Nobody has time to fixate over clothes like you do, Jem." Sharae had finally stopped laughing when she reached out to run a hand over Jemel's hair.

Jemel hadn't combed her long curls out yet; she'd just pulled off her scarf and headed over to save Rita from burning her house down. Not that it would've gotten that far, but Rita could see how it might've looked from their standpoint.

"Obviously," Jemel replied, with a nod down at Sharae's blue Crocs. "Those shoes look awful with the hem of her dress pants resting on top of them."

Sharae looked down, then back up at Jemel and shrugged. "I've got court in—" She paused and twisted her wrist to look at her watch. "Oh shit, I have to be downtown by eight, and it's already twenty after seven. Traffic's gonna be a bitch!"

"Sorry again," Rita said when Sharae started to head out of the kitchen.

Stopping, Sharae wrapped an arm around Rita. Jemel joined in by easing an arm around Rita's waist. These were her sisters-of-the-heart, her ride-or-die BFFs and most favorite cousins in the world. If there was ever a time she needed their hugs and good thoughts, it was now.

"Don't apologize. I'm here whenever you need me. Even when you don't call me to give a heads-up that you're about to start an inferno in your driveway." Sharae smiled and leaned in to kiss Rita on the forehead.

"Me too, even though I'd like for you not to burn our neighborhood down before I can gain more equity in my house," Jemel said and added a kiss to Rita's cheek.

"Gee, thanks, you two," Rita replied, but she looped her arms around them until they all came together for a tight group hug. "I don't know what I'd do without y'all."

"You don't have to find out," Sharae said when they broke apart. "I'm gonna call you after I finish up at court, and you can tell me how it went with the lawyer."

Rita nodded and walked out of the kitchen.

"And I'll be at the shop, but y'all can FaceTime me so I'll be on the call too. I want to know how much of McCall Motors' assets you'll be adding to your portfolio." Jemel was big on saving and preparing for a stable financial future. Probably because she'd been so short on funds growing up and hated working for anybody long enough to make any real money.

Jemel had taken cosmetology in high school and had done hair in Aunt Ceil's basement to make money. It had taken her a few years on the road with her boy-band boyfriend and then another couple of years at community college to finally find her niche in floral design. Now she owned her own florist shop and was pleased as punch about it.

"How 'bout I just call you both later tonight. I've got an HOA meeting I need to prepare for and some more purging to do. Plus, I just need some time to think." Truth was, she needed a *lot* of time to think. Her life was going to change, and she had no idea if that was going to be for the better, but she had to figure it out, and it was best if she did that on her own.

She opened the front door, and the smoky scent filtered into the house on a balmy breeze. The fire truck and police cruisers were gone, but Willow Grove was fully awake, and a couple of cars slowed in front of the house as neighbors got a peek at what Rita knew was going to be the talk of the development for the next couple of days.

Sharae stepped outside first. "That's fine, but do me a favor, don't burn anything you purge this time. Just put all his shit in trash bags and put 'em in the garage."

"That's right," Jemel said as she walked out the door. "Trash day's not until tomorrow. But you can be ready to drag all his crap out here bright and early in the mornin' 'cause you know sometimes those jokas like to roll up at the crack of dawn."

Rita laughed and Jemel smiled back at her. It was those smiles and their encouragement that guided Rita back into the house to close the door. And it was the weight of her world barreling down on her shoulders that had her leaning against the door and sliding down until her butt hit the floor.

Chapter 4

THIS DAY JUST KEEPS GETTING BETTER.

Sharae showed her badge and walked through the metal detector at the courthouse.

"Lookin' good this mornin', Sarge." Meadows, one of the sheriff's deputies that secured the building flashed his toothy grin and sexy green eyes.

"Hey, Meadows," she replied, continuing to use the last name printed on the pocket of his uniform shirt. She knew his first name was Rodney, his favorite drink was cranberry juice and vodka, and he sucked at darts. In fact, he still owed her forty dollars from the last night she and some of the other law enforcement workers had been at the pool hall talkin' shit and gettin' drunk.

"How many you got today?" he asked when she'd made it through the detector and stood at the front desk across from him.

"Just the one; then I'm heading back to the station." Captain Hall had already sent her a text saying he wanted to see her as soon as she finished in court. She wasn't looking forward to that confrontation. It wouldn't be the first time they'd butted heads, and considering Floyd Hall thought she'd be better off sitting behind a desk, Sharae knew it wouldn't be the last.

"You got Tempton or Fray this time?" Meadows asked.

Judge Mabel Tempton had been on the bench for twelve years and was known for giving a defendant every ounce of time the law allowed on any given charge. While Judge Abby Fray leaned more on a rehabilitative course rather than looking only toward punitive recourse. As the guy Sharae and her partner had investigated, questioned, and arrested was beyond guilty because he couldn't aim worth shit and missed his intended target—a rival gang member—killing two innocent teenage bystanders in the process, she'd hoped the case would be heard by Tempton.

Unfortunately, as disappointment seemed to make a beeline for her on a daily basis, it was Judge Fray's courtroom number that was typed on her summons to appear.

"Fray, but we've got a lot of evidence, including eyewitnesses, so we'll see how it goes."

The courthouse was already busy at eight in the morning, with employees coming in, citizens reporting for jury duty, and others showing up for whatever judicial matter was going on in their lives at the moment. Beeping from the metal detector had continued to sound while she'd stood talking to Meadows, as two other deputies worked at the opposite end of the desk either checking employee IDs or giving directions to courtrooms.

"You off this weekend?"

Smiling, she gave Meadows a knowing gaze. He'd been asking her about a second date every week for the past eight months since their first date. "Yeah, but I'm not comin' out. Got some stuff to do around the house and with my family." That was only a partial lie—she did have a new desk being delivered on Saturday, and she needed to clean out the second bedroom she used as an office before it arrived. But her family knew she hated impromptu visits and was likely to leave them outside pressing the buzzer to get into her apartment building if they ignored her wishes.

"Or you're just brushin' me off again," Meadows replied. His grin never faltered, nor did the look that said he was still picturing their night in the back seat of his 4Runner as if it'd just happened yesterday.

That had been a very interesting night. He'd asked her out at least half a dozen times before Sharae had finally given in. Meadows was a good-looking guy with his tawny-brown complexion. The temple fade with sponge twists hairstyle he preferred coupled with those seductive eyes only added to his charismatic charm. So many women in the courthouse, in law enforcement, and probably all around the city wanted to date him. Sharae had only wanted to fuck him, and so she had.

"One and done, Meadows. You know that." And before he could say another word, Sharae waved a hand at him and walked away.

She could hear his deep-throated chuckle as her four-inch heels clicked across the marbled floor, toward the elevator.

Minutes later she was on the third floor sitting on the bench outside Judge Fray's courtroom. She'd already checked in with the state's attorney and was now just waiting for the trial to begin. Pulling her file out of the black Tory Burch Perry leather tote she carried, she settled back and opened it to read over her notes. The bag looked like new even though Jemel had given it to her two birthdays ago. Sharae only carried big fancy purses on special occasions, but that didn't stop her from having a collection of them that she kept carefully stored in the special shelving she'd had installed in the second-bedroom closet at her apartment. While she was working out in the field, a functional cross-body bag about the size of two cell phones side by side was all she needed to hold her phone, wallet, keys, and notepad. But on the Sundays she could make it to church, and whenever she had to attend some other function that the Aunts deemed necessary, she pulled out her pretty bags and carefully coordinated them with her outfits.

Jemel called that progress, considering those outfits were hardly ever skirts and dresses like she and Rita preferred to wear. Sharae had always been the tomboy of the trio, and as she crossed her legs and flipped through the file, she smiled at the thought. From early on they'd each had a place in their little clique, serving a purpose to the others and forging their bond. As if being first cousins wasn't enough.

"Hello."

Sharae looked up at the sound of the man's voice. "Hello."

Similar to down on the first floor, there was the usual morning commotion in the hallway. Lawyers rushing to their assigned courtrooms, the sound of the wide, heavy oak doors that matched the antiquated design of the one-hundred-year-old courthouse being opened and closed with a bang echoing throughout the long hallways. The hum of multiple conversations and a combination of keys and the chains shackling an inmate's ankles as deputies escorted them to courtrooms joined the chorus.

"Mind if I sit here?" he asked before nodding at the empty space left on the bench to her right.

He was a lawyer, of course. A high-priced defense one, no doubt. His suit wasn't off the rack, not at any place like the Men's Wearhouse or Macy's. No, the navy-blue slim-fit pants and jacket were definitely high quality and had been professionally tailored. There was no way a guy over six feet tall, as he was, with his athletic build could go into any type of store and find a suit that would fit him as perfectly as this one did.

She shrugged. "Sure." It was a public bench, and she'd settled at the end closest to the courtroom door. Her hope was to get in and get out as quickly as possible.

As he took a seat, she returned her attention to her file, reading the original report she'd filed and the photocopy she'd made of the notes on her pad since she didn't like flipping through her pad in the courtroom and she never tore the pages out. After nineteen years on the police force, she knew the drill with court appearances. Last week she'd met with the state's attorney to go over her testimony. Routine stuff, no surprises there. But six years as a homicide detective, ten in narcotics, and three as a beat cop had shown her just how smart and divisive defense attorneys could be. It was always better to be prepared than be caught off guard by some slick legal strategy.

"I'm Desmond Brown," the lawyer said from beside her.

Sharae barely spared him a glance and a curt nod.

"You're Sharae Gibson."

Now she let her gaze settle on him. His beard was low cut and well maintained, as was his wavy black hair. His lips were of medium thickness, his eyes an interesting cognac color. Not only was he wearing an expensive suit, but he also wore an eight-hundred-dollar Movado watch—she knew because her cousin Tariq sold knockoffs down at the flea market on Saturdays.

"Okay," she replied finally, not bothering to hide the questioning tone.

It wasn't odd that attorneys knew her, and as much as she'd been in this courthouse, she was certain there were more lawyers and other staff who knew her than who didn't. So, the slither of alarm that now danced along her spine wasn't normal.

He reached into the leather messenger bag he carried and pulled out a thick brown file folder. Unwrapping the band from the file, he opened it and extended a picture toward her.

That alarm swirled up her back to wrap around her neck and tighten until she gasped. She looked away from the picture of herself at the age of four sitting on her father's lap, grinning like life was all rainbows and cotton candy, and stared at him. "Where'd you get this?"

"My firm represented Sanford Gibson in multiple matters." He spoke slowly, as if he were measuring his words, watching her every reaction as he continued. "I'm handling his estate."

"His . . ." Sharae paused, swallowed, and blinked. "His estate." The word stuck in her throat as its implication settled in her mind. "He's dead."

"Yes. I'm sorry to tell you that your father passed away last Wednesday from sarcoidosis."

She shook her head. "He's in jail. I mean, he *was* in jail." Since she was thirteen. Ten weeks before her fourteenth birthday, to be exact.

"Yes." Desmond nodded. "At the Jessup Correctional Institution."

Where he'd been serving a life-without-parole sentence for killing her mother.

"Ms. Gibson, I have some things to discuss with you about your father's estate."

Sharae held up a hand to stop him from talking. She didn't want to hear anything else, yet those words weren't readily falling from her lips.

Desmond continued. "I understand that this has come as a shock to you, and I tried to reach you at the precinct but was told you were in court today. There are some things we need to discuss."

He was still talking, his words floating around that black void that had settled into the farthest recesses of her mind. Sanford Gibson was dead. Just like her mother had been for the past twenty-seven years. "I can't." The words came out raspy. Her throat felt tight, her chest filled with some unnamed emotion that threatened to crush her.

"Ms. Gibson," Desmond said.

She didn't know what he'd done with that picture, but he was now reaching into the file folder again. Sharae shook her head. "No. Don't. This isn't . . . um, it isn't for me."

Behind her, a clicking sound followed by the creak of rusted hinges echoed. "We're ready for you now, Detective Gibson."

Turning in the direction of the new voice, Sharae saw the state's attorney's law clerk standing by the door. That's right, she was here to testify. In another murder case. Not her mother's. She let out a breath she hadn't been aware she was holding and stood. "Right. You're ready for me to testify."

Intending to walk away leaving Desmond Brown and his big folder of news she didn't want to hear behind, Sharae took the first step on unstable legs. She stopped, just to take another cleansing breath and focus her mind on the present, the case outlined in the folder she now carried in her hand.

"As his only child, you would be the executor of his estate." Desmond continued as if they hadn't just been interrupted and she wasn't attempting to walk away from him. "There's the matter of three properties he owned and some other investments that need to be dealt with. Here's my card. You can call me when you're finished here today. I have time that we can meet this afternoon."

She turned back slowly, until she was facing him again. He stood now as well and extended his arm to offer her the white business card tucked between his fingers. Sharae looked down at that card, then back up to him to see that he was staring intently at her.

"This is important business, Ms. Gibson. And while I offer my sincerest condolences to you and your family, there are a few time-sensitive issues that need to be addressed." He paused and lowered his voice when he spoke again. "Please, take my card and call me later."

Sharae didn't know what to say. This wasn't a case she'd taken notes on, investigated every aspect of, and knew like she knew her name. No, this was totally different and unexpected and . . . she didn't know what else. What she was certain of was that she couldn't deal with it right now. Snatching the card from his hand with a little more force than she'd intended, she stared at Desmond Brown. "He wasn't my father," she said. "He was the man who killed my mother."

She didn't stick around for a response, didn't give a damn what Sanford Gibson's attorney thought about what she'd just said. When Sharae stepped into the courtroom, she pushed everything that had happened in the last fifteen minutes out of her mind and walked up to the witness stand.

For what seemed like an eternity, but was really only an hour and a half, she testified about her case. About the murder she could prove and the bad guy she wanted to put away for taking two innocent lives.

Her mother, Justine Johnson, had been thirty-five when her life was brutally taken. She'd been innocent too. Guilty of only one thing—falling in love with the wrong man.

Chapter 5

ELEVATOR MUSIC IS THE SPAWN OF THE DEVIL.

Rita slowly set the phone down on its base. She closed her eyes, clenched her fingers into fists, and held back the scream that burned for release. Why was this happening to her? Why now? And how was she supposed to do this?

Her parents hadn't taught her how to do divorce. Hale and Vi had taught Rita many things; her father made sure her soul was saved and that she loved the Lord, while her mother taught her how to love and take care of a husband and a household. Nowhere in between was there a chapter on getting rid of the trash that was supposed to be her partner for life. Sure, infidelity was covered in the Bible, but so was forgiveness. Rita was tired of forgiving Nate.

Opening her eyes, she walked toward the dresser across the room. Nate's dresser. At Sharae's suggestion, Rita had brought the box of trash bags upstairs and had started packing up Nate's stuff before her call with the lawyer. Thinking back on the forty-minute call with Sharon Raymond that had just ended had her temples throbbing.

Always prompt, because it was professional and respectful, Rita had called at exactly two o'clock. Only to be put on hold for fifteen minutes filled with the most dreadful elevator music ever recorded. She'd been just about to hang up and compose a very strongly worded email to Sharon when she came onto the line.

"Hey, Rita. Sorry for the delay. Had a last-minute issue to tie up from my court appearance this morning. What's going on?"

Rita had known Sharon since they were in high school, when Sharon's parents moved to Baltimore from Brooklyn. They were the strongest altos on the young-adult choir back then; now they sang on the Glory choir and were often on the same committees at the church.

"It's okay." It really wasn't—Rita couldn't stand people disrespecting her time—but she'd wanted to get to the gist of the matter. "I wanted to talk to you about starting divorce proceedings." The word *divorce* still sounded foreign, and doubt continued to surface. Was she really doing this?

If Sharon was shocked, she didn't let on. Instead, she'd gone straight into what Rita suspected was her professional lingo. "I'm so sorry to hear that. Are you sure there's no chance of reconciliation?"

Doubt be damned. The answer to that was a resounding no. Enough was enough. Then the details began. How long had they been married? Too long. Grounds for divorce? Infidelity times four or five, but who was counting? How many children? Alimony or child support? Assets?

Rita had rattled off all the answers like she was a robot, all the while the last piece of her heart that had once belonged to Nate shriveled up and died.

They were scheduled to meet in person on Thursday, when Sharon would have a draft separation agreement. Rita needed to get her own accountant to valuate the car dealerships and the two vacation homes her name was on with Nate's. She'd have to talk to Necole and Taryn before then. Maybe she'd call them and have them both come over for dinner tomorrow. She could fix crab cakes, fried shrimp, and fresh-cut fries—they both loved that. And then she could tell them that their parents were breaking up because their father was a lying bastard.

The thought had her pulling open the top drawer of the dresser, grabbing everything inside, and then tossing it into a trash bag that was already half-full with his clothes. With each stack she dropped into that bag, she wanted to toss them out the window and burn them too. But she wouldn't do that to Sharae. Guilt still nagged at her, and she'd texted Sharae twice already trying to find out if she'd gotten her into trouble at work. Sharae's reply both times had been a curt "Don't worry about it."

Rita did have other stuff to worry about. After twenty minutes and six trash bags full of crap, she realized she had a *whole lot more* to worry about. One being how she was going to haul these heavy bags downstairs and out to the garage, where she planned to leave them until Nate came home.

A triple beep and then a low buzz sounded as the house alarm gave notification that someone had used a key and an approved code to get in. Necole and Taryn had gone to Ocean City for the weekend and weren't expected back in Baltimore until late tonight, and even then, they were going to the apartment they shared in the city. She sighed heavily, knowing that only meant one thing—Nate was home.

"Rita! What the hell happened in the driveway? Did your tacky-ass cousin Cedric try to light fireworks again?"

Cedric was her uncle Jimmy's son, and he had been here last night, but without fireworks because he'd been working double shifts at the warehouse and hadn't had a chance to drive up to Pennsylvania, where he could buy them cheap. Over the years Nate had developed a decent relationship with most people in her family. He had no real choice, since the Johnsons were always together for one occasion or another, or just church and dinner on Sundays. But Ced and Nate had had a tense relationship for seven years, ever since Ced had set off fireworks in Rita and Nate's trash cans and sent them soaring through the air to land in Mr. Myerson's prize rosebushes. Ced had refused to pay the eight-hundred-dollar bill Mr. Myerson had taped on their front door, and Nate had never forgiven him for being what he called "a reckless and cheap-ass idiot."

Nate yelled her name again, and Rita moved to the bed they'd shared. She reached for the box of trash bags and pulled out another one. There were two more dresser drawers to empty, and then she had more boxes in the closet. Turning away from the bed, she pulled the opening of the bag apart, then stuck one arm deeper inside to spread it open. Walking over to the dresser, she rolled the top of the bag down a couple of inches and set it on the floor next to her. Then she started taking the stuff out of the second drawer from the bottom. That's what she was doing when Nate walked into the bedroom.

"What the hell are you doing? Didn't you hear me calling you?"

Nate didn't like being ignored. In fact, thinking back on their life together, she now realized just how much he'd coveted being the center of attention. Whether he was talking about the dealerships, improvements being made to the house, his newest car, or investments, Nate always found a way to bring any conversation back to him. Funny how that had never bothered her before.

Truth be told, it didn't bother her right now either. Especially since there was a part of her that had planned to never speak another word to this man again. With a heavy sigh, she realized that part must've resided in some delusional world, one where Rita had always told herself she'd never venture. She was a realistic woman, a sensible, God-loving woman. There wasn't anything she couldn't face—not even the man who'd once held her heart.

"Packing," she replied without sparing him a glance.

She smelled his cologne—a crisp, woodsy scent that immediately reminded her of the fire that had burned bright at the crack of dawn this morning.

"You're packing my stuff?" He came closer as he talked, grasping the arm she'd just reached into the drawer for another stack of clothes.

The way Rita's body instantly tensed and her head moved slowly to turn so that she now stared at him felt like something out of a movie. She'd been feeling that way all day long—like this had to be someone else's life she was experiencing because there was no way this was how her life was meant to turn out. Nate must've finally gotten a clue to her mood when he stared back at her two seconds before hurriedly releasing her arm.

"What's going on, Rita?"

She took that stack of clothes out of the drawer, leaving it empty now, and dropped it into the trash bag before standing up straight.

"You should live with the woman you got pregnant. A child deserves to have both parents in their household," she said, her voice much calmer than she felt. "So I'm helping get all your things together. It won't take much longer, and since you're here now, you can take them right down to your car and be on your way."

"What the hell are you talking about?" He took another step back away from her when she shot him a quick searing look. The good Lord must've been whispering some sense in his ear.

Nate hadn't grown up in the church like she had, but he was no stranger to the culture, and since day one of meeting Rita's parents, Nate had been attending NVB every Sunday that he wasn't out of town. She'd never been sure how much of the Bible teachings he'd taken in, but one thing was for certain—he was going to need all the Holy Spirit's help if he wanted to get out of this house unscathed.

Not that she was capable of violence. Rita liked to believe she was too levelheaded to resort to such basic actions. But honestly, there'd been a rage brewing in her all day that she didn't realize the full intensity of until the moment her gaze rested on Nate's familiar one.

"Your little slut called me this morning to tell me the good news," she continued and then turned her attention back to the bottom drawer. "Now you could've just told me yourself, but that's fine. It's over now."

"Rita," he began, "listen to me."

"I can hear you just fine, Nate," she told him but didn't stop emptying out that bottom drawer.

"It's not what you think," he said.

She'd just dropped another scoop of his socks into the bag when she stood. Grabbing the bottle of cologne from the top of his dresser hadn't been what she'd planned, but the second her fingers wrapped around it, she turned and hurled it at Nate. He ducked out of the way, and the bottle crashed against the wall, breaking on contact.

"Not what I think?" she yelled, her fingers trembling. "Who even gives that ridiculous excuse anymore?"

"You need to calm down!" he fired back.

"Calm down?" Rita reached for another bottle from his dresser and threw that one at him too. "Oh, I'm calm, you simple bastard! I'm as calm as I'm gonna get!" Another bottle went flying across the room and another, until Nate was ducking from one direction to the next, bobbin' and weavin' around their bedroom like a cartoon character. While she was aiming and throwing like she was trying to win the biggest, ugliest teddy bear at the church carnival.

Nate moved fast, crossing the room and grabbing her wrists just as she was about to reach for whatever else she could find on his dresser to throw at his lying self. He held her tight, walking them both away from the dresser. Fury still bubbled inside her, and now he was too close. And he was touching her with the same hands that had touched that woman and countless others.

She wrestled to get free of his hold. "Get your hands off of me!"

He released her with a little push, and she bounced back onto the bed. But she didn't stay down. Jumping up again, she reached for the lamp on the nightstand, stopping just as her fingers wrapped around the stem. What the hell was she doing? Was she really going to destroy her house for this fool?

"Are you gonna listen to me, or do you just want to break up everything in this room?" He had the audacity to sound annoyed.

Staring at her fingers for what seemed like endless moments, Rita took a steadying breath and let them slip away from the lamp. She cleared her throat and ran a hand through her hair before turning to face him again.

He was wearing brown khaki pants and a yellow polo shirt. His white tennis shoes were crisp, not necessarily brand new because Nate kept all his shoes looking like they were fresh out of the box. Diamond studs sparkled in each of his ears as she looked at the familiar round face. The umber tone of his skin and thin beard he'd begun wearing a few years ago. His eyes were a very dark brown, so sometimes they looked black; his hair, the same color, was cut close, the odd line-up he always had still receding.

Nate had broad shoulders, and the twenty-five pounds he'd picked up over the last twenty years looked good on him thanks to the time he spent working out. A gold watch shone at his wrist as he stood back, licking his lips in that way that said he was thinking hard about something. Probably about what lie to feed her next. Well, he need not think too hard on that one. There was nothing he could say that she'd ever believe again.

"No," she said solemnly. Her voice was lower than it had been just moments ago, the rage that had her trembling on the inside slinking back a bit. She stood straight as she looked at him now, arms at her sides, fingers extended so that she wasn't holding in anger there. "I'm not going to destroy everything in my house."

He raised a brow. "*Our* house."

"This stopped being our house when you started stepping out of it and slipping into another woman's bed." The declaration came easily, the burning in the back of her throat at the words not so much.

He shook his head. "You're too old to be believing everything you hear. Now, I don't have time to stand here explaining to you that some jealous bitch is playing games with you, because we've been down this road before." He turned away from her and knelt down to pick up one of the bottles that hadn't broken in her hit-the-jackass target practice.

All the more reason why he should've known better than to take the denial track, but it was what it was. "And we'll never walk this path again," she told him. "I want you out of my house. And yes, I said *my* house."

She circled around him to the dresser again and grabbed the last of his socks, but he stopped her with another hand to her arm. This time he squeezed harder as he yelled, "Stop it! I'm not playing this game with you. Put my shit down!"

Yanking her arm from his grasp, she threw the socks in his face and pushed him back so that he was no longer invading her personal space. "Make that the last time you put your hands on me, Nate." Now her tone was tinged with something Rita hadn't heard in a very long time—possibly ever—since she'd never been faced with this type of hurt and betrayal before.

The other affairs, they'd been what they were—just affairs. Or at least that was what she'd told herself each time Nate insisted the affairs were over. Immediately after those declarations Nate would swear he was dedicated to their marriage. And, every time, Rita would believe him. It was a foolish belief, she knew that now, and had most likely known it on some level then. But today was a different day, and she wasn't the one Nate McCall wanted to mess with.

"Now, I've already contacted my attorney. I gave her Chris's name since I figured you'd call him to represent you, so she'll be in touch with him later this week. For now, I want the house and my car, and we'll work the rest out. I've got a meeting to go to, so you have three hours to get the rest of your crap out of here." She didn't know how much longer she could resist the burning urge to cry.

It'd plagued her all day as well while she'd moved about the house gathering his stuff. Every room she walked in held a memory of their life together. Everything she touched in this house, every picture, every scent, it all circled right back to him—her husband—and the life they'd built as a couple. The life that was in shambles right now. But she hadn't cried, hadn't shed one tiny tear. Instead, she'd reminded herself that this was something she should've done a long time ago and that she wasn't going to look back. The past was done, and she didn't know what the future held; all she knew was that she wasn't spending another day pretending to be the happily married Rita McCall.

"You're out of your mind," he said and ran a hand down his face.

"No," she told him. "I'm finally in my right mind."

"She's lying, Rita. That's not my baby," he implored, his tone softer than it had been before.

The chuckle came abruptly from her as she continued to swallow back tears. "You're so pathetic. You didn't even have the good sense to say 'I didn't sleep with her' this time. No, you just went right for denying paternity."

He frowned. "Rita, let's sit down and talk."

"No, Nate. I'm done talking. Get your crap and get out!"

She left him standing there, walking out of the room as normally as she possibly could, and headed down the hall. Her hand held tight to the banister as she made it to the stairs and took them one by one. She didn't trust her legs, nor the tears that now stung her eyes. Biting her bottom lip, she prayed long and hard that they wouldn't fall. She couldn't cry over him. Not today. Not ever. Crying wasn't going to change what he'd done, and it wasn't going to stop the tightening that had been in her chest since that phone had rung at 5:18 this morning.

Walking into the living room, she found her purse and checked inside to make sure she had her keys and her cell phone. Then she went to the garage and climbed into her car. There she sat for she didn't know how long, just staring through the windshield trying to make sense of all that had happened.

Three weeks ago when Nate had returned from a business trip, Rita had been in the bedroom removing the plastic from the clothes she'd picked up from the cleaners. Nate had come up behind her, wrapping his arms around her waist in that way he always did, pulling her back against him. She'd immediately leaned into him. From day one he'd been her rock, someone she could go to and talk about anything—her hopes, dreams, plans.

She'd missed him more during that last trip than she ever had before and had inhaled deeply of his scent, folding her arms over his at her waist as he kissed her temple. He'd whispered something about missing her and needing her, and Rita had mimicked his words. When he'd lowered his hands to unbutton the jeans she'd been wearing, Rita hadn't stopped him, and moments later he'd been pushing deep inside her, filling her in that way that only Nate had ever been able to do. He'd been her first lover, her only lover, her entire life.

Letting her forehead rest on the steering wheel now, she cursed herself for being such a fool. Nate had probably been with one of his hoes that time as well, and he'd come home to her, having sex with her in the same way . . . the same way he had their entire marriage. With no condom.

And now he had another woman pregnant, so he'd likely been with her with no condom. Fury mixed with pain, and she gripped the steering wheel while closing her eyes tightly. She wanted to kill him. Not only had he cheated on her and humiliated her, but he could've possibly infected her with any number of sexually transmitted diseases with his irresponsibility. She groaned and lurched back in the seat, this time slamming her fists onto her thighs.

With jerky movements, she pulled her phone from her purse and dialed her GYN's number. It was just after four, so she'd be cutting it close to the time the office would close for the day. After scheduling an appointment for next week, she tossed the phone onto the passenger seat and took out her keys to press the button that opened the garage door. She started the car, backed out of the garage, and heard the tires squeal over the asphalt as she drove as fast as she could out of Willow Grove and away from all the memories of what her life had been there.

Chapter 6

NEVER LET THEM SEE YOU SWEAT.

Thankful for the well-known roads that she could travel along without much thought beyond safe driving, Rita let her hands rest on the steering wheel while sitting at a red light. "It's Not Over," a familiar gospel song, played on the radio, and she hummed along with the verse, feeling the power of the inspiring words wash over her. Help was on the way, that was what the lyrics said, and she let them resonate. Her fingers clenched the wheel when she wondered about the form that help would take.

She'd been created to be a wife, a mother, a woman of faith. What happened when she failed at one? That would surely be her mother's topic of conversation when Rita told her about the divorce. Had she done everything she could to save the marriage, to be all that Nate needed so he'd never have a reason to stray?

With disappointment and irritation still bubbling in the pit of her stomach, the words to the song blurred, and she stared down at her hands. At the left ring finger to be exact, where the light spot from her rings basically shouted out to her. There'd never been a day in her twenty-three years of marriage that she'd even considered being unfaithful to Nate. And there'd been plenty of times during those years that he'd been less than what she needed from a husband. She wouldn't shoulder the blame for his infidelity; it just wasn't going to happen that way.

With a shake of her head, she eased a hand from the steering wheel and changed the station on the radio. R & B singer Monica's soulful voice blared through the speakers now as she declared she was still standing after trials and tribulations. Rita turned up the volume before easing her foot off the brake and proceeding through the light.

This wasn't her fault. She wasn't going to allow anyone to tell her any differently. She made a left turn at the next light and continued down a long narrow road. Mature trees and miles of fresh grass lined the path, and Rita took in a deep breath, releasing it slowly. Rolling her neck on her shoulders, she tried to refocus her thoughts, to look toward the future, telling herself it would be as bright as the sun shining through her windshield.

Jolting at the sound of her phone ringing through the music playing on the radio, she used one hand to insert her earbud into her ear and answered the call.

"Hey, Rita, it's Phyllis. I had a few additions to the menu for next week."

Rita rolled her eyes, grateful that this wasn't a FaceTime call, which Phyllis was known for. Phyllis Wyatt's daughter was pregnant with twins, but the baby shower Phyllis was planning was fit for five or six babies. If Rita had a dime for every addition Phyllis had made since hiring Rita to cater this shower two months ago, she'd be well on her way to purchasing a new diamond ring to fill in the empty space she couldn't stop staring at on her left hand.

"We've already finalized the menu, Phyllis." She spoke in her best professional tone because it would never do to let anyone know what she was really going through.

Something else her mother had taught her: *Never let them see you sweat, Rita. People don't need to know what's going on in your personal life for you to fulfill your purpose.* Vi lived by the words, as nobody at NVB ever knew what was going on in the pastor and first lady's household. All they saw was the unity of the couple in church and their unwavering faith. Anything less would've been worse than a scandal, as far as Vi was concerned.

"I know, but, see, I've got family comin' in from Atlanta, and my uncle Carl loves fried green tomatoes and vegetable soup. So I figured we can have that on the buffet as well. And then red velvet cake, my grandmother loves that. She'll be so tickled to see we remembered," Phyllis continued.

To Rita's way of thinking, this last-minute adjustment wasn't really based on Phyllis wanting to do something nice for her family. It was Phyllis's way of showing said family she could throw the biggest, most elaborate baby shower any of them had ever seen. She'd seen it before, this endless need to impress people that didn't have much more than Phyllis did just to feel superior. It was annoying, especially on a day when the last thing Rita wanted to think about was fried green tomatoes and vegetable soup.

Rita used her finger and thumb to pinch the bridge of her nose and released a slow breath before replying, "You already have three meat selections, four salads, green beans, collards, and spinach on the buffet. I really don't think there's room to add anything else." Unless they were having a soul-food-dinner feast instead of the early-afternoon baby shower, which was the original plan.

How had she gotten roped into taking this job? Oh, she knew how, because for the past ten years she'd been catering for the church and all of Nate's business functions. Word of mouth could be the best form of publicity or the devil wrapped in foil in a lightning storm. Outside of those two places and her family functions, Rita had begun getting calls to do private events at least a few times a year, and because she hadn't been doing anything other than taking care of her family, tending to her church duties, and keeping an eye on the management of the car dealerships she and Nate owned, she'd accepted the jobs. The money she earned from them had gone into a bank account with only her name on it, something she'd felt guilty about for a while but now, with her uncertain future ahead, she was thankful for.

"Nobody counts how many food dishes are on a buffet, Rita." Phyllis's tone was filled with a bit of haughtiness and a splash of annoyance. "Everybody will talk badly about an event if there isn't enough food."

Rita had been doing this for a while, so she knew how to prepare for the 148-person baby shower without a problem. Adding more dishes to the menu wasn't the answer. But the customer was always right. Not really, but she was in no mood to argue with Phyllis over some tomatoes and red velvet cake when she needed to figure out how she was going to navigate being a single woman after all this time.

"I'll see what I can do, Phyllis. I like to use a specific type of tomato when I fry them. If I can get to the farmer's market and find some, I'll add it to the menu."

"And the soup and the cake, 'cause Granny'll love having a big slice of red velvet after dinner," Phyllis added.

There was already a three-tier Thing One and Thing Two lemon yogurt cake and a parade of vanilla cupcakes continuing the Dr. Seuss story theme, not to mention the full candy bar that three weeks ago had been a must-have. Granny wasn't going to lack for anything sweet to eat at this shindig.

"I can contact the same baker who's doing the cake and cupcakes to see if they have time to add a red velvet cake. Just a ten-inch round cake should suffice because we have all the other dessert items and the goody bags everyone will go home with," Rita said. Goody bags on top of the candy bar was way more than she thought was necessary, but again, she aimed to please her clients. "The soup shouldn't be a problem at all." Just another thing she'd have to prep the night before, but that was fine. The shower was next Friday evening. On that Thursday, she was supposed to go with Nate and a few of his business associates to dinner in Annapolis. She mentally scratched that off her calendar.

"Great! I knew I could count on you!" Phyllis sounded happy and, in the end, that was all that mattered. A happy client paid on time and referred her to others.

Was that what she wanted? To continue being referred for catering jobs where clients asked for way more than was needed at over-the-top events? Shaking her head, Rita admitted she had no clue what she wanted right now.

"Yes, you can," she told Phyllis and said her goodbyes before disconnecting the call. Phyllis loved to talk, and the more she talked the more things she was likely to add to this shower.

Rita frowned as she pulled the earbud from her ear and glanced down at the time on her phone screen. She'd been out driving around for much longer than she'd anticipated. Now she had about a half hour to get back to Willow Grove and the HOA meeting she definitely didn't feel like attending.

Twenty minutes later, Rita walked into the Clubhouse—a redbrick building located at the farthest end of the Willow Grove development. The space, which on the inside resembled the VFW hall her uncle Jimmy's crab feasts were held at every August, could fit up to sixty people in its main room. There were three other smaller rooms that they sometimes rented out to members of the community, and a kitchen. This main area could also be rented by residents, but the HOA board had voted that no liquor could be consumed on the premises, which was why Rita had never rented it for her large family gatherings. If there was something the Johnson family liked just as much as they enjoyed good food, it was good liquor. It was a wonder Vi's holy lifestyle withstood that family trait.

A few residents had already shown up for the meeting, and Rita made her way to the front of the room, where two six-foot-long tables were pushed together. Six chairs, one for each member of the board, were positioned behind the table. Ethel, the president of the HOA board, was already settled in the center seat, her infamous black binder and pen on the table in front of her. The woman's reproachful gaze found Rita as she made her way behind the table to take her seat to the right of her.

"I was starting to think you wouldn't make it." Ethel whispered the comment, making sure her ruby-red lips barely moved so that no one in the audience would know she was chastising her vice president. "I mean, considering all the excitement this morning, it would've been understandable if you'd opted to stay home and recuperate."

Rita pulled out the chair and sat down. "I'm not sick." And she wouldn't dare give Ethel the pleasure of issuing a fake sympathy report at the meeting.

"Oh, I know. I just meant—"

"It's fine," Rita said, holding up a hand to stop the rest of Ethel's sentence. "I know what you meant."

Normally, Rita exercised the patience of a mother dealing with her toddler children whenever she was in Ethel's company. She spoke in a gentle but firm tone, making sure to afford the older woman respect while still giving the impression that she would in no way tolerate her getting out of pocket. Ethel had a mean streak that Rita, the other members of the board, and some of the residents had been witness to on more than one occasion. If she could've kept her distance from the woman, Rita certainly would have. But Nate loved to brag about how Rita was active in their community, taking where they lived and the environment they'd raised their children in very seriously. While all he took seriously was sleeping with every woman he could without his wife finding out.

Frowning, she looked to the other end of the table and greeted the remaining board members. When she looked out to the audience again, it was to see that more people had begun to file in and take their seats.

Jemel and Omar came in, sitting in the back row, which Rita knew was Jemel's preference.

Omar Kelly lived in the house next to Jemel's with his husband, Jason Corbet, and their lazy but adorable English bulldog, Trixter. Omar and Jason were fashion stylists who'd instantly become like family to Rita and Jemel when they moved into Willow Grove a few years ago and received more staring and judgmental whispers than was necessary. The bighearted couple was also good for Jemel, in that they tended to keep her a little more grounded than she was used to being. At least that was before Jemel's on-again, off-again boyfriend, Marc, came back into the picture. Now, Rita and Sharae, as well as Omar and Jason, were keeping an eye on that relationship, all of them prepared to pick up the pieces when or if it went south.

Moments later, Ethel called the meeting to order and efficiently moved down the agenda, passing the microphone to whichever board member was responsible for the next report. Kemp Webster presented the financial report, and Rita almost laughed as she noticed Jemel frowning as Kemp went over the importance of everyone paying their eighty-five-dollar HOA fees on time. Sharae thought it was a sin and a shame that people had to pay for others to dictate how homeowners in this upscale neighborhood would take care of their homes. Jemel agreed, but on the other hand, loved that she didn't have to do any land-scaping if she didn't want to because the association paid for someone to do it on a weekly basis.

The meeting dragged on while Rita's thoughts continued to stray. Why was she even here? Why couldn't she have barricaded herself in her bedroom and focused on her next steps? Because she was expected to keep going, no matter what. All Black women were. Square her shoulders, hold her head up high, and never—ever—let them see her sweat.

"I'm just mentioning that having events on the property that invite an unsavory element into our community might be an issue," Ethel was saying when Rita's attention zoomed in on Jemel once more.

"And by *unsavory*, what exactly do you mean?" Jemel—who was standing now, with one hand on her hip—asked.

Ethel was in her early fifties. She was just a whisper taller than Jemel's short stature, with a deep mocha complexion and black hair that was often styled in big tight curls—the kind only made by those ancient sponge rollers Aunt Ceil and her mother used to put in her, Jemel's, and Sharae's hair when they were little. "I mean, persons with a criminal history," Ethel replied.

The condescending tone was nothing new where Ethel was concerned. Ethel thought she knew everything about everybody and led the perfect life that gave her the authority to correct anybody she chose. It was why so many people in the development referred to her as a loudmouth know-it-all.

Rita had missed the conversation leading up to this point, but she recalled something in the meeting notes and the attached police report Ethel had emailed her earlier today about Janice Spencer's flowerpot being stolen.

"So you think somebody who was at my family's cookout last night stole a flowerpot? You do know that I own a florist shop. If somebody in my family wanted a flowerpot, they could've easily come to me to get one."

Wait, was that what was going on here? Was Ethel really accusing them of being responsible for the theft?

"First of all," Rita said. She cleared her throat just to give herself another few seconds to keep a handle on her composure. "The police report says the pot was stolen two days ago. There's no way someone who was at my house last night could've taken it."

Ethel lifted her chin in defiance. "This isn't the first time those persons have been at your house."

Now Rita stood and stared down at Ethel. "Those persons are my family," she said.

This could go one of two ways: If Ethel backed down from this ridiculous accusation in the next few moments, Rita could walk out of this meeting with the same general irritation that Ethel always provoked in her. But if this high-and-mighty loud-and-wrong excuse for an adult continued down this path, Rita wasn't so sure she could hold on to the calm demeanor she was known for. Too much had happened today, and try as she might to keep it all together, she could feel something inside her starting to shift right now.

"Well," Ethel replied before tossing a look out to the crowd and shrugging, "we all have to come to terms with certain blemishes in our bloodline. And really, Rita, after what happened this morning, I'd say there are a lot of unwanted behaviors that may need to be addressed from your residence."

"Oh, I've got something to come to terms with," Rita said and took another step toward Ethel. Meryl Ripley, the board's secretary, who'd been sitting on Rita's other side, jumped up from her seat then, moving to stand between Rita and Ethel, while Kemp cleared his throat loudly and grabbed Ethel by the shoulders the second she popped up from her seat. Out of the corner of her eye, Rita could see Jemel hurrying out of her row and heading to the front of the room. No doubt, her cousin was ready to put hands on Ethel if that was what Rita was planning to do. If there was one thing that didn't go over well with any of the Johnsons, it was somebody speaking ill of their family members. Rita had never been one to rush into fistfights with members of her family, or outsiders for that matter, but that didn't mean she couldn't handle her business.

"I'm going to wait for an apology from you for those offensive and baseless remarks," she said in lieu of actually tossing out the first blow. As an adult and a cousin of two cops, she had a basic understanding of what constituted assault. Even if she'd been blurry on the arson or destruction-of-property ordinances earlier this morning.

"I am just stating general facts. Everyone knows you have lots of gatherings here with your family members. We also know that those family members aren't from the Willow Grove community, which means they haven't been properly vetted," Ethel said.

"Properly vetted?" Rita questioned, and started to lean more toward just punching Ethel in her loud mouth.

Omar and Jemel appeared at her side then, both of them taking hold of one of her wrists.

"Let's go," Jemel said.

"No! She's got something she wants to get off her chest. Well, so do I!" Rita yelled back at Ethel.

Jemel shook her head and held tighter to Rita's arm. Omar did the same from the other side.

"When they go low, we go high, Rita," Omar said.

"No," Rita snapped back. "We go upside their head." She was tired of taking the high road.

Jemel started pulling Rita back at that point. "That's enough. You know she's full of herself. Let's just go."

"She's not gonna accuse my family members of stealing some stupid flowerpot and get away with it!" Rita yelled.

Rita never yelled. Not even at her daughters, who could certainly push the envelope on her nerves. The rest of the attendees had stood as well, some of them turning and walking out the door. Others came closer to the table as if they were ready for the entertainment an altercation between Rita and Ethel was sure to be. May Young, a twentysomething who'd just moved in about a year ago with her boyfriend and two loud and annoying shih tzu dogs, had her phone out filming everything.

It took a few more minutes for Omar and Jemel to get Rita outside, and when they did, she pulled away from their grasps. Wiping her hands down the front of her blouse and pants like she'd somehow gotten dirty by just arguing, Rita shook her head.

"You cool now?" Omar asked.

The glare she tossed at him was enough of an answer as Omar threw up both his hands in mock surrender.

"How 'bout we go to my place and have a drink?" Jemel asked.

"I don't need a drink," Rita replied and lifted a hand to fix her hair.

It was probably just fine, not one strand out of place, as usual. Just like the black capris and crisp white T-shirt she wore with cute velvet, black jeweled sandals was a casual-chic outfit. The hair, the outfit, her attitude (sans Ethel stepping way out of line), all of it was Rita's signature, along with her steady and relaxed attitude. Today just wasn't her day. And something deep inside warned tomorrow and the days that followed weren't going to be much better.

Taking a deep breath and letting it out with a quiet sigh, Rita continued, "I'm going home."

"We'll come with you. I'm sure you have something left over from last night we can use to calm our nerves after that little incident." Omar rubbed a hand over his mouth and gave an exaggerated look back at the clubhouse.

"I don't need a drink." Her response was quick and sassy, as her mother would've said if she were here. "I'm going home. I'll call you tomorrow." Before she turned away, she glanced at Omar. "Both of you."

That was her apology to Omar for biting his head off . . . twice. He wisely accepted it in silence and stood by Jemel as they both watched her walk away.

Chapter 7

Go for the balls, and squeeze until he passes out.

"So, you dodged a bullet," Malik Jennings said the moment Sharae climbed into the passenger side of the car and closed the door, a little after one o'clock that afternoon.

Reaching for the seat belt, she frowned and said, "Barely."

Malik's wry chuckle seconds before he pulled out of the station parking lot was familiar. They'd been partners for three years, had investigated over a hundred murder cases together, and had spent more time in each other's company than Sharae had with any other man—not related—in her life.

"His comments were basically 'I should write you up,' and 'Get your shit together,' all tied in with that I-expect-nothing-less-from-a-woman-like-you glare. I swear I hate it here," she groaned.

Both of them knew that last part was a lie. Sharae didn't hate her job; to the contrary, she loved every second of being a cop. She was living her dream.

"Hall's old school," Malik said, referring to the captain of the homicide division. "But he can also be an ass."

One of the things she admired about Malik was his ability to see through all the crap in their business and get right down to the truth. At least he'd been that way until a case they'd worked a few months back where Malik had gotten caught up with his high school sweetheart who'd also been a suspect. They'd spent weeks after the case was closed going over all the reasons why he should've backed out of investigating it, so his next comment was no surprise to Sharae.

"You could've just called me and had me go over there," he said before making a left turn. "I mean, you had to know it was gonna come down to this."

Unable to hide her defensive tone, she asked, "How was I supposed to know what was going on before I got there? She's my cousin, and she never even double-parks, let alone breaks any laws. It freaked me out to hear her address coming over the scanner."

Glancing over, she saw Malik nod. His complexion was a shade darker than hers, and he sported a thin mustache-and-goatee combo lined as perfectly as his close-cropped wavy black hair. They were going to follow up on some leads, so he wore a light-gray suit, white shirt, and a gray-and-white tie that she knew was probably silk and ridiculously expensive. Malik loved clothes, casual and dress. He looked good in all of them and knew it too.

"I get that, but what'd you tell me before? A few seconds to think things through would've saved a couple of hours of misery."

"That's not what I said, and this is not the same." She looked out the window. "You were sleeping with a suspect."

"And this time you'd been at the suspect's house hours earlier, drinking and line dancin' in the grass. Same personal link."

Shaking her head, she continued, "Different circumstances entirely. Rita isn't a murder suspect."

He chuckled. "From what I heard, she killed those clothes and tennis shoes. Jordans, Sharae? Your cousin was burnin' classic Jordans in her driveway!" His incredulous tone had continued from when she'd called him after leaving the courthouse to tell him what had happened.

"When a guy rips your heart out, you go for the balls and squeeze until he passes out," she replied. "I bet Nate's trifling ass will wanna die the second he finds out those shoes are now a big black ash stain on the cement." She wished she could have seen his face when Rita told him what she'd done. The look of shock and rage would be pure enjoyment for her—that is, if she could've restrained herself long enough without punching that bastard in his lying face.

"How would you know? When you never give a guy your heart to rip out?" Malik asked.

"Damn right," she replied with no remorse. "They don't deserve it."

Malik grinned. "You might be right about that."

Their topic of conversation switched to a comedian host on a radio show and some silly comment he'd made that was under heated debate between his cohosts. That foolishness managed to take Sharae's mind off Captain Hall's dismissive attitude toward her this afternoon. She should probably be thankful that a big break in a high-profile robbery-homicide case had come in about half an hour after she'd arrived back at the station from court. She'd gone into Hall's office to deliver her report on the incident at Rita's, knowing he was on his way out to a press conference, hoping he'd take the report and go on about his business. To her chagrin, he'd stuck around for the longest five minutes of her life to bluster and berate her before stomping off.

It was just as well. She'd been there and done that same dance with him on a few occasions before. And Hall was definitely one of those leopards who was never changing his spots. Sharae just didn't have the time or inclination to deal with his old-school misogynistic mentality toward women on the force.

Malik parked the dark-colored sedan with the front facing the curb. This break in one of their most recent cases had led them to a townhome development where all the houses were neat and basically identical—except for a three-color pattern of doors and matching window shutters. Sharae reached into the inside of her jacket pocket for her notepad.

"Alicia Watkins has lived here for seven years with her aunt and uncle. She has two daughters, who go to the local elementary and middle school a few miles from here. Two DUIs and four trespassing charges in the past eighteen months. Currently on a three-year probation plan, which includes weekly drug monitoring." After reciting the notes she'd jotted down before leaving the precinct, she closed the notepad and stuffed it back into her pocket.

"Well, if this tip pans out, she's violated that probation in the worst way," Malik said before climbing out of the car.

Sharae followed him, grimly agreeing with his assessment. The narcotics division had picked up two junkies and a handful of low-level dealers during a raid in Ellicott City last night. One of the dealers was looking for a deal and dropped Alicia Watkins's name as an accomplice to Sharae and Malik's double homicide. They were going into this house to question Alicia and, if need be, arrest her.

After they rang the doorbell three times, a girl who looked to be no older than eleven or twelve opened the door. Her sandy-brown hair was styled in box braids and hung past her slim shoulders. She wore a school uniform—light-blue polo shirt and navy-blue pants.

"Hey." Malik spoke first while the girl continued her blatant perusal of them both. "I'm Detective Jennings, and this is my partner, Detective Gibson. We're looking for Alicia Watkins. Is she home?"

The girl shook her head. "Nope."

It was a little early for them to be out of school, but their district could've had a half day today. Sharae had no kids, and the nieces she was closest to were adults, so she wouldn't know that for certain. "Are your aunt and uncle home?" she asked, trying to sound a little friendlier than Malik had.

Keen golden-brown eyes zeroed in on Sharae and held her gaze. There was no fear in the depths of those young eyes, only intense sadness that rang all too familiar for Sharae. She took a deep breath before continuing. "If they're home, we'd like to speak to them."

"They ain't here either," the girl replied and folded her arms across her chest.

"Are you home alone?" Sharae asked. She thought about bending over so she would be eye to eye with the girl, but she wasn't sure that would be helpful. Whatever her age, this girl was more mature than she should be. Sharae could tell by the way she opened the door and stood ready to answer any questions and protect whoever was in that house with her. Narrow shoulders were squared, one foot extended farther out than the other, as she waited impatiently for them to be finished here.

"Why?" was the girl's response.

"Maybe we can come in and talk to you and your sister," Sharae suggested.

Malik, whose demeanor was obviously better with women his age—whom he'd been intimately involved with—than with this younger girl, sighed impatiently. "How old are you?"

The girl rolled her eyes in his direction. "Eleven," she said and then sucked her teeth. "Y'all gotta come back when somebody else is home. I can't keep this door open long."

Before Sharae could ask another question, the little sister she'd suspected was there came into view. She eased next to her older sister, staring at Sharae with almost identical eyes, except hers were filled with innocence and acceptance. "Hi," she said in a tiny voice and gave a little wave. "Did my daddy send you here to pick us up?"

"Shut up, girl! These are police. They not here to take us to Daddy's house," the older sister yelled.

They were waiting for their father. Sharae's chest instantly hurt, and her breaths became a little more labored as she tried to keep her focus.

She'd never waited for Sanford Gibson to pick her up. She'd known he would be in jail forever, and she hadn't given a damn about it either. That was where he'd belonged after the way he'd torn her family apart. Yet she couldn't keep her mind from circling back to the lawyer's business card she slipped into her pocket earlier today.

This time she did bend down until she could stare into the younger girl's eyes. "What's your name, sweetheart?"

"Destiny," the girl replied.

Sharae extended a hand. "It's nice to meet you, Destiny." The girl happily reached out to shake Sharae's hand. "Can we come in to wait for your aunt and uncle to return home?"

"Y'all can be lyin'," the older girl said. "You ain't show me no badge or nuthin'."

Malik pulled out his badge, eased it close to the older girl's face, and then stepped forward. "We're coming in under suspicion that the two of you are too young to be left alone in the home of a convicted felon."

Sharae didn't agree with the way he used his size and position to step around the older sister and into the house, but she followed him, her attention focused on both girls as she closed the door behind them.

"Our daddy's on his way to get us," Destiny told Sharae as she now stood in the living room.

The scent of cigarette smoke mixed with a cotton-scented air freshener she suspected was plugged into one of the outlets assaulted her nose. The Aunts loved using plug-ins throughout their houses, which was how Sharae knew the varying scents. Fresh cotton was one of Aunt Rose's favorites.

"Stop tellin' all our business," the older girl snapped and walked away. "Besides, he was 'sposed to be here hours ago."

Destiny crossed the room to where her older sister now stood at the window. "He's late again, Jazzy?"

Jazzy nodded in jerky movements. "Yeah, Des. He's late again."

But Jazzy's tone sounded more like she didn't expect her father to come at all. Sharae sucked in a sharp breath as she realized she'd never expected to hear from Sanford again. Or to find out he was dead.

"We can't touch anything 'cause we don't have a warrant, but I'm gonna look around," Malik said, his words pulling her out of her thoughts. "You give social services a call. I don't want to leave them here alone."

She didn't either. Their father wasn't coming to pick them up. Jazzy knew that, but she was trying to give Destiny hope. As Sharae pulled her phone out of her pocket, Desmond Brown's business card came out with it. She stared down at the lawyer's name and number and knew instinctively that any hope she'd ever had of letting her father rot in jail forever was gone. The memory of the man who'd taken everything she loved away from her was coming back in forceful dark waves, and she didn't have a moment to catch her breath because she had a job to do. There were two young girls who needed the attention that Sanford hadn't been able to give Sharae because he was a cold-blooded killer.

Chapter 8

STARVE A COLD, FEED A ... PISSED-OFF DAUGHTER.

Humming was in no way as satisfying as cooking; still, Rita was doing both on Wednesday evening. Taryn and Necole were coming over for dinner, so she'd changed out of the old sweatpants and tank top she'd been walking around the house in all day, and slipped on black ankle pants and a red blouse. In the back of her mind, she could hear Sharae chuckling and asking why she thought she had to get dressed a certain way for her daughters to come over. But for Rita, her clothes, her hair, the personality she showed to everyone, were all part of the complete package. The carefully put-together woman who was determined not to shatter. At least not again, since yesterday's driveway scene was still fresh in her mind.

She didn't put on shoes, but instead slipped on a pair of Cruella de Vil ankle socks because they matched. And she was a Disney villains fan, now and forever. That was probably the one wild streak she allowed herself in life, and she planned to hold on to it tightly.

The russet potatoes had been cut into long slim strips and now waited in a bowl of warm water while the oil in the double-basket deep fryer heated. She'd cook them first and then add the crab cakes so in case a fishy tinge was left in the grease, it wouldn't seep into the fries.

Going to the refrigerator, she retrieved the glass bowl that contained the pound of lump crab meat she'd carefully picked this morning.

Her humming continued as she took down another bowl and began adding the ingredients to her binding mixture. The old Natalie Cole tune had been on her mind all day. Vi loved her some Natalie Cole and used to blast that in the house almost as much as she did her gospel music. Natalie sang about an everlasting love, but Rita had already started to believe that was an impossibility.

She was just about to scoop out the amount of mayonnaise she needed to start the binding mixture when the alarm sounded, signaling that someone with a key and who knew the code had entered the house.

"You put Daddy out of his house?" Taryn asked the moment she walked into the kitchen, and Rita's humming stopped. The heels to the white sandals she wore clicked loudly over the gray tile. "He stopped by our place this morning and told us what you did and that now you're ignoring his text messages. Don't you think that's a little immature?"

Rita continued to scoop the mayonnaise, dropping it into a second empty bowl. She closed the container and reached for the yellow mustard. At least Necole, her youngest child, came over to kiss Rita on the cheek before she started with her interrogation.

"Is it true? Are you really divorcing Daddy?" Her tone was much calmer than Taryn's, which was the norm since Taryn was boisterous and extroverted like her father, and Necole was compassionate and easygoing like Rita. At least that's what Aunt Ceil always said.

Both Taryn and Necole had Rita's honey complexion. Taryn even shared Rita's narrow nose, easy smile, and high cheekbones. Today, her eldest wore a lavender shirtdress, belted at the waist. Her hair hung past her shoulders in a light, wavy style. She, like Rita, loved to dye her hair, and today's color was a soft bronze highlight that mixed well with her natural dark-brown tresses. Necole wore her caramel-brown natural curls pulled up into a high puff. Her yellow jumper highlighted amber eyes that were the same as Rita's.

"Hi, baby," Rita said to Necole and then looked over to where Taryn stood at the end of the island as if she needed space. "Hello, Taryn."

Rita watched as Taryn placed her small purse with its chain strap on the island and stood with one hand on her slim hip.

Thoughts of when Rita had considered herself grown enough to stand in her mother's kitchen with her hand on her hip crossed her mind. That had ended with Vi reminding Rita that there was only one woman in that house that was grown enough to stand that way, and Rita wasn't that one. Rita declined to say the same thing to Taryn because she'd thought it a foolish statement when her mother had said it. After all, it didn't matter how old she was, she had hips just like her mother did. Still, the sentiment alluded to disrespect, and the instant tinge of irritation at her daughter's tone and posture could attest to Vi's instincts.

"I'm just mixing up the crab cakes. Necole, you can start the fries," she said, deciding it was best to keep talking instead of thinking. Rita measured out the mustard, dropped it into the bowl, and closed that container. She picked up the ground mustard and shook the desired amount into the mixture as well. A few years ago, she'd written down her recipe for crab cakes, just in case her daughters might want it in the future. But she never pulled it out when she was actually cooking. Years of being in the kitchen with the Aunts and her grandmother had taught her to measure with sight and taste.

"I'd hoped to have a nice dinner with you two and tell you first, but since your father beat me to it, yes, we're getting a divorce." And she hated Nate a little bit more for rushing over to see the girls before Rita could talk to them. Clearly, he'd wanted them to hear his side of the story first. She refrained from sighing, just kept moving and kept acting as if everything would be all right. There really was no other option.

"You think food fixes everything!" Taryn huffed. "Well, it doesn't. And my father is hurting. He's staying at a hotel, you know."

She did know, because one of his many text messages she'd received told her so, but she'd decided not to care. Actually, she'd thought he would do what she said and go back to stay with the hoochie he'd impregnated, but in the end, it was better not to think about that either.

Rita went to the refrigerator and retrieved an egg. She cracked it, and while it dropped into the bowl, she glanced at her daughter. "Food doesn't fix everything, but it calms your nerves while you figure out what to do."

Grandma Patty used to say that whenever Rita joined her in the kitchen. Her grandmother's kitchen was half the size of this one, which Rita had painstakingly designed to her specifications. But as far as her grandmother and great-grandma Fannie were concerned, food was everything to their family. It was the glue that had held them together throughout the hard years of slavery and into the world that still didn't want Black people there.

"If you sit down and take a breath, you could calm your own nerves." Rita went to the sink and dropped the eggshells into the garbage disposal.

"You know *calm*'s not in Taryn's vocabulary," Necole said. She'd done as her mother had told her and was now lowering the first basket full of uncooked potatoes into the hot grease. The sizzling sound of contact filled the kitchen, but Rita still heard Taryn suck her teeth.

"Now's really not the time to be a kiss-up, Nikki," she said and rolled her eyes at her sister.

"Don't talk to your sister that way." Rita had never stood for bickering or teasing between her daughters. "Look, I know this isn't easy for either of you to hear, but your father has been seeing another woman. I found out because she called me to inform me that she's having his baby." She waited a beat, looking from one daughter to the next to see if Nate had left that little tidbit of information out of his talk with them.

"And you believe her?" Necole asked.

Because discussing this deeply personal situation with her daughters was more than a little uncomfortable, Rita went back to her cooking. She picked up the plastic bag full of bread crumbs she'd shredded to a fine texture earlier today and poured them into the bowl. This was the secret to the best crab cakes—the less filler that was tasted in the cake, the better. So, chewing her cakes was like tasting a mouthful of even more flavorful meat than was fresh out of the shell. After the bread crumbs, she added Worcestershire sauce, salt, pepper, and of course, a healthy dose of Old Bay Seasoning. She used a fork to stir the mixture and was either so focused on the task or too deep into her thoughts to stop, because the next thing she knew, Necole was touching her arm, whispering, "Mama, are you okay?"

"What?" she asked and then looked down at the wet mixture that had been mixed almost to a liquid status. "Oh. Dang it. I'm sorry, got carried away." She reached for the bowl of crab meat and dumped it into the bowl with the wet mixture.

"You didn't answer her question," Taryn said. "Do you believe this chick that called you?"

Rita had thought about this all last night and then a good portion of today. She was actually tired of thinking about it and hoped this would be the one and only time she'd have to discuss it again. Well, except for whenever she decided to tell the Aunts.

"I do," she said and then began combining the meat into the wet mixture. Out of the corner of her eye she saw Necole removing the first baskets of fries and refilling them with the rest of the potatoes.

Rita loved potatoes, but she could stand to cut down on her starch intake, so she only planned to eat a crab cake.

"Just like that? You don't even know her." Taryn was beyond upset, and the hurt tingeing her angry tone broke Rita's heart. "And who even calls the wife anymore? That's not what side chicks do nowadays. They know how to play their position."

Rita frowned. "Meaning she decides to be a tawdry secret for the rest of her life." Rita could never, ever live that way.

Necole shrugged. "It's a real title with benefits for some women. But I never thought Daddy would . . . I mean, I still don't know if I believe it. Why don't you wait for a DNA test?"

"Thank you! Now you see what I'm saying," Taryn said to her sister before turning her attention back to Rita. "I feel like you rushed to a conclusion and just did what Aunt Sharae and Aunt Jemel told you to do."

That stung. "What do you mean by that? I don't do what anybody tells me to do, Taryn. I make my own decisions." Except that wasn't entirely true. A good portion of Rita's life was exactly as her mother had told her it should be, and look where that had led her.

Taryn didn't look like she believed Rita's words any more than Rita expected her to. Despite Rita trying to be a different type of parent than her mother had been to her, Taryn and Necole had been brought up in the same church, listening to the same rhetoric that Rita had as a child. They'd also sat at the same dining room table with the Aunts, hearing them give one lecture after another about how Black women should act, what they should wear, and whom they should love.

"I believed that woman because I know your father." It was on the tip of her tongue that this wasn't the first time that Nate had cheated on her, but it really wasn't her goal to tear down the father her daughters knew and loved.

"Obviously you don't. If you'd just waited and talked to me and Nikki first, we could've helped you see the truth."

"I don't need any help seeing the truth. And talking to you and your sister first wouldn't have changed my decision," she replied. "You and your sister have a right to your opinion; after all, this affects you too." Not nearly in the way that it affected Rita, but she wasn't going to totally count them out of the equation.

"Then why aren't you listening to us? It's like you're just hell-bent on doing your own thing. What is it? Do you have another guy?"

Rita turned at Taryn's words, staring into root-beer-brown eyes she'd gazed into when they were just three days old. Taryn had been five weeks premature, her four-and-a-half-pound body so light in Rita's arms. But when she'd cried, as Aunt Rose used to put it, "all hell broke loose." The thought almost had Rita smiling, but for the disgusted look that the adult Taryn was now tossing her way.

"I hear the concern and the hurt in you and your sister's voice, and I'm sorry for my part in the pain that you're experiencing." Hearing the disappointment and despair in her daughters' voices was breaking a part of Rita, another barrier she hadn't even realized she'd placed around her carefully manicured life. "But you obviously aren't listening to me."

With all the ingredients mixed, Rita pinched a piece and put it into her mouth to taste. It needed more Old Bay and mustard. She added them both before doing another taste. That was better, and she began patting handfuls of the mixture into cakes and placing them onto an empty plate while she waited for the fries to finish cooking. Rita preferred her crab cakes broiled, but her family had always loved them deep-fried. While she waited, she opened a cabinet and took out some plates.

There were no paper utensils used in Rita's house unless it was a cookout or other function that drew a crowd of people to her house. For the smaller dinner parties that she'd often hosted for Nate's business associates, she used the good china. Today, she used her everyday dishes, which were still very nice considering the hefty price tag they carried.

"We heard you say you kicked our father out of his own house."

Could a person dislike another person who'd been born from their very own body? She was starting to think so. How easy would it be to yell that she didn't owe Taryn or Necole any explanations? What happened between Rita and Nate was *their* business; it was *their* marriage that had fallen apart. None of that had anything to do with the daughters they shared, except, yeah, on some level it definitely did.

"It was time for him to go," Rita said quietly. She stood with her back to both her daughters now. "I wish he would've left years ago." She'd never admitted that to anyone before.

The shock of the statement had Taryn gasping and Rita moving quickly to put back all the ingredients she'd taken out for the mix.

"So, you checked out on the marriage a long time ago?"

"No, Taryn," Rita said, raising her voice louder than she'd intended. "Your father checked out each time he went home with another woman."

"He said that happened one time years ago and you've never let him forget it. What happened to forgiveness? I know you know what that is because Granddad's constantly yelling it from the pulpit, and you swear by everything he and the Bible say."

Spare the rod and spoil the child.

That wasn't the exact scripture—Rita did have Proverbs 13:24 and many other scriptures committed to memory—but that wasn't the point. The point was, she was dangerously close to shaking some sense into her oldest child.

Forgiveness was a slippery slope. She'd forgiven Nate so many times before, and he'd taken that as permission to do it again.

Rita had brought her daughters up in the church the same way her parents had done with her and Benny. While there'd been many strict rules and teachings her parents had pushed on Rita and her brother, there'd been some that she'd decided not to inflict on her children. The part where she would've been smacked in the mouth for taking this sassy tone with her mother had been one of them. For a brief moment, Rita regretted that decision, because the flippant way in which Taryn was speaking about things her mother had done was starting to piss her off.

"Look," Rita told her. "Your father shouldn't be talking to you about our personal business. And before you say it, this *is* personal, Taryn." She turned back to look at her daughter, who had her glossed lips turned up in consternation. Then she looked at her youngest child, who was moving slowly, taking the fries from the baskets and putting them in a towel-lined bowl. "The relationship between your father and I is personal. We're your parents, yes, but that's where it stops. I didn't invite the two of you here so you could question me or my motives. I called you both here to tell you what I'd decided. Now, you need to respect my decision."

"How can we when you're not even trying to fix this?" Taryn asked. Rita swore this was her most tenacious child.

"I don't want to fix it," Rita said evenly. "I don't want to be married to your father anymore." And she couldn't even say that was totally because of the affairs. Rita had been grappling with this all night.

"But why? He's a great guy!" Taryn really sounded like she didn't understand what was happening, and for a minute Rita understood.

"He really is, Mama. Maybe you should give him another chance," Necole added.

Her daughters' whole world was Nate, Rita, and the family unit they'd built. Sure, NVB and the Johnson family were extensions of that, but the girls had always turned to Rita and Nate. Mainly because Rita had made a point of telling them that what happened in their house was their business. They weren't allowed to tell anybody about things that went on in their house, and if they had a problem, it was expected that they'd bring it to Nate or Rita.

There'd been many nights that Rita second-guessed carrying that rule over from her childhood. Those were the first nights she'd discovered her husband was a lying, cheating fraud of a man.

"He's a great father," Rita said. She moved to the basket and put three large crab cakes in each before lowering them into the grease.

Then, she grabbed one of the dish towels that hung on the pewter cabinet handles. Wiping her hands, she turned so she could see both of her beautiful girls. After dropping the towel to the counter, she took Necole's hand and then walked over to the island to take a very reluctant Taryn's.

"That's all you and your sister need to worry about. How good a father he's been to you," she said softly.

"You've both been good parents," Necole said softly. "I never thought you'd break up, and I don't know how to deal with that now."

Rita nodded. "I know, baby. I'm not so sure I know how to deal with it either. But we will." That's what Black women did—they adjusted to whatever hands were dealt them, and they did so with their game faces on. Rita took a deep breath and released it slowly. "Let's sit down and have a nice dinner. You can tell me all about your trip."

Unfortunately for Rita, that wasn't the direction the dinner conversation took. About halfway through the meal, it'd been Taryn who'd asked, "What're you going to do now? Without Daddy to take care of you? Cook yourself into old age?"

Again, Rita had been stunned at the edge to her daughter's question, and after the day she'd had yesterday and the fitful night of sleep she'd endured, she really was ready to toss Taryn's smart-mouthed ass out of her house. Instead, she'd given the question the same thought she had last night and replied, "I don't know."

But hours after Taryn and Necole had helped clean the kitchen and left, Rita sat in the center of the bed she'd once shared with a loving husband and thought about Taryn's question again.

What was she going to do?

It wasn't that Nate had taken care of her. Sure, he was the one the girls saw leaving the house every day to work, and he was the face of McCall Motors, but he wasn't the only one who worked in their household. The car dealership had been started three years into their marriage when Nate and Rita were involved in a car accident. Their car had been totaled, and Nate had sustained mild injuries. But it was Rita who'd had a dislocated shoulder and required surgery and months of physical therapy to be whole again. When the settlements from both the personal-injury cases they'd filed came in, Rita's was for ten times more than Nate's. That was the money they'd used to start the dealership.

Aside from the money that fell into the what's-mine-is-yours-and-what's-yours-is-mine category so early on in their marriage, Rita had used everything she'd learned from her two years of evening business classes at community college and built the foundation of the dealership, while Nate took his charming persona out to the showroom to make the big deals that brought in even more money for them to eventually open more dealerships up and down the East Coast.

Jemel and Sharae were right each time they said McCall Motors was just as much hers as it was Nate's. Arguably more hers than his, if they were being technical. Which she wasn't. Rita had never thought that way. Everything they had always belonged to them, their family. The family that Nate had shredded with his wayward dick.

Shaking her head, Rita unfolded her legs and crawled across the bed to grab her iPad from the nightstand. Pulling up the online-banking website, she typed in her password and waited for the screen to change. She knew the balance in each of her and Nate's bank accounts, not because she counted their money obsessively, but mainly because she was the one who paid the household bills. But Taryn had said something else tonight that had stuck with Rita. *What're you going to do now? Cook yourself into old age?*

Rita had another account with the same bank, the one that she'd opened when she'd started receiving her catering payments. That was the account she was interested in tonight. It was a silly thought—one she'd brushed off yesterday after speaking with Phyllis about her larger-than-life baby shower—but one that had taken hold in the last few hours. Had she saved enough of her catering earnings to start something official? Could she really "cook herself into old age" by cooking for other people? She'd started a business before. Could she do it again? Or better yet, did she *want* to at this stage in her life?

All her thoughts and considerations stalled as she stared at the screen that showed the balance of all accounts with her name on them. The two at the top of the screen, the joint checking and savings accounts she shared with Nate, had a zero balance. Her heart thumped slowly, like it wasn't sure it wanted to keep going, and Rita blinked repeatedly. Praying, hoping, begging that this wasn't true. Her eyes had to be deceiving her. It was late. She'd eaten two crab cakes and a slice of carrot cake, and had drunk three glasses of wine before coming to bed. This could not be happening.

But when she opened her eyes again, those zeroes were still there, and a mixture of panic and anger shot through her chest like a flame-tipped arrow.

"Nate McCall, you lowdown sonofabit . . ." The last word gave way to a scream Rita felt as if she'd been holding in for a hundred years.

Chapter 9

TALKIN' SHIT.

"You still can't shuffle worth a damn," Tariq said, a frown marring his face.

One of Aunt Margaret's—who was actually Sharae's great-aunt—grandchildren, Tariq was five years older than Sharae and had been responsible for teaching her and Rita how to smoke when they were in high school. Tariq had been in the streets all his life, at least that's how the Aunts put it. Meaning, whenever Sharae, Rita, and Jemel wanted to know something the Aunts had forbidden them to do or learn about, Tariq was their go-to. He was also the Spades guru of the family. Nobody ever sat down at the card table to play without going through Tariq's crash course of Spades for Black folk, a set of rules he swore by and would freak the hell out about if others didn't follow. Dressed in a white T-shirt and dark-blue denim shorts, he'd reluctantly removed the Miami Heat fitted hat from his head when Aunt Ceil had come into the room and given him a warning gaze, followed by, "Hats off in the house. You know better." Tariq did know better, and Sharae had grinned before shaking her head, because as old as he was, he was still down for breaking whatever rules he possibly could.

"Man, shut up, I shuffled the cards," replied Ivan, Tariq's younger brother and Spades partner.

"Nah, I'm gettin' all the same cards 'cause you didn't shuffle good enough," Tariq countered.

Rule one for playing Spades with Black folk—know how to shuffle so the players won't receive the majority of their cards in the same suit. Tariq looked like he was about to flip the damn table over as he picked up each card and sorted it in his hand. Ivan, the more laid back and scholarly of the brothers, looked as unbothered as usual.

Organizing her cards by suit in her hand almost managed to relax Sharae completely. But too many things had happened this week to make that possible.

"Are y'all 'bout to be arguing all night?" Jemel asked from across the table. She'd pulled her wavy dark-brown hair back with a pink-and-white-striped satin band tonight. The band matched her tank top, and her white shorts were—as always—short, short.

"Girl, don't start. Just bid," Tariq replied. "I don't know why you're in such a hurry to get this ass whuppin' anyway."

"Oh boy, here we go," Sharae said. "You talkin' shit already."

Tariq folded his cards into one hand and slapped the palm of his empty hand to his chest. "That's what I do, bay-bee!"

Sharae couldn't help but laugh. Tariq was always entertaining, even when he was trying to get under somebody's skin for whatever reason. Talkin' shit was farther down on his list of rules, but he never forgot to bring it out in full force.

"What you got, Jem?" she asked, ignoring Tariq's glowing glare.

"Five and a possible," Jemel replied, eyeing her cards carefully.

Sharae followed up with, "Okay, I got six," and set her hand of cards facedown on the table.

"You bet' not come up short, either, after this trash-ass hand you dealt me," Tariq told Ivan.

The second rule was to bid confidently. The last thing a teammate was going to stand for was a predicted book being set by the opposing team. Hence the warning look Tariq was now sending his brother.

As expected, and without a care in the world, Ivan gave his low bid, and Jemel grinned. "And y'all plan to win."

When Tariq playfully pushed her shoulder hard enough that she leaned over in her chair, Sharae chuckled. "Don't start abusing my teammate."

"Oh, don't worry, I've got something for yo' ass, too," he continued and pushed her in the same way he had Jemel.

Three hands later, Sharae was focused on the game. She and Jemel were up in score, but she wasn't cocky enough to believe that meant anything. Tariq liked to play ten games before declaring an overall winner, so they still had a ways to go. There was no doubt that Tariq and Ivan were good; part of the fun was simply getting Tariq hyped up and watching how seriously he took a simple card game. Rita didn't find that entertaining, so she'd done as she usually did during card nights—hid out in the kitchen with the Aunts.

Across the room at the second card table, Uncle Jimmy yelled "Uno!" with the exuberance of a lottery jackpot winner. Ever since she could remember, this was how card nights went down in her family— with good food and competitive playing.

That would be why the house smelled like fried lake trout. The Aunts always had fish on Fridays. Without having been in the kitchen at all tonight, Sharae already knew there'd also be homemade potato salad, fresh green beans cooked in bacon fat with chunks of bacon included (because this was Aunt Rose's house, and that was the way she loved to cook them), and Aunt Vi's honey cornbread. If there was one thing the Johnson family did well, it was cook, and so they made sure to do it often. Another thing some of them excelled in was cards.

With that in mind, Sharae took the last book and folded it neatly into her pile. Across the table, Jemel did a fist pump, and Tariq scowled.

Shaking her head at her surly cousin, Sharae was about to join the talkin'-shit bandwagon when her phone began to vibrate. She reached into the back pocket of her jeans and pulled it out. Jemel had her phone on the table and was constantly checking her emails and texts—something else that got Tariq into a tizzy. He didn't like any distractions during the game, especially when his team was down by a hundred points.

Not necessarily giving a damn about Tariq's mumbling about her paying attention to the game, Sharae frowned down at the screen when she saw the caller's name. She definitely didn't want to talk to him again, not now, or ever if she could help it. Huffing, she swiped her finger over the "Decline" button.

"You good?" Ivan asked.

Shaking her head, Sharae glanced at him while slipping the phone into her pocket again. "Yeah. Just somebody I'm not in the mood to talk to right now."

"Well, that's good, since we're in the middle of this game," Tariq added.

Sharae sighed and tried to pick up her hand of cards, but her fingers were shaking now, and the cards flipped right through them, tumbling faceup on the table.

"Yoooo, what you doing?" Tariq asked, obviously irritated. "We don't need no help winning this game."

"You sure you're okay?" Jemel asked while Tariq continued to eye the cards Sharae had inadvertently revealed.

Cursing, Sharae began gathering the cards back into her hand. At the same time, not waiting for a response, Jemel stood and came around to her side of the table.

"I'm good," Sharae said, but her voice hitched on the last word, and she cursed.

"We're taking a break," Jemel said.

"There's no breaks in Spades," Tariq complained.

"Shut up!" Jemel and Ivan said simultaneously.

Jemel took Sharae's arm, easing her up from the chair. It would've been no problem to pull away, continue to protest that she was fine, and keep on playing. That was why she'd come here tonight, to get sucked into a card game and familiar family banter. It's what she'd sworn she'd needed all week long—to cleanse her mind from the haunting memories and irrefutable reality. But Sharae was a realist: that plan wasn't working.

Following Jemel out of the room was probably best. She should've called her and told her earlier this week. Then, maybe by now she would've found some distance from this situation. As it was, she currently felt like she was drowning in pain, guilt, and obligation, and she didn't like it one bit.

They were at Aunt Rose's house—a row house on Northern Parkway with a stone front porch and a yard full of healthy patches of hostas that the Aunts spent at least half an hour looking at and commenting on whenever they were all here. Rose Johnson had never married or had any children of her own, but Sharae, Rita, and Jemel had spent many weekends with her.

The card tables had been set up in the living room, but now Jemel marched Sharae into the dining room, stopping at the door that led down to the basement. Aunt Rose was a pack rat but kept her stash limited to the basement, which was full of boxes and bags of stuff—new and old—that she probably didn't need and most assuredly didn't use. If she'd ever bothered to clean out that space, they could have card nights there instead of in the living room, already cramped with her bulky three-piece floral-print furniture set.

"What's going on with you? And don't you dare tell me nothing, because you've been acting weird all week." Jemel folded her arms across her chest and tilted her head as she surveyed Sharae.

"I wasn't going to say that," Sharae replied.

"Well, good." Jemel nodded. "Because I knew the other night when you didn't want to come over for drinks and to press Rita for answers on how she was doing, that something wasn't quite right with you."

She had blown that off on Wednesday night and not just because she'd worked a twelve-hour shift on Tuesday. Memories of Jazzy and Destiny had lingered way too long in her mind after meeting and turning them over to social services. Then, when she and Malik had finally talked to Alicia Watkins, who was in a rage on Thursday afternoon when she found out they'd taken her children, the woman had given them an alibi that they'd spent most of this morning trying to nail down.

But, for Sharae, talking about her emotions wasn't her favored pastime; that was Rita and Jemel's. Those two would talk about a zit on their noses and act like it should be a headline story. Sharae preferred to keep all her heavy personal stuff—and some of the lighter fluff that she just didn't want to deal with—to herself. It wasn't because she didn't trust them. They were the closest to sisters as she was ever going to get, and she loved them. She just never wanted to burden them, not in the way she'd become a burden to her aunt Vi and the rest of the sisters after her mother died.

Sharae leaned back against the burnt-orange painted wall. She let her head fall back and sighed heavily. "What's the one thing I never, ever talk about, to anyone?" she asked.

"What exactly you do to pleasure yourself, and why that's your preference to real dick," Jemel replied without a second's hesitation.

Sharae's eyes popped open, and she lifted her head so she could stare at her cousin. Jemel seemed serious even though her response was ridiculous. "Really? That's your answer?"

Jemel shrugged and blinked with a *What?* expression.

"Her father," Rita said as she entered the room. "Sharae never talks about her father."

"Sanford," Sharae corrected. He may've provided the sperm that created her, but all he'd ever been was a burden. A bottomless black spot that marred her heart and brought tears to her eyes in the dark of too many nights to count.

"What about San?" Aunt Vi said, following behind her daughter to enter the dining room.

Rita was wiping her hands on a black-and-white-checkered dish towel while her mother carried a glass bowl filled with potato salad. Aunt Vi set the salad on the table, and like clockwork, Aunt Ceil and Aunt Rose came through the kitchen door seconds later, the two of them stopping behind where Aunt Vi now stood staring at Sharae. They looked like an assembly line of gorgeous and formidable Black women, or a firing squad, depending on how you came at them.

"What's going on?" asked Aunt Ceil, who became the youngest of the Johnson sisters when Sharae's mother, Justine, died.

"San did something to Sharae," Aunt Vi said.

Sharae stared blankly at the Aunts for a few seconds. Aunt Rose had the darkest complexion, with her deep-mocha skin tone, which coincidentally Sharae shared. Like the other two sisters, Aunt Rose had a full face, but deep dimples punctuated her cheeks when she smiled. Aunt Vi had been married to Uncle Hale for over forty years. She wore her golden-blonde-streaked hair in a chin-length bob and never left the house without a complete face of makeup. And Aunt Ceil, who was quick to laugh with her cap of silver-gray hair, had married right out of high school and traveled the world with her military husband, until he'd decided a wife and kid weren't in his future plans.

"Oh, baby." Aunt Rose's voice snapped Sharae out of her thoughts as she came close enough to put a hand on Sharae's shoulder. "What'd that evil spawn do to you?"

"Now, Rose, he *is* her father." Aunt Vi was always ready to chastise. It was as if she thought being the oldest and having the title of first lady of NVB gave her the authority to keep everyone she knew in line. The apple didn't fall far from the tree where Rita was concerned, but Rita had a softness that Aunt Vi rarely showed anyone that wasn't family—and even then, Aunt Vi's gentle side was shown sparingly.

"He's also a homicidal maniac," countered Aunt Rose, the blunt one.

Aunt Ceil, the only one of the six women standing in this room who had a naturally forgiving spirit, shook her head. "He's paying the price for that now, Rose."

"He didn't pay the highest price," Rose snapped back.

"He's dead," Sharae blurted out.

Silence fell like a heavy blanket, leaving each woman blinking and speechless. It was a first. The Aunts loved to talk. Whether they were on a three-way call with each other at the crack of dawn or into the late evening hours, sitting on the same pew in the sanctuary, or on Aunt Vi's back porch in the Adirondack chairs they'd each picked out during a sale at Home Depot. They always had something or someone to talk about.

"C'mon and sit down," Aunt Rose said, guiding Sharae to one of the cherrywood chairs pushed under the dining room table.

Sharae did as she was told, sinking into the chair, ignoring the crunch of the plastic that still covered the cushioned seat. Aunt Rose and her sisters all took a seat at the table, while Rita came to stand at Sharae's right, resting a hand on her shoulder. Jemel came to her left, kneeling down beside the chair and taking Sharae's hand in hers.

"An attorney, Desmond Brown, approached me at the courthouse on Tuesday. He said Sanford died in jail—sarcoidosis—and that I'm now the executor of his estate." Saying the words out loud didn't make them any easier to digest.

Her chest still burned each time she thought about it, like she'd had that spicy chicken from Del Alto's on the Avenue.

"San had an estate?" Aunt Rose asked. "He could never keep a job, as far as I can remember. But I guess his preferred occupation of selling drugs was the cause of that."

"Anything can be part of an estate," Rita chimed in. "Bank accounts, an old trunk, a car. Anything he owned at any point in his life is now part of his estate."

Sharae nodded at Rita's very accurate description of an estate, like she was a lawyer instead of a stay-at-home world-class untrained chef. "He apparently owned three houses—two in the Lake Clifton area and one down in Ocean City. There're some bonds and two bank accounts that he at some point added my name to without my knowledge."

"Uncle San was an OG; he must've kept his business going from behind bars." Jemel said what Sharae had assumed. That was the only way Sanford could've purchased properties and stashed money. "But how could he put your name on bank accounts without you knowing?" Jemel asked, still clutching Sharae's hand. "Wouldn't he have needed your ID and signature?"

With her free hand, Sharae rubbed the back of her neck. "He got a copy of my ID somehow and had someone forge the signature."

"Hmph. A criminal 'til the very end," Aunt Rose said.

Aunt Vi closed her eyes briefly and whispered, "Lord have mercy."

"So what are you going to do with it all?" Aunt Ceil asked.

Sharae shook her head. "I've talked to Desmond twice since Tuesday." And she'd been even more annoyed each time. But ignoring this legal situation with him wasn't going to make it go away. "He says first things first—I gotta figure out whether I'm having a funeral or simply cremating him. Sanford had thought of everything else, but as far as what to do with his body, he left that up to me." The sorry sonofabitch. How could he leave this kind of burden on her after all he'd put her through?

How many times had Sharae asked herself that question? Just as many times as she'd told herself it didn't matter. Nothing Sanford had ever done or intended to do where she was concerned mattered to her. The only thing she'd ever remember and never forgive was him killing her mother. She closed her eyes to the pain of those words flitting throughout her mind.

"I don't want anything to do with him or his belongings," she said through clenched teeth. "I could care less about anything he owned. It can all go straight to hell with him."

"Justine wouldn't want that," Aunt Ceil said quietly. "She'd want you to have anything that could help you in your life."

Sharae's eyes shot open for the second time tonight, and her gaze zoomed in on her aunt. "Not like this. Not anything that had to do with him. You know what he put her through, Aunt Ceil. Even before he finally . . . finally . . ." The word caught in her throat.

All her life Sharae had only been able to think of the man who'd offered his sperm to create her as the one who'd killed her mother. But she'd never been able to say it. Even now, the word just wouldn't fall from her lips.

"No, baby," Aunt Ceil said quietly. "None of us will ever forget that."

"My sister loved that sorry bastard," Aunt Rose added. She folded her plump hands in front of her and heaved a heavy sigh. "From day one, she loved him. Said he was the best thing that had ever happened to her. At least, until you came along." Aunt Rose turned her attention to Sharae, the look in her warm brown eyes solemn and still grief stricken.

Sharae knew that look well. She'd seen it often staring back at her in the mirror.

"She loved him to death," Aunt Vi added in an abrupt tone.

"I don't know what to do," Sharae admitted.

"You do whatever you want to do," Rita told her. "Whatever is best for you."

"Like you're doing pursuing a divorce that you know is going to get plenty nasty." The rows of lines that appeared on Aunt Vi's forehead exacerbated her displeasure.

"You told them?" Jemel asked, her question echoing what Sharae was thinking.

They both looked up at Rita, who replied to them with a nod. "When I got here earlier today. It didn't make any sense to keep it a secret."

"Divorce is not the end of the world, Vi," Aunt Ceil said. And she would know, since she'd divorced Jemel's father about three seconds after he said he didn't want to be a husband or father anymore. Two days later, Aunt Ceil had packed her bags and traveled from Hawaii back to Baltimore, where she and three-year-old Jemel moved in with Aunt Vi until she could get her own house right down the street.

"I'm not saying it is. All I'm saying is, going to a lawyer who goes to our church wasn't such a good idea. What if she talks about the case? Details of the divorce, of all the years they've been married, will be all over the church." Aunt Vi shook her head. "Such a mess. Hale's gonna have a fit when I tell him."

"I'll tell him myself, Mama. And it's my business that'll be spread all over the streets—not just the church. But that's just the way it has to be. I'm not staying married to a man who clearly doesn't want to honor his vows to me anymore," Rita said.

That was an understatement considering Nate had a whole baby on the way. Sharae sighed heavily. This was exactly what she didn't want to happen. Now her problems were front and center when it was clear that she and Jemel needed to be throwing all their support at Rita and what she was going through right now.

"Look, it's cool. I think I'm just gonna cremate him and get it over with," she blurted out. When everyone in the room stared at her, she shrugged. "It's no big deal. I'm his next of kin, so I'll do what I'm required to do. Just because he couldn't manage to do that doesn't mean I have to follow in his footsteps." That sounded so noble of her. Too bad she wasn't sure it was nobility she was going for, rather than just the quickest possible resolution she could think of.

She could call a funeral home first thing Monday morning and tell them what she wanted. They could pick up the body from the morgue and cremate him the same day. Then it'd be over. Simple as that.

"Okay," Aunt Ceil said. "Well, we'll help. You need me to go to the funeral home with you?"

Sharae took a steadying breath. "No. I'll call on Monday. Hopefully they can get it done the same day, and I can move on."

"No memorial service?"

All eyes zoned in on Aunt Ceil at her last question.

"Well," Aunt Ceil continued, unbothered by their quizzical glares, "it's a formality, but it's also closure. It doesn't have to be anything big. We can have it right at the funeral home and—"

"No," Sharae said adamantly. She slid her hand out of Jemel's and stood. "I'm not bothering with any formalities. I'll cremate him and sell whatever he owned. Then it'll be done. It'll be over. Finally."

With that, Sharae walked out of the dining room. She passed Tariq and Ivan still sitting at the card table obviously waiting for her and Jemel to return, from the expectant gaze Tariq shot her. She ignored it and kept right on walking, until she was through the front door and on the porch. There she stopped and sucked in a gulp of humid pre-summer air.

"It'll be over. Finally." She repeated her words, determined to convince herself that they were true.

Chapter 10

ISN'T IT IRONIC?

"This ain't over," Rita said to Nate. It was the closest she'd come to a threat in the fifteen minutes she'd stood in his office late Monday afternoon. "What you not gon' do is clean out our accounts and then sit here looking smug like this is all my fault."

The man she once thought she loved sat back in his black leather office chair and shrugged. "You made a personal decision for your future, and I made a financial decision for mine. I don't see the problem."

"Oh, you definitely see the problem. You ain't slick!" she yelled, and didn't give a damn if every other salesperson and whatever customers might be on the sales floor at the time heard her. Although none of their employees had ever heard her raise her voice, Rita figured it was a good day for them to learn that she wasn't the one to push. "And Sharon has assured me we'll get every penny of it back in the final settlement."

It had taken all the strength she possessed and a couple more glasses of wine for Rita to wait until a respectable time to call Sharon. She'd actually gotten up on Thursday morning and called the bank to make sure what she'd seen wasn't a security glitch. Her lawyer hadn't been totally surprised, although she admitted she'd thought Nate was a better man than to do something so cliché, but the entire reason why Rita needed Sharon in the first place was cliché. Nate had already shown them both who he really was.

"Calm down, Rita. I'm not trying to leave you high and dry," he said. Like she was really going to believe a word he said right now.

"That's exactly what you've done, Nate. There's no money in the household account or the primary savings account."

"But there's money left in the second savings account, the one we use for vacations, and you still have the power to take a draw from the dealership. So you can stop all this drama."

"Drama?" Was this fool serious? Stepping back from where she'd had her hands planted on his desk while she yelled at him, she folded her arms across her chest.

Today she wore a fitted navy-blue dress with a wide ivory belt and matching pumps. Pearl studs were at her ears, and she gripped her ivory-and-gold clutch tight between her fingers. "You dare to talk to me about drama? You're the one with the stray women calling my house at all hours of the morning. And I'm certainly not the one going through a midlife crisis and creating babies when my youngest is in college. Don't you dare talk to me about drama."

He stood up so fast the chair slid back on its wheeled legs and smacked into the credenza where his printer and a few family photos were. "This was your idea, Rita," he said tightly. He was trying not to yell and probably praying they didn't draw the attention of their staff. Wasn't that cute. "I told you I wanted to talk about this, to work through our issues."

She was already shaking her head. "I don't have any issues, Nate. Unless you count the sorry, disrespectful man I chose to spend my life with. I've never cheated on you!" That wasn't what she'd planned to say to him when she came here today, but now that the words had fallen from her lips, she waited for Nate's reaction.

For the moment he seemed speechless, but then he shook his head. "I never thought you would."

"Same," she said through clenched teeth and then huffed. "I married a man that I loved and trusted. It never occurred to me that he would do something as trite as have an affair. But you did, on multiple occasions."

When he came around the desk and stopped about a foot away from her, Rita took a slow step back.

"Listen," he said, his voice notably lower than either of theirs had been thus far during this conversation. "I really do want to talk about this. I want to sit down and have a heart-to-heart, the way we used to." He reached for her hand then, but Rita pulled back.

"We're not who we used to be." And that was the truth.

Sharon had told her to let her handle the money situation with Nate, and Rita had agreed to do that. But over the weekend, she'd had more time to think and more time to destroy another couple of boxes of Nate's stuff from the basement. He owed her so much and not just on a monetary level. He owed her for the time and care she'd taken with him and their family, for the visits to his mother in Boston and all the calls Rita took from that complaining woman in between. For the stretch marks now marching across her stomach and down her thighs, and for the missed opportunities to continue her education and receive her bachelor's, possibly even her master's degree, in business. Something she'd never pursued after he'd complained so extensively about her taking the evening courses for two years.

Managing another slow step back, Rita realized that each of those sacrifices were choices she made. She'd never given Nate any indication that she'd wanted to be anything other than his wife and the mother of his children. Mainly because she'd been so sure that those were the two most important titles in her life.

"Let's go to dinner," he said, and before she could stop him, he continued. "I'll make reservations at Ruth's Chris. I know you love how they cook your filet."

Nate's hands were on her shoulders then, holding her in a way that was both familiar and, to her complete dismay, desired.

This man had been everything to her for so very long. She'd shared all her hopes and dreams for a family and a beautiful home with him. He'd shared her love of Christ and had carried out the role as head of their household, just as he'd vowed to do. There'd never been a moment that she'd thought of being with another man; his touch had always soothed and aroused her. He was the love of her life.

"Sure," she said and nodded. "Make the reservations and text me with the details." She gave a weak smile and eased out of his grip.

He smiled. "Good. I'll take care of that in a few minutes. But why don't you go and visit your mother or go to that spa you love so much. I'm sure they can squeeze you in without an appointment."

She nodded. "Yeah, I might just do that."

When he touched a hand to her arm and started to lead her toward the door, Rita almost laughed. He was hurrying her out. She'd obviously made enough of a scene for him today. Well, this silly bastard had no idea what she was about to do to him.

Leaving the dealership without further incident, Rita slipped behind the wheel of her car. She pulled out of the parking lot and drove toward the funeral home where she and Jemel were scheduled to meet with Sharae to help her take care of the final plans for her father. Her phone chirped just as she pulled up in front of the funeral home, and she waited until after she parked her car to look at the text.

Ruth's Chris, Odenton 730 tonight

Nate was still as handsome and as charismatic as he'd always been. For just a sliver of a moment his touch on her shoulders had reminded her of all the things that had made her fall in love with him. The mesmerizing scent of his cologne, those warm and intriguing bedroom eyes, the way he always licked his lips and lowered his tone when he was trying to be extra sexy. Yeah, he'd done all that in his office a little while ago, and as she'd watched him, she'd imagined all the times he'd probably done the same thing with other women.

She deleted his text.

"You'll be having a well-done filet by yourself, you ignorant piece of crap," she said before stepping out of the car.

Moments later she walked through the tinted glass doors of Medwin Harris Funeral Home, her heels moving quietly over the beige carpet in the reception area. Unfortunately, the place was familiar, with its mauve wallpaper and dark-brown crown molding. A large pink-and-brown floral arrangement set in a gold vase was on the mahogany console table directly across from the front doors, and to her right was the antique gold-leaf reception table. The woman sitting behind the table was Dinah Rodstram, who'd lived around the corner from the Aunts during their childhood years. She'd also been a member of NVB for as long as Rita could remember. Between Dinah and Medwin Harris, Sr., who'd been a long-serving and dedicated deacon at the church before his death twelve years ago, there was an inexplicable link between NVB, the funeral home, and the Johnson family.

"Margarita. It's such a pleasure to see you." Dinah came to her feet and walked around the desk.

Rita ignored the snooty way in which Dinah always insisted on using her full name. It was no secret that some of the members of NVB had wondered about the pastor naming his daughter after an alcoholic beverage. But none of them were so bold as to ask the first lady how that came to be. Not that Vi liked talking about still being so worn out after a thirty-seven-hour labor that she'd spelled her daughter's name wrong on her birth certificate—so that it was Margarita instead of Marguerite. Rita had been thankful for the mix-up, as she preferred her nickname over what Vi had intended.

She closed the space between them and easily smiled. "Hi, Ms. Dinah. It's nice to see you as well."

How weird was it to be exchanging such niceties when the reason they were seeing each other this time was because someone had died?

"Missed you in church yesterday. Is everything all right?" Dinah asked, arching a very badly drawn-in eyebrow.

Of the hundreds of members at NVB, at least 20 percent of them were nosy women waiting with bated breath to sink their teeth into the next morsel of juicy gossip. As the divorce of the pastor's daughter would no doubt qualify for that title, Rita had been in no hurry to announce her new situation to the congregation, nor had she felt like addressing any questions about where Nate was. Even though he was out of town often and she'd said that more times than she could recall to various members of the church, repeating that task for two and a half hours wasn't something she'd wanted to do yesterday.

Today, however, she had no choice. Sharae had asked her and Jemel to meet her here this afternoon to finalize the arrangements for her father, and Rita wasn't about to let her down.

"Well, no, everything's not all right," Rita replied. "Sharae's father passed away."

"Yes, I took her call this morning." Folding one arm across her chest and letting the free hand move to her chin, Dinah shook her head. This was the infamous sorry-to-hear-that stance that she always took upon discussing someone's death. "Margarita, I have to tell you that was such a shock. I mean, I didn't even think any of you still kept in touch with Sanford."

"We didn't," Rita told her. "He was in jail."

There was no doubt that Dinah knew all these facts; this was just her way of keeping the conversation going in the hope of drawing some more scandalous gossip out of Rita.

Dinah nodded. "That's right, he was." She made a tsking sound. "A shame what happened between him and Justine. They were such a beautiful couple in the beginning."

Were all couples beautiful in the beginning? Rita could envision her first date with Nate—dinner at the Rusty Scupper and then a romantic walk around the Inner Harbor. He'd held her hand the entire time, and she'd had to practice steady breathing to keep from swooning at his dreamy eyes and every word he said to her. Wasn't it ironic that all these years later, she was planning to stand him up for a dinner date and then go after every dime she could get from him in a divorce?

"Hey, am I late?" Jemel came over to where Rita and Dinah were standing.

"No. I just got here," Rita replied.

Dinah turned her wrist to look at her watch. "Sharae's not here yet. But it's only a few minutes after four."

Which in Dinah's sarcastic terms meant she considered her late.

"She probably got held up at work. I know she said she had another meeting with her captain today. I hope that goes well." Rita was still worried about how her impulsive actions last week might affect Sharae and the job she cared about more than almost anything in the world.

Jemel, most likely knowing what Rita was thinking, rubbed a hand over Rita's arm. "It's fine, I'm sure. We've got enough on our plates to worry about right now. Don't add to it."

"Well, there's no need to worry about the arrangements," Dinah chimed in, reminding them that she was there, ear-hustling as best she could. "As y'all know from previous dealings with us here at Medwin Harris, we know how to take care of our families. And the Johnsons are definitely family. Even though we haven't seen you here since your great-uncle Paul died last year."

"This ain't Target," Jemel said dryly. "We prefer not to make a stop here every week."

Dinah's spooky-looking brows raised again, and this time she added a weary gaze at Jemel. There'd never been any love lost between these two. Jemel thought Dinah was disrespectful and low-key jealous of the Aunts while Dinah had made it her business to tell anyone who'd listen about Jemel and her—as Dinah called her—"fast behind" during Jemel's partying days.

"Still got a fresh mouth, I see, Jemel. I pray for Ceil every week."

Jemel waved a hand in Dinah's direction. "Don't waste your prayers on me. The Lord knew what he was doing when he made me; I am what I am."

"Okay, well, we'll just go have a seat over here and wait for Sharae," Rita said, looping her arm through Jemel's and guiding her away from Dinah.

"Maybe you should give her a call. The purpose in making an appointment is to have time allotted for everyone who requires our services."

"And I could see when I pulled up that you've got a line of people waiting to get in here and buy these overpriced caskets and gaudy flower arrangements you keep paying that tacky Yolanda Camp to design."

That was the other point of contention with Dinah and Jemel and probably the biggest issue for Jemel, since she'd never cared what anybody thought about her or her life's choices. Unlike Rita, who'd always tried to do the right thing to please everybody. But Jemel was proud of the florist shop she'd built over the years, so whenever she saw arrangements that she considered subpar, it grated on her nerves.

"We go with the most economical price and the person who does more for the community. We like to give back around here, not take all the time," Dinah replied with a huff.

Rita was glad the woman turned and walked away because Jemel, as always, was down for a fight or a spirited argument when she knew she was right.

"Stop egging her on," Rita chastised when they were across the room. She sat in one of the guest chairs, crossing one leg over the other.

Jemel sat in the chair to Rita's left, leaned back, and crossed her feet at the ankle. "She's so annoying with her nosy-ass self. And they are cheap in here; it ain't got nothing to do with giving back to the community. All Yolanda does is host a car wash in the summer and says she's donating the proceeds to the rec center. Nobody knows if she's really doing that. Plus, how much is she really making on a car wash?"

Rita worried the clasp on her purse, her thoughts more on where Sharae was rather than how much money could be made at a car wash.

"You could do some type of fundraiser for the community if you wanted to. It wouldn't hurt to get that exposure for your shop," she said absently.

Jemel didn't generally take advice about her shop. Her stance was that she'd worked her butt off to get that place off the ground without anybody lifting a finger to help her, so she didn't need anyone's input now that it was doing well. Anybody other than Rita and Sharae, who both knew it was still smart to be very selective in what they said to Jemel about her business anyway.

"And you'd be the one to help with that since you've chaired just about every fundraising committee at the church." Jemel sighed. "Look, I'd just like to take people's money by selling them pretty flowers. I'm not into tricking them to give me money that I'll send off to someone who's probably lying about what they intend to use it for. You know half the money that's earmarked for rec centers never makes it there. Hence the reason so many of them are closing."

Rita could agree with that and could go on and on with this discussion with Jemel about the demise of their communities and people's reluctance to help. But she was more concerned with the fact that Sharae was now fifteen minutes late. Sharae was never late.

Chapter 11

MEN AIN'T SHIT.

It didn't matter how many times she said it, committed it to memory, or had it engraved on her mirror so she'd see it and be reminded every morning—men just weren't shit.

She doubted they even tried to be anything better.

At least Captain Floyd Hall with his too-loud voice and irritating laugh had never tried to be anything more than the obnoxious chauvinist he was.

"Now look, this is your second fuckup this year. I'm not gonna write you up for not letting the first responders take the official statements at your cousin's house last week, but one more slipup like that and you'll be back writing reports in narcotics. You investigate murders; you don't show up at crime scenes just because you want to and pull rank over the people there to actually do their jobs."

That's what he'd yelled when she'd sat in his office half an hour ago. This had been the second meeting they'd had on the same subject, since the first one had been cut short and subsequently delayed for a few days while he dealt with a high-profile case. Still, it was just as much a waste of time as the first one, no matter how brief it had been.

Actually, it was his way of establishing his perceived control over her one more time. And while in this case the captain would've had every right to file a written complaint about her behavior, he wouldn't because she'd always been too much of a liability to him and the department. She hadn't considered this at the time, because truthfully, it wasn't something she thought she'd ever have to do. Floyd Hall was an asshole, but he wasn't stupid.

The first fuckup he was referring to had happened in January when he'd commanded her to work overtime one weekend. She'd put in her request for time off months prior, and it'd been approved. Besides that, there were already four more detectives than necessary for a regular shift signed up to work—he didn't need her there. This was just another way to cover up the egregious and unsubstantiated overtime he was authorizing to some of his favorites on the force. Sharae didn't want to be a part of the scam, and she especially didn't want to be used to help make the whole sordid plan look more legitimate.

When he pushed her, threatening to fire her if she didn't show up, Sharae had pushed back, swearing she'd report all the times in the past he'd scheduled more than enough detectives for unnecessary shifts. He'd slammed his beefy hands on his desk so hard that day, the lamp had fallen over the side, breaking on contact as it hit the floor.

Today, when Hall had called her into his office, she'd sat in the guest chair across from his desk, watching him in silence the way she often did. He wanted to intimidate her, had wanted that since she'd applied for this job, but he had the wrong one. Sharae didn't intimidate easily, and this blustering idiot wasn't going to be the one to crack her shield.

It hadn't mattered that in the last week, her testimony—coupled with the investigative work of her and her partner—had convicted a man on two counts of manslaughter and multiple handgun violations. Nor had the fact that she and Malik had the most closed cases in their department for the past three years. No, what mattered most was that she'd once again bruised some fragile male egos in the department.

Boo-the-fuck-hoo.

She couldn't stand a whining-ass man, and despite the appearance of a pool of testosterone, the police department was full of them.

On top of the nonsense he'd been spouting, the captain had made her late for an appointment she really didn't want to keep.

She pulled up to the corner and stared at the burgundy-painted 1920s Victorian-styled house that had been the Medwin Harris Funeral Home for the last fifty years. That was what the bronze plaque on the side of the building stated.

Grabbing her purse from the passenger seat and pulling out her phone, she noted that it was four thirty. She was half an hour late. There were also multiple missed calls and text messages from Rita and Jemel. Cursing, she switched her phone from vibrate to sound. She hadn't wanted to hear beeping and ringing as she sat in Captain Hall's office, but then he'd pissed her off so badly with that ridiculous threat that she'd forgotten to turn it back to normal.

Climbing out of the car, she told herself she had lots of apologizing to do once she got inside. But before that could happen, the phone rang.

Dammit. It was Desmond again.

This time he'd actually called at a great moment. She was more than ready to cuss somebody out right now, and he'd just picked the short stick.

"Hello," she answered, not bothering to hide the irritation in her tone.

"Sharae?"

"Ms. Gibson to you."

"Really?"

Silence. She huffed and decided that was probably a bit much. "What do you want, Desmond?"

"See how that works. You call me by my first name, and I call you by yours. You know, since we're both adults."

"I was taught only your family and friends should be able to use your first name freely. Others have to earn that right of familiarity. And as you're just a . . . um . . . you're just a lawyer . . ." She purposely didn't complete that sentence.

"Are you finished?" he asked after a few seconds.

Why didn't she like this guy? Maybe because he'd been the bearer of bad and then worse news last week, and ever since then he'd continued to call and email her with even more news that she could live without. Nobody cared what Sanford owned or what his wishes were. Nobody cared about Sanford. At least she didn't, and she never would.

"Can you just tell me what you want this time so I can get on with my day. I'm already late for an appointment."

"Fine. I need your signature on the paperwork for the estate," he said easily.

"What estate?"

"The one I told you we need to open for your father. Everything he left to you will go under the estate, and you'll manage it as the executor."

She held the phone to her ear and walked toward the black wrought-iron gate that surrounded the funeral home. No matter how many times she came here, the first thing she noted was how out of place this very regal gate looked on the corner of one of Baltimore's busiest inner-city streets. For that matter, the blast-from-the-past house that was the funeral home was in stark contrast to the three-story row houses that continued down the rest of the block.

"I don't want to bother with an estate. Can't I just get him cremated and sell all the things he owned?" The sooner she could be done with this situation, the better.

"The estate paperwork must be filed in order for you to do business regarding the properties, bank accounts, and investments. All you have to do is sign, and I'll take care of getting everything filed," he said.

Standing at the narrow double doors to the funeral home now, she turned away from the glass windows. She took in a slow breath, then released it in as calm a fashion as she could muster and said, "Fine."

Her voice sounded much smaller than she'd intended, and for that she was just a little more pissed off. Truth be told, she'd been pretty irritable in the days since Desmond had first approached her in the courthouse. Her daily routine had felt off-kilter since that day, and try as she might, it didn't seem to be getting better.

"I know this isn't easy for you, Sharae. But I'm here to help. Once you get everything squared away at the funeral home, I'll need you to send me a copy of the death certificate."

For a minute, Desmond's tone had also lowered, hinting at real compassion. Was that what she needed? Someone to feel sorry for her and this new situation she'd been thrust into? If so, she had her family for that. Desmond had a job to do, and he was hell-bent on doing it, so she squared her shoulders. "Yeah, sure. I'll get that right to you. Listen, I gotta go."

"Can I bring the paperwork to you tonight to sign? I've got court first thing in the morning, and I can take care of the filing then." When she didn't immediately answer, he continued. "The sooner we get the ball rolling, the sooner you'll be able to unload everything and move on with your life."

He wasn't lying about that. So, against her own rules about not inviting people—especially lawyers who tracked her down to deliver bad news—to her apartment, she sighed and said, "Sure. You already have my address. I should be there around seven."

"I'll see you then."

"Yeah, I guess I'll see you too." She disconnected the call before he could say anything else.

"Dammit," she whispered. This was draining and uncomfortable, and she wished it were happening to someone else.

Not that she gave a damn about Sanford dying. She hadn't seen him in twenty-seven years. Had never spoken to him or received a single letter from him in that time. Her chest burned with that realization. Had she wanted him to reach out to her?

Of course not. He was dead to her, the same way her mother was, long before he took his last breath in that prison hospital. Then what the hell was going on with her? Why was she having such a hard time digesting this situation? Letting herself lean back against the door, she lifted her fingers to her temple and massaged the dull ache that had started to form.

Two seconds later she was trying to keep her ass from hitting the floor as the door opened behind her.

"You gonna stand outside all night?" Jemel asked, then extended her arms to catch Sharae as she stumbled.

"Dammit, Jem!"

"What? You can't yell at me after I've been sitting here for a half hour with Ditzy Dinah over there," Jemel complained.

They moved inside and Jemel closed the door. Sharae had two seconds to take another breath before Dinah was in her face.

"Well, I'm glad you made it. You know I had to push some things back for you, but it's okay. Let's just get started." Dinah spoke quickly as she glared at Sharae.

Rita stood behind Dinah, shaking her head as if to tell Sharae not to even bother replying to Dinah's sarcastic tone. Admitting to herself that she was tempted, Sharae took another breath and managed, "I apologize for being late. I was held up at work."

Rita was beside her now, touching a hand to her shoulder. "Oh no, was it about the other day?"

"It's fine," Sharae told her for what felt like the billionth time. "I took care of it just like I told you I would."

Even if her taking care of it meant her boss was now on her ass, waiting for the barest slipup so he could send her back to narcotics. He hadn't wanted her in homicide in the first place, but when she'd applied, there'd been a shortage of detectives and a surging crime rate in the Columbia area where she worked. It'd been almost impossible for him to turn her down, especially if he wanted to avoid a discrimination lawsuit against the department. None of that mattered because there was no way she was going to let those cops question Rita last week. She hadn't known what was going on with her cousin, and she wasn't going to risk her saying something incriminating. Was that unethical? Hell yeah. Did she care? Absolutely not.

If Rita had been standing over a dead body, that may've been a whole different ball game. But just a pile of scorched clothes wasn't that big a deal, especially not after learning why she'd burned some of Nate's clothes.

"We don't have any more time for conversation, ladies. There's a family hour starting at six and funeral following." Dinah led them into a room with crimson leather chairs and a glossed conference table.

Minutes later they were joined by Medwin III, who shook their hands and spoke in that slow, calming tone of an undertaker. Thirty-five minutes later, Sharae had signed all necessary paperwork to have Medwin and his staff pick up Sanford's body from the morgue and cremate him.

"A three-hundred-and-seventy-five-dollar urn?" Jemel was saying as they walked out the front door.

"It's natural stone and will coordinate well with the furniture in her living room," Rita replied.

Sharae had been walking a few steps in front of them, but at that comment, she stopped. "Wait? What? Who said I'm keeping that in my house?"

Rita raised a brow. "It's your father's ashes, Sharae."

"It's the ashes of a man who took away the most important person in my life. Hell no, he's not living with me for the rest of my days." Why hadn't she thought about what to do with his ashes before now? Because she didn't want to think about this mess at all.

While Rita appeared stunned, Jemel smirked. "I can't believe she didn't just donate his body to science," Jemel said.

Sharae resumed walking to her car. That headache that had been brewing when she first arrived was on full blast. She needed something to eat, a couple of aspirin, and a drink.

"I shouldn't have to deal with any of this," she said, surprising herself and apparently Rita and Jemel as well.

They'd both been on their way to their cars but looked up at her outburst.

"He never did anything for me," she continued as Jemel and Rita now walked toward her. "Nothing."

No phone calls. No birthday cards. No hugs.

Those words lodged in her throat.

"It's okay to be angry with him, Sharae. Nobody's saying you have to be beside yourself with grief." Rita took her hand. "But I know you, and I know you don't have it in you to hate anyone."

"But I *should* hate him, Rita!" Her fingers clenched at her side. "I should hate him and the air he breathed all these years. I should've told them his body could rot in the morgue for all I cared. And all this other estate shit, I should just let that go however it needs to go without my help. Because he was nothing to me. Nothing!"

What was that saying about protesting too much?

She couldn't think. Her mind was a flurry of past events, mingling with the present. Sanford pushing her on a swing in the backyard when she was nine; her mother lighting the candles on her birthday cake while Sanford carried her over so she could blow them out when she was five; the Christmas morning when she was ten and Sanford took her outside in the freezing cold to teach her how to ride her brand-new bike; and the night she'd sat at the police department crying and confused until Aunt Vi and Uncle Hale had come to pick her up.

Her chest hurt so much she thought for just a second that it might be better to simply not breathe.

Jemel was on her other side then, her arms going around Sharae's waist, while Rita's circled her shoulders. Sharae couldn't do anything but lean into them. How many times had they stood like this when one of them was going through something? A lot. Most recently, last week at Rita's when she discovered her husband was an ass.

Now it was Sharae's turn, and she hated it. She despised the raw emotion that had been bubbling inside her all last week and through the weekend. Not one day had passed since learning of his death that Sanford didn't cross her mind. Him, her mother, and all Sharae had lost.

"I don't want to hate anybody," she said honestly. "I just don't want to care either."

"You're not built that way," Rita said. "And I'm glad for that. You've got a good heart, and your mother would be so proud. We're all proud of who you've become."

"If you don't want to keep the ashes in your house, Rita will keep 'em in hers," Jemel said.

Rita looked around Sharae to glare at Jemel. "Excuse me?"

Sharae chuckled. She loved these two women. They were hers. Maybe they weren't sisters, but they were blood, and they'd always belonged to her, especially Rita, who'd let Sharae climb into her bed and cry herself to sleep on countless nights after she'd come to live with them.

"I'll take that expensive-ass urn," she said, giving them both one last squeeze before breaking their embrace and stepping toward her car. "I might put it on the floor in the back of my closet, but I'll keep it."

Or she'd leave it in some alley to rot the way she'd wished Sanford would've rotted in prison.

Chapter 12

Do you share?

Sharae held a receipt in one hand and a fourth of the giant Italian cold-cut sub she'd picked up from Jersey Mike's in the other. The total funeral home bill had come to $1,217.84. Money that wasn't in this month's budget. Who was she kidding? She never made a budget, despite the numerous times Rita had offered to create one for her.

She was single, loved purses and shoes, but could live off the leftovers she packed from Rita or either of the Aunts' houses on any given day. Since she'd opted for the police academy over college like Jemel and Rita, she had no student-loan debt. Jemel had a gripe with her tossing her money into the abyss of a rental apartment, but Sharae was fine not having the weight of plumbing and other expensive household repairs on her shoulders. Still, last week when June was about to come rolling in, she hadn't imagined she'd be shelling out this type of money on a man she didn't even like.

The knock at her door had her dropping the receipt and looking over her shoulder toward the living room. Her dining room table was positioned near the window so she could stare outside while she ate. Skylines had always been her favorites. Interruptions, however, were not.

Setting her sandwich on her plate, she grabbed the napkin beside it and stood to answer the door.

First thing she noticed when she opened it was that this man was too damn fine. Did that matter? Of course not, but still. It wasn't just the crisp lines of his beard and haircut, it was also the cheekbones that were too sharp and too perfect for a man. The eyes that weren't extraordinary in any way, but when they fixated on her, made her heart stumble and her palms sweat.

"Oh, you did say you were coming over." She tripped over the words as her mind tried to readjust to the business reason Desmond would be at her door.

"I did, and I'm on time too." The edge of his mouth tilted in that barely-there-but-still-potent-as-hell smile, and she frowned.

"Well, come on in, and let's get this over with." Backing up, she left enough space for him to walk past and into her apartment.

He smelled good too. She already knew she didn't like this guy, or the reason he was here. Slamming the door shut, she circled around him and led the way to the dining room table. Without turning back to him, manners had her extending her arm for him to sit across from where she'd been. "Just let me get a pen so I can sign the papers."

"I've got a pen," he replied.

Was his voice deeper? Silkier?

Exhaustion must've been making her mind mush. This man wasn't here for her to consider taking to her bed. *Was* she even considering that? "I like to be in charge," she blurted out.

"Excuse me?"

Heat rose in her cheeks, and she clenched her fists to keep from cursing. "I like signing documents in blue ink."

There was a hint of disbelief in the way he nodded, those clever eyes still watching her. His gaze moved boldly from where she knew her rapid pulse could be seen in the hollow of her neck, down to the swell of her breasts on display, thanks to the very low-cut tank top she'd pulled on after her shower. How in the hell had she forgotten that he was coming over?

Because she was bone tired and had wanted to eat, drink wine, and climb into bed. Now the bad-news lawyer got to see her in tiny black shorts with the words *hot buns* scrawled across her ass and a tank top that had lost all its elasticity from too many trips through the washing machine.

He held up a pen as she continued to work through her irritation and embarrassment. "I always have my clients sign in blue as well. That way we know which one is the original."

She nodded as he said that last part. Another lawyer had told her that years ago, and the concept had stuck. Actually, she preferred writing in blue ink anyway, but he didn't need to know all that.

"Good. I can sign and then you can—" She was about to say he could leave, but after he pulled two blue pens and a small stack of papers from his bag, Desmond set that bag on the floor and parked his too-sexy-for-her-senses self down like he'd been invited to dinner.

Well, she had directed him to the chair.

With a heavy sigh, she moved to her seat, grateful that at least the table hid her long and very exposed legs from his view. There wasn't anything she could do about her parade of cleavage without drawing attention to the fact that she knew she was displaying too much skin in the first place. Getting him out of here fast was the best option.

"Okay, where do I sign?" A curse almost followed the question as she watched him pick up a pen, remove the top and place it at the other end, and then let the pen slide into an easy grip between his fingers. Her traitorous thoughts had her imagining those same fingers moving with identical efficiency and purpose over her . . .

"Do you share?"

She gulped and forced her gaze up to his. "Excuse me?" Parroting his former question must've made her appear unfocused or uncouth. Neither of which she was known for being.

"I said, do you share?" And he looked down at the crumpled Jersey Mike's paper that held the other three-fourths of her sub.

She frowned. "You always roll up in strange women's houses and ask for their food?"

He chuckled. "Only when I'm hungry."

Obviously, he was also damn alluring when he was hungry. She used a napkin to pick up a piece of the sandwich and set it in front of him.

"I've never had a client so out of sorts about dealing with a parent's estate." He took a bite of the sandwich and reached for another napkin.

The stack she'd grabbed at Jersey Mike's was in the center of the table where a real napkin holder and store-bought napkins probably should've been.

"Are they normally jumping for joy over having to pay to cremate someone they barely knew?"

"I told you you'll be reimbursed for all expenses once the estate is opened," he said after chewing the second big bite he'd taken. He hadn't lied, he was hungry.

"How, if I haven't sold the properties yet?"

"Didn't you read all the paperwork I sent you in the mail?"

No, she hadn't. And no, she wasn't watching this man chew, at least not anymore. Turning her attention to her own sandwich now, she picked it up and took a bite, hoping the flavorful meats and cheeses would redirect her thoughts. "They just came on Saturday," she replied when she'd finished chewing.

His brows arched. "Today's Monday."

"I don't read on Sundays."

"Really? What do you do on Sundays?"

None of your business. "Sometimes I go to church with my family. Other times I sleep in late, roll out of bed around noon, and eat cereal right out of the box while staring out of this window."

He looked out of the window. "Nice view."

There was a park across the street from her apartment building. Mature trees and rolling grass created a serene skyline that she enjoyed after being in the trenches with murder suspects ten to twelve hours a day. On Sundays, people walked their dogs, or pushed their kids in strollers through the park. Toddlers ran around giggling, new couples held hands, normal-type stuff. The stuff Sharae had never envisioned in her future. Her past was too dark and dismal to ever consider having a family of her own.

"So you're a church girl?" He was just about finished with his piece of the sandwich.

She took another napkin and gave him a second piece. Then it dawned on her that he might be thirsty after feasting on her dinner. Of course, her glass of pink Moscato was on the table a few inches away from her plate. Getting up, she went into the kitchen and grabbed a can of Coke from the refrigerator. She offered it to him when she returned, and he accepted it with a nod of thanks.

"My uncle's a pastor. I lived with him, my aunt, and my cousins after Sanford went to jail. But even before that, church was as regular as going to school." And it'd taken years after her mother's death before sitting in a sanctuary felt normal again.

"I used to go," he said after pulling the tab back to open the can. "When I was younger, I mean. Not so much once I got to college and grew older."

"Too grown for the Lord," she said with a chuckle. "That's what my Aunt Vi would say." She'd said it to Sharae whenever she missed too many Sundays.

"Nah, never that," he replied. "Just got busy and then never took the time to find a church home. What church does your uncle pastor? Maybe I'll stop by."

Oh, please don't. The words almost fell from her mouth. If a man showed up at NVB and said he came because he knew Sharae, the Aunts would be halfway to picking out wedding invitations and thinking of baby names before the service was over. "New Visionary Baptist," she told him, figuring if he lived in the city, he'd have heard of it before.

His immediate nod said she was right. "That big church right off 83?"

She nodded too. "That's the one."

"Okay, yeah, I've heard about it. Maybe I will stop by one day."

"The doors are open to all," she said and then reached for her glass. After taking a gulp, she put the glass down and pointed to the papers. "Are you going to tell me where to sign now? I mean, you've just about eaten half my sandwich. If you sit here any longer, you might start thinkin' about spending the night." Her lips clamped shut once the words were out.

He wiped his hands on his napkin, that half smile ghosting his face once more. Turning the papers around so they'd be easy for her to read, he pushed them the short distance across the table toward her. Then he picked up the pen and reached over to place it in her hand. His touch was warm, and he moved slowly, wrapping her fingers around the slim tool with deliberate movements.

"You sign right where the yellow tab is on each," he said, his voice gruff with an emotion she didn't even want to explore.

Sharae signed each one of those pages so fast she didn't even think she'd spelled her name correctly. Then she hurried that too-fine, too-distracting man right out of her house before she did something totally out of order, like insist that he spend the night.

"I don't know why Marc didn't just ask us to cook for this gathering," Aunt Ceil said as she stood near the jug at the end of the table and fixed herself a cup of fruit punch.

It was a gorgeous Saturday afternoon, perfect weather for the community celebration of Baltimore's own R & B singing group, The Squad. Marc Miles, Jemel's boyfriend, was the lead singer of the group that fifteen years ago had been at the peak of their career. This morning, they'd all attended the ceremony at Morgan State, Marc's alma mater, where the music department had honored the group with its Humanitarian Award. Jemel had beamed proudly as her man was on that stage, while Sharae and Rita stood beside her clapping and sharing in the happy moment with her.

Now they were sitting at one of the many tables positioned under a reserved pavilion at Druid Hill Park, the first place The Squad had performed all those years ago. The Aunts, who'd complained about just about everything at the ceremony, were apparently ready to do the same at this supposedly festive community function.

"I mean, if you're gonna put burgers on the grill, you could at least use fresh ground beef," Aunt Rose chimed in. "I don't like no beef patties." With her face fixed in a frown, she picked up the hot dog she'd taken from the grill area instead and took a bite.

Aunt Vi nodded as she used her fork to push pieces of the shrimp away from the small scoop of seafood salad she'd put on her plate. "And use shrimp big enough that I can actually taste in the salad."

Sharae grinned and shook her head. She was smart enough not to respond when the Aunts were carefully dissecting a menu.

"I made way too much potato salad for the baby shower I catered last night, so there's a bowl in my cooler over there," Rita told them.

Aunt Ceil perked up as she set her cup in front of the spot where she'd been sitting. "Oh really?" She made her way over to the cooler without wasting another second.

Rita unpacked one of the many bags she'd had Sharae help her carry from her car when they arrived. "And I've got sandwiches, chips, fruit salad, and some crab balls too."

"That's my girl," Aunt Vi said and pushed the plate she'd already fixed to the side.

"I don't know why they even took that other food. They know they never like anything anybody else cooks," Sharae whispered when Rita sat a bag in front of her to unpack.

Rita shook her head. "Girl, you know how they are. Gotta taste everything."

"And critique it down to the brand of salt used to season it," she replied with a chuckle.

There were at least two hundred people out here today, all milling around the tables they'd claimed upon arriving. About twenty feet from the pavilion was a stage with a DJ situated in its center. Music played from huge speakers while smoke billowed up to the brilliantly sunny afternoon sky as three grills worked to cook a variety of meats. Hot dogs and hamburgers for sure, but she thought she could also smell some barbeque—chicken and ribs, most likely.

"The tuna sandwiches are in that container in the cooler," Rita told them. "But the others are over here."

Sharae opened the plastic container Rita had just pointed to, knowing there'd be a variety of sandwiches inside. Rita's sandwiches could put Jersey Mike's out of business with the assortment of breads she used and the different ensemble of deli meats and cheeses. She also made her own seasoned oil that Sharae loved eating spread across fresh baked bread without anything else.

"Now, this is good picnic food," Aunt Rose said. She'd put what looked like a sandwich with two types of ham, turkey, and Muenster cheese on rye bread onto her plate. Rita had set plastic bottles of condiments in the center of their table, along with a platter of lettuce, olives, and pickles.

"There're two pound cakes—almond and lemon—wrapped in that foil at the other end of the table too," Rita told them as she continued unpacking and making sure she hadn't forgotten anything. Which she never did.

It was a private Johnson-family smorgasbord.

Sharae chose the tuna sandwich because she loved the way Rita chopped the celery so fine and used a bit of Old Bay Seasoning for a tangy punch to an old favorite. Adding a few crab balls and some BBQ chips to her plate, she sat next to Aunt Ceil on the bench. Aunt Rose was on the same side of the bench while Aunt Vi and Rita sat across from them.

"Jemel's not here yet?" Aunt Ceil asked after a few minutes.

"I think she was going to stop home to change first," Rita said.

Aunt Vi shook her head. "She should've put another outfit in their truck and changed at the school. It doesn't look good that one of the guests of honor is late."

"I don't think you can count this as being late, Mama," Rita replied. "It seems pretty informal to me, and besides, the group's not supposed to play until around four, I believe. That's when the media people are set to arrive."

"If there's a schedule, it's not informal," was Aunt Vi's haughty retort.

Aunt Rose popped an olive into her mouth. "That child never did have a grasp on time."

"Yeah, she's always had that adventurous spirit," Aunt Ceil added.

"What's that got to do with being on time, Ceil?" Aunt Rose snapped.

Aunt Vi shook her head while spreading mayonnaise on one slice of her bread. "It just doesn't look good."

It was possible to get whiplash at how fast the Aunts could go from complaining about one thing to another.

"Maybe Marc's proposing, and that's what's taking them so long." The hope in Aunt Ceil's voice was unmistakable. Just as the quick oh-no look Rita passed Sharae was totally understandable. Aunt Ceil had been planning Jemel's wedding since the girl had gotten her first period. It was like that milestone had ushered Jemel into the available-wife status, and Aunt Ceil was watching the clock and the front door for Jemel's husband-to-be to finally appear. As Marc and Jemel had been heavily involved in an on-again, off-again relationship for the past fifteen years, there were currently bets on whether he was the one. Tariq, of course, had coordinated the pool of gamblers on their cousin's love life.

"She don't need to rush into no marriage," Aunt Rose added. "Matrimony ain't meant for everybody."

With that remark, the Aunts' full attention landed on Rita. Sharae watched sorrowfully as Rita realized this too, but took her time slicing a crab ball in half on her plate.

"How're the girls dealing with you and Nate's separation, Rita?" Aunt Ceil asked, her tone soft, as if she didn't want anyone else to hear about the big bad divorce in the family.

These women were Sharae's role models. After her mother, there'd never been any other women she loved and admired more. Because Rita and Jemel were her age, the bond between them had always seemed on another level entirely separate from the Aunts. The Johnson sisters had a confident and regal air to them, despite their very humble and tumultuous upbringing during the years of segregation and the Civil Rights Movement. But there was no mistaking that they could also be the most critical and sanctimonious women she'd ever met.

Rita cleared her throat. "It's going to be an adjustment for all of us."

That was the official statement. Rita had said it a couple of times over the phone when Sharae had asked how things were going with the divorce. Sharae knew she was holding back, but she and Jemel hadn't figured out when they were going to pressure her about it.

"They need to respect the decision, even if they don't like it," Aunt Vi began. "Taryn was over the house the other day, and I had to tell her she wasn't too old to get smacked in the mouth."

Sharae felt the quick wave of rage that crossed Rita's face as if it were a physical slap and immediately spoke up. "It's still new," she said. "Give them time to get their bearings."

Not that she didn't think Taryn and Necole could be a handful. For all that Rita was a good mother, those girls could be on the mouthy side, but Rita and Nate had insisted their children have the freedom to express themselves. Sharae, Jemel, and Rita hadn't been raised that way. Any expressions they had that differed from whatever they were told to do were best mumbled behind the closed door of their bedroom. And even then, the Aunts' super hearing abilities sometimes led to another scolding.

"It's not their business," Aunt Rose said.

"Well, Nate's their father. I guess they are entitled to feel some kind of way about him leaving," Aunt Ceil added.

"He didn't leave, he was put out," Aunt Vi clarified.

"Because he was cheating on me and got another woman pregnant," Rita countered, bringing the tension at the table to a fever pitch.

"Hey, y'all!" Sharae had never been happier to see Jemel prancing over to the table, waving like she hadn't just seen them forty-five minutes ago.

Marc walked beside her, holding her hand and grinning just like Jemel. They really did make a cute couple. If they could actually get their act together long enough to remain one, it would be cool. At least, Sharae figured that was the way it should be. Relationships weren't her thing, so knowing who should be together and who shouldn't didn't come as easily to her as it did the Aunts.

In the next moments, Marc was embracing each aunt, and Sharae watched the older women hug and kiss him. Each congratulating him and wishing him well as if they hadn't just been talking about the woman this man loved and her tardiness.

"Girl, you came right on time," Sharae said to Jemel, who was standing at the end of the table where she and Rita sat. "They were just starting to go in on Rita about the divorce."

"No," Rita said and rolled her eyes. "They were just critiquing my parenting skills."

Jemel glanced at Sharae, and Sharae gave a quick, short shake of her head, warning her to not go there right now.

"Well, this party is lookin' dry," Jemel said. "Let me go over there and tell the DJ to play something jumpin'."

And that was just what Jemel did. The next song that came on was the "Cupid Shuffle," and in true Black-cookout fashion, just about everybody got up from their seats and formed a couple of lines in the grass to dance every step to the song. By the time Sharae, Rita, and Jemel returned to the table, the Aunts had found another subject to dissect, and the afternoon progressed without any further family discussions.

That worked out well for Rita, who looked tired but continued to smile and chat with whoever came by their table. Jemel was in her element, beaming with pride as Marc and The Squad finally took to the stage to sing one of their early ballads and then standing by Marc's side as he was interviewed by reporters. It was moments like this that Sharae felt a little left out. She wasn't the socialite, nor had she ever wanted to be the center of attention. All she'd ever aspired to be was a cop, but today, she wondered if that was really enough. If the life she'd created for herself had somehow become a box she didn't know how to break out of.

Where those thoughts came from she had no idea. Perhaps because Sanford was dead. The man she'd blamed for all her unhappiness growing up was gone, so now whose fault was it that this feeling of discontent had suddenly crept up on her? She didn't have any answers, nor did she feel like hunting through her mind to find them. Instead, she went to Rita's second stash situated under the table, grabbed a wine cooler, and stood by herself drinking and swaying to the nostalgic sound of rhythm and blues on a balmy summer's night.

Chapter 13

A New Day.

"That sleazy, no-good bastard!" Jemel picked up, then punched, one of the throw pillows on the beige sectional in Rita's living room. She'd been sitting at one end, her legs tucked under her, white-painted toenails winking at the world. Now she clenched the pillow between her hands like she was strangling it . . . or someone.

From the other side, with her legs stretched out along the extended end of the furniture, Sharae shook her head. "I'm not even surprised. When you're already considered dirt, there's nothing you can do to take you any lower."

Rita sat comfortably with her hands resting on the wide arms of the chair across from them. One leg was crossed over the other, comfortable fluffy purple socks on her feet. "I'm over it," she said, her even tone depicting the peace she'd come to feel about the situation. "And I sold every piece of jewelry he ever gave me."

Sharae's eyes widened. "All of it?" She waited a beat. "Even that ruby-and-diamond necklace-earring set you hated wearing because you thought it was gaudy and over the top?"

With a slow nod, Rita said, "That twenty-two-thousand-dollar perfectly ugly ruby-and-diamond necklace-and-earring set."

"That's right! Get your money!" Jemel added. "But you still need to get back half of what that asshole took out of those accounts."

"My lawyer's taking care of that," she told them. "I considered emptying the second joint savings account but decided playing tit for tat wouldn't make me any better than him."

Jemel shook her head. "You always taking that high road, I swear. I would've taken every penny out of any other accounts left with both our names on them."

Why didn't that response shock her? Rita chuckled as Sharae shrugged. "I don't really see nothin' wrong with that. I mean, it's only fair."

"My lawyer said she'll get it all back and then some. I'm trusting her to do that," Rita told them. Clearing her throat, she prepared to tell them the real reason she'd invited them over here on a Sunday afternoon. "I also had some money of my own that I've been saving for the past few years or so." Six years, to be exact. When she'd looked at the account with only her name on it with more detail, she saw that every catering job she'd been paid for in the last six years, she'd deposited the checks into that account and hadn't thought about them again. Over time, that money had gained considerable interest.

"Oh no, Miss Prim and Proper wasn't keeping a secret stash from her husband." The smile on Jemel's face said she totally approved if that were the case, which it was not.

"Nate knew I'd started getting paid for the jobs that I did outside the church and the dealership. In fact, he and I had discussed what I should charge when the school board asked me to cater their appreciation dinner." They'd gone to dinner down at Little Italy that night, and he'd told her she should definitely start charging for her time and services. He'd even told her to contact their business attorney to get a contract drawn up that she could use for future clients. Funny how the good moments with Nate were much harder to remember now than the bad ones.

"And last year, he'd decided I would start being paid by the dealership to plan and cater the holiday party each year."

"But you didn't put that money in your joint account?" Sharae let the question linger in the air even though Rita was certain she wanted to say something else.

"No, I didn't," she replied. "And you know what? I don't know why I didn't." Rita had believed her marriage was a partnership and that whatever she had, Nate had also and vice versa. For years she'd listened to Aunt Rose go on and on about being independent, owning her house and having her own money. It was no family secret that her aunt loved men—loved sleeping with them and using them for whatever else she wanted at the time—but never kept one longer than it took to get what she could from him.

Aunt Rose's stance was that she could take care of herself and would only tolerate a man if he was bringing something extra to the table. From what Rita could remember, Aunt Rose never lacked for a man in her life, regardless of those terms. What her aunt also never experienced, as far as Rita could tell, was a broken heart.

"I guess deep down you always knew you'd need a safety net," Sharae was saying, snapping Rita from her thoughts.

"I guess." She shrugged. "Anyway, what I called you over here for was to tell you what else I've decided to do."

Jemel sat up straighter, tucking the pillow under her arm this time. "We rollin' up on this chick that slept with your man? 'Cause that was mad disrespectful, and she needs to know that."

"Nate's the one who's married. It was his responsibility to be loyal to her," Sharae said.

"Still, that heffa knew he was married. I just can't get with women who're okay with sleeping with men who're already in a committed relationship." Jemel was shaking her head. "Even if he tells you they're 'having problems' or 'separated,' whatever, until he's *dee*-vorced and can show me them signed court papers, he can skip his happy little dick on off to somebody else."

It could never be said that Jemel minced words about how she felt on any given subject. Rita admired and respected her cousin for that trait.

"Well, at least she's letting him go on and be with whoever he wants to now," Sharae said after nodding at Jemel. She looked back to Rita and continued, "Now it's time for you to start over, and we're here for whatever you need us to do to help."

New day, new me. That was what Rita had whispered to herself when she'd gotten out of bed this morning. "That's exactly what I wanted to tell you. I couldn't talk in church, so I figured we could just chat here."

"You should've also figured we'd eat dinner here too," Jemel chimed in with a huge grin.

Shaking her head, Rita could only smile. "You already know I cooked."

"I sure do. I can smell that roast baking in the oven," Jemel said. "But I was tryin' to be polite and wait for that invitation too."

"Since when have you ever been polite?" Sharae asked.

They all laughed.

"I'm going to start a catering business," Rita said a few moments later, cutting through the laughter.

"Well, it's about damn time," Jemel snapped.

Sharae clapped. "I second that."

Rita felt the bubble of anxiety she'd been walking around with most of last week subside a bit. After speaking with Sharon about Nate emptying the accounts, she'd mentioned the possibility of wanting to start her own business because she needed to ask how that would play out during the divorce. Sharon didn't think it was a problem as long as Rita wasn't asking for alimony, which Rita had already decided she wouldn't. Her plan was to take care of herself and to take half of everything she and Nate had built. Sharon had happily directed Rita to a business attorney.

Sighing loudly, Rita rubbed her hands down her thighs. "I've been thinking about what you were going to say all week." Even though she'd known neither of them would try to talk her out of it. The Aunts, on the other hand, were going to be a totally different ball game. But Rita was ready. She had to be.

"Girl, please. You know we got your back," Jemel said. "Besides, I know all about wanting to be your own boss. I can take you right down to the bank where I got my small-business loan, and you can get started right away."

"I don't need a loan," Rita said. "I told you I had money saved up, and besides, I think I'm just going to redecorate my basement to act as my office, at least for now. That'll cut out costs." She'd drafted a business plan and had done a cost-analysis report, which the business attorney was looking over this week.

"You've really thought this through," Sharae said. "I'm proud of you."

"Me too," Jemel added. "And I'd like to be your first official client."

"What?" Rita hadn't expected that. Then again, Jemel was known for her impetuous nature, so Rita shouldn't have been all that surprised.

Now, Jemel let her legs fall off the chair and sat up so that she could lean forward, elbows resting on her knees. "Remember when we were at the funeral home and Ditzy Dinah was talking about how Yolanda liked to do stuff for the community?"

"Was that before I arrived? 'Cause I don't remember that conversation," Sharae said.

Rita nodded. "Yeah, it was before you got there. Yolanda does all the flowers for the funeral home, but Jemel doesn't like her because she's cheap," she said by way of a recap.

It was Sharae's turn to nod now. "Got it."

"So I was thinking that maybe I could do like you said and have a fundraiser, then donate the proceeds. Marc and I were talking, and he suggested supporting the music programs in the city schools. You know they never give enough to the music or any of the arts programs, and kids need a way to showcase their talent." Jemel should've been out of breath at that quick spiel, but she wasn't.

Instead, Rita saw a gleam in her cousin's eyes that she hadn't seen since Jemel had announced she was opening her flower shop. It was that same look that Rita had felt when she'd decided it was time for her to open her own business. "Let's do it," Rita said. "We'll rent the Rowing and Water Resource Center down on Waterview and invite all the politicians that come to the church. They won't say no because they know you're Daddy's niece, and they don't want him on their bad side because they'll eventually need him to rally his members into voting for them again."

"And I can get the sheriffs and maybe the FOP to show some support, too," Sharae added.

Even more excited now, Jemel clapped her hands together. "Necole's good with graphic design," she said. "She helped me with my website. We can have her do some amazing invitations and tickets."

"Email blasts," Rita said, feeling her own excitement grow. She loved planning and executing events. Not as much as she loved cooking, but in this instance, the two would go hand in hand. "We should do a massive email blast."

"Right," Sharae added. "It'll announce the opening of your business and promote the event."

Was this really happening? In the midst of all the turmoil she'd been going through these last two weeks, was she actually sitting here feeling the giddiness of planning what she already knew was going to be a spectacular event? Why, yes. Yes, indeed, she was!

Rita smiled nervously. "I'm opening my own business, and you're gonna be my first client." She squealed and jumped up out of her chair to run over and hug Jemel. "Thank you!" While she hadn't thought it would be a problem to get clients because she'd been booking between three and five catering jobs throughout the year already, having this fundraiser be the first from her new company could be huge. And she owed it all to Jemel.

"No," Jemel said, standing to return Rita's hug. "Thank you for the initial idea. You're always so full of good ideas, Rita. I'm glad your next one is to start your own business."

"Wait, don't leave me out," Sharae said and then joined them for another hug.

Rita held on to them tightly, reveling in the sisterhood that they shared and the rejuvenating spirit she always found when she was with them. For the next hour they talked about plans for the event, tried out names for her business and for the event, and Rita didn't think about how anybody else would feel about her new venture in life. As long as her girls had her back, she had nothing to worry about.

It was well past midnight, and Sharae's mind still buzzed with all the plans she, Jemel, and Rita had made tonight. Her cousins were both doing something new, while Sharae . . . well, she was still Sharae. And amid those plans were the worries that had been steadily creeping into Sharae's mind every day since she'd learned Sanford had died.

Sitting in her car across the street from the cemetery, she let her head fall against the headrest and sighed. It was too late to visit her mother's grave. Besides, that was something she usually did with Jemel, Rita, and the Aunts. She'd never gone alone, and whenever she went with them, she never said a word. The Aunts always talked to her mother as if she were standing right there with them, giving her a recap of things that had happened in the family over the previous year as if she cared. If what the Aunts had told her all her life was true—that her mother had been looking down on Sharae, watching her grow up and keeping her safe as she interacted with criminals on a daily basis—then they shouldn't have had to tell her anything. At least Sharae always used that as her excuse for remaining silent.

"Are you watching me now?" She spoke into the silent interior of the car. "Do you know what he's doing to me?"

Sharae didn't really know, or she couldn't figure out why it was such a big deal that Sanford was dead. She hadn't loved him. Not anymore. And she'd barely thought about him in the past years. At least she cursed herself each time she did. So it didn't matter.

Yet, it did. Because of him she was the woman she was today. The woman who was so hell-bent on being the best cop she could be that she never took a moment to consider there could be something else in her life. Or someone else?

With a heavy sigh, she shook her head. "You are not thinking about that guy again."

"That guy" being her attorney. Why Desmond kept popping into her mind, she had no idea. Their only interaction had been about the business of Sanford's estate. Except when she'd shared her sandwich with him. Well, no, that was still business. It hadn't been her intention to feed the guy. And yet, she'd watched him chew and hadn't balked as he'd unnecessarily touched her hand as he gave her a pen.

"Foolish!"

She lifted her head and slammed her palms against the steering wheel.

"You're sitting in a car talking to yourself. That's the definition of being foolish."

Or was it just that she didn't trust her thoughts or—apparently—her cousins enough to share any of this with them. Jemel would have opinions. Jemel always had opinions. And Rita would rationalize the situation. But in the end, it would be Sharae who decided what she would do, how she would make it through this new scenario. Because it *was* a scenario. One where she had to again push Sanford out of her life and at the same time confront what her issue really was with being attracted to Desmond or any other man, for that matter.

"I wish you were here," she said, more quietly this time.

If her mother were here, she'd talk to her the way they always used to talk. And Justine would tell her what she should do. Sharae had missed that most of all. Talking to her mom and hearing her mother's voice in response. That couldn't be done at the grave site, and it wasn't going to happen as she sat here in her car alone.

Still, before she started the engine and pulled off, she whispered one more time, "I really wish you were here."

Chapter 14

THE CURSE.

"How you gon' look at me crazy 'cause there're spots on your glasses?" Vi frowned. Her caramel-toned sixty-four-year-old skin didn't show one crack as she continued to shake her head. Using the napkin that had been folded neatly on the table when they were seated, she cleaned every utensil before setting them on one of the new napkins she'd already requested.

The server had looked at her like she'd spoken a different language when it was clear as day that the glass had spots on it, most likely left over from the detergent they used in the dishwasher. Still, Vi had a tone to her voice that could immediately offend. Rita had watched her use it endlessly at church whenever somebody thought they were gonna come at her sideways about anything.

"She'll bring you another glass, Mama," Rita said, already regretting agreeing to have lunch with her mother today.

But it was something that had to be done, and handling things sooner rather than later was Rita's new mantra. It had taken her way too long to decide to leave Nate and to realize she wanted to open her own business. But there was nothing she could do about that now. Nothing but move forward. She wasn't putting off doing anything anymore, and scratching items off her always lengthy list of things to do was a new hobby.

She had no other choice, really. After the many hours she, Sharae, and Jemel had spent talking about and planning her new business and Jemel's fundraiser, she had a ton of things she needed to do to get ready. Streamlining and prioritizing were the only ways she was going to survive the next few months. That, and finally getting on even ground with her mother.

Her purse hung on the side of the chair, but she set her phone on the table and placed her napkin neatly in her lap.

"That meeting went well past an hour, and they knew it would," Vi continued, her lips curved upward at the corners as she did one of the things she loved to do—complain about church stuff.

Rita had often wondered why her mother had married a preacher when it seemed she rarely found anything good about being in the church. Sure, she could spout a scripture for any circumstance, and for the most part she walked the saved-and-sanctified line pretty well, but there'd been tiny glimpses of another side of Violet Leanda Johnson Henderson that had given Rita the barest space to breathe. Because as long as her mother wasn't the saint she sometimes proclaimed to be, Rita could justify all the times she'd dared to stray from the generational curses being passed down from one Johnson girl child to the next. Unfortunately, after the demise of her marriage, Rita wasn't sure she'd strayed far enough.

"There was a lot on the agenda because it's the anniversary celebration. I think it went well, all things considered." With "all things" being the fact that her mother had tried to spearhead the meeting, circumventing the two committee chairs that had been elected.

She opened the menu and stared at it to avoid the chastising glare she could feel Vi tossing her way. Disagreeing with her mother wasn't something Rita did often—at least not to her face.

"Well, I'm glad it's over. I'll talk to Carol about keeping more to the meeting guidelines established during our leadership training later tonight. She'll be at choir practice by the time I get finished at the hairdresser, so I'll have to put an alarm on my phone to remind me." Vi did that while Rita continued staring at the menu.

She wasn't really hungry. In fact, she hadn't been eating much in the past two weeks. It would've probably been another stroke to Nate's humongous ego if the reason for her loss of appetite had been because of him moving out of the house, but that wasn't the case. That blame rested solely on her Aunt Rose, who'd commented on Rita looking "fat in the face" a few weeks ago. Not that any of the Aunts could talk with their very round, full faces and bodies that matched, but that had never stopped any of them from remarking on how she or any of her cousins looked.

A few minutes later Vi had put down her phone, and they'd both ordered grilled chicken Caesar salads.

"I don't know when was the last time I've had cold chicken. I hope they heat it before putting it on the salad," Vi said as she surveyed the new glass the server had brought her.

"I made rotisserie chicken salad last week when we had all those chickens left over from the women's ministry meeting. I took the sandwiches down to the shelter the next morning," Rita said. Thinking back on it now, it was a really good thing she'd decided to make a business out of doing something she loved, because she really did have a serious cooking regimen. She'd baked cookies and brownies for the youth ministry meeting a couple of days ago and had cooked pork chops, onions, and gravy for the fellowship after morning service yesterday. And that had been in addition to the dinner she'd cooked for her house.

"Did you add some vegetables? You know you could've done some mini carrots and cauliflower. You could just drop them into a plastic bag. That'd be a good way for people to get their vegetables. I used to always do a nice vegetable scramble for you and Benny so you got your daily dose."

Rita sipped from her glass of water. "Mm-hmm. I do the same every time I fix eggs. Whatever I have in the fridge at the time—scallions, red or green peppers—I just chop them up and toss 'em in."

"Mmm, that sounds good."

The one thing Rita and Vi could always talk about was food. It was their common link, and rightfully so. She'd learned so much standing at her mother's elbow watching her cook. And the way food had always brought her family together had inspired Rita early on to do her very best in the kitchen. She'd wanted nothing more from her family than to be held tight by the same threads that had been weaved so intricately through the Johnson clan. Through the good, bad, and the worst—Aunt Justine's death—they'd always stuck together, using food as a reason for fellowship while showering love and support on each other.

"So," her mother began after she'd taken the first forkful of her salad, chewed, and decided the chunks of grilled chicken were warm and therefore acceptable.

Rita had just finished her first bite as well when the one word had her tensing.

"You really going through with this divorce?"

Rita had already swallowed the food, but it sat in the back of her throat, threatening to come back up, and tension immediately hovered over the table.

"Yes," she answered after clearing her throat and willing the food to stay put. Just in case, she took another drink of water.

"I don't know when the last time we've had a divorce in the family," Vi continued and gathered more salad on her fork.

"You mean after Aunt Ceil?" It was knee jerk and sassy as hell. Rita took another sip of her water.

"That man ain't want a family. Ceil didn't have a choice," Vi countered.

"Nate left me each time he found his way to another woman's bed. And as long as I forgave and forgot, he was going to continue," she said. "I don't have it in me anymore."

"What? The ability to forgive? Because you know that Jesus forgave . . ."

"Yes, ma'am. I know all that Jesus did and how his life was given for my sins. I thank the Lord for all that every day. But I can't be thankful for a man that doesn't respect me or our marriage enough to stay faithful. Even the Bible said a man should keep only with his wife."

Vi snatched up her napkin, dabbed it to her lips, and continued to hold the crumpled cloth tightly in her hand. "Well, I see you brought the attitude with you today. I thought this was gonna be a nice, simple lunch."

Nothing was ever nice and simple when her mother had something on her mind. "Mama, I'm forty-two years old. Just because I counter something you say doesn't mean I've got attitude. I'm old enough to have a different opinion."

"You're also old enough to know that people make mistakes," Vi continued.

"Are you gonna sit here and tell me that I should forgive him for getting another woman pregnant?" Lord, please say that wasn't what her mother was telling her.

"Do you know if it's his? Was there a DNA test?"

"Mama." That was all Rita could manage before a heavy sigh.

"Don't 'Mama' me. Do you know how many women have chased behind your father? Wanting the first-lady title without doing any of the work. You can't trust every word that comes out of a woman's mouth."

She wasn't lying about that, but Nate had a track record, one Rita had ignored too many times before. Whether or not that woman was really carrying Nate's baby, Rita didn't care. It was the infidelity that mattered to her. The blatant disrespect time and time again, and then the insult of him not even bothering to give a credible excuse, other than to accuse her of overreacting.

"I'm just tired, Mama. Have you ever been tired of Daddy and all the church drama that comes with being married to a pastor?" That question had crossed Rita's mind so many times in the past. Today seemed to be the day to ask, since, as her mother put it, she'd brought the attitude.

Vi shook her head. Her hair was perfectly bump curled at the ends, so Rita didn't know why she was going to get it done this afternoon. Then again, she did know—Vi had a standing weekly appointment at the hairdresser and nail shop. She wore the most stylish skirt suits and shoes because she had a title and a reputation to uphold. And according to the Aunts, Vi had always been the too-cute sister. Rita had taken after her to the extent that she did like to look nice whenever she came out her front door, and most times while she was walking around the house too. Sharae had often joked that Rita went to sleep pretty and woke up the same way. Grandma Patty always said Black folk had to be better and work harder. That started in the mind and translated in their presentation. Rita took that advice seriously.

"I know how to play my position, Rita. That's what you've got to learn to do. You worked hard being Nate's wife, raising those girls, and building that business. Now you're just pushing it all out the door."

"My daughters will always be with me." Even though Taryn was still a bit salty about the situation. "And the business, well, it was always more Nate's than mine." This would've been the perfect time to announce that she was opening her own business, especially considering her new stance to just get things done. But she, Jemel, and Sharae had decided they'd wait to announce the new business when they had all the preliminary things ready to also announce the fundraiser. The two were going to be highly marketed together, so they'd thought dropping it all on the Aunts at one time was the way to go. And it gave Rita a little more time to ponder her mother's reaction, which was probably dangerously close to the one she was having now about the divorce.

"Nonsense," Vi continued. "You worked your butt off in those early years. I know because I was the one keeping those girls while you spent hours at the dealership getting all the paperwork in order. And Nate knows you're the backbone of the business too. That's what he told your father anyway."

"Nate talked to Daddy? When?"

"Last week. Your father called him as soon as I told him about the divorce."

Her father had called Nate but hadn't said a word to her about the divorce. How did that make sense? Then again, looking back on her life, there'd been so many things that just didn't make sense to her right now.

"Look, Mama, I'm doing what's right for me."

Vi raised a brow. "And to hell with everybody else?"

"No. I don't wish hell on anybody. But I'm finished putting Nate's feelings, Taryn and Necole's feelings, yours and Daddy's, everybody except my own feelings first." She wanted a drink to back those words up. That was how she'd been coming to terms with all this nonsense in the past couple of weeks—sit, think about it, make a decision, and then have a glass of wine, or two, to chase away the doubts. So far, it'd been working just fine.

Her phone chimed, stopping Vi from making her next statement. Rita glanced at it and swiped the screen when she saw it was a text message.

"Wendy's bridal shower is this weekend in Ocean City," she said, reading over the reminder filled with pink, gold, and white hearts and balloons, which seemed to be the theme of Wendy and Ivan's wedding.

"Yeah, Rose was talkin' about that last night. Y'all don't get too out of hand down there." Vi gave the warning and settled into another bite of her salad.

Considering the discussion of her divorce over and thanking the heavens, Rita continued. "It'll be good to get away for a couple days." She sent a separate text to Sharae and Jemel, asking which one of them was driving down, and then pushed her phone to the side.

"I still have to get her a gift, but I really don't know what to buy."

"She's got everything. The way she spends Ivan's money is shameful."

Rita chuckled and shook her head. "You know she has a job. She's spending her own money."

"Hmph." Lifting a hand, Vi waved away Rita's comment and continued. "She works at Walmart, and Ivan's got that good finance job. She ain't buying Gucci on her paycheck."

"There's nothing wrong with workin' at Walmart, Mama."

"Never said there was. All I said was she likes spending Ivan's money." Vi shrugged. "And hey, if she's gonna marry him and take care of him, then she gets to do that. No complaints over here."

Rita wisely kept her mouth shut, deciding to focus more on her salad than her conversation with her mother, because if there was one thing for sure, it was that Vi Henderson wasn't ever gonna change. Her mind was set in the ways she'd been brought up and the life she'd created for herself, and Rita didn't begrudge her that. Sure, there was a part of her that wished she'd made some different choices in her early adult years. Perhaps she didn't have to take her mother's teachings so seriously. What would've happened if she'd listened to Sharae when she'd insisted Rita hadn't even experienced being an adult before she was diving into being a wife?

She'd thought about this repeatedly in the past weeks, coming to the conclusion that shoulda-woulda-coulda thoughts were pointless. The past couldn't be undone, and she needed to focus on the future.

With that in mind, two hours later, Rita walked into her house. After changing out of the pantsuit she'd worn to the meeting and lunch, opting for comfortable knit capris and an oversize T-shirt, she grabbed her tablet and returned to the living room. Dropping down onto the sectional, she pulled up the lists she'd made last night and began reviewing the one for the contractor she needed to hire. Besides converting the front of her basement to an office where she could receive clients, she also wanted to make some changes to her kitchen. When she'd first moved here, she'd designed the perfect personal cooking space for her. Now she needed to reimagine the space into the most efficient working space.

A part of her wanted to err on the side of caution where this new business and the changes to her house were concerned. To make the least amount of changes to the place she'd considered her safe haven, just in case things didn't go the way she planned.

Faith over fear.

Those three words echoed in her mind as she recalled reciting them last night and on so many other occasions in her life. She had to have faith that God's will for her life would be done, and that needed to be bigger than the fear of making yet another mistake.

It had occurred to her after her lunch with her mother that she'd self-consciously tried to play it safe all these years. That was why she'd married the first man to ask her and why she'd stayed even when she'd known he wasn't who she'd thought he was. But that couldn't be the only reason she'd stayed with Nate. He wasn't her safety net—she had her family for that. But he had been a huge part of the life she'd always imagined for herself, and now that things had drastically changed, all she had was her faith in a brighter future.

The chime of the doorbell startled her, and the tablet almost slipped off her lap as she turned to look toward the foyer. She wasn't expecting anyone, and there was no one else in the house to answer the door. Nate hadn't been here in two weeks, and she'd told herself every morning when she got up that this was a good thing. Change was good, her life was going to be better, she could do this.

Those same words rolled around in her head as she walked to the door and pulled it open. New—less flattering—words came to mind as she stared at Ethel's frowning face.

"I've been calling you all day," she said without any other form of greeting, and stepped forward as if she'd already been invited inside.

"I was out," Rita replied, still blocking her entrance. "You could've tried calling my cell." But that would've been too much like right, and Ethel so often preferred to take the most difficult route to a task. At one point, Rita had thought she and Ethel could be friends. But that was long before she saw Ethel's true personality. Ethel only wanted two things from people—to know all their business so she could judge them and their circumstances accordingly and to have them kiss her butt even when she was woefully undeserving of the praise. Still, Rita had always tried to remain as pleasant as possible when dealing with the woman. At least she had before their last HOA meeting.

Working alongside her on the HOA board had been less than thrilling in the past two years, and Rita couldn't wait until it was time to vote on new board members. When they'd first moved to Willow Grove, she and Nate both thought it a good idea to stay involved with the community, not only to plant roots here for their family but to establish communal ties and to really be an active part in their surroundings. Over the years Nate's involvement had been streamlined, but like with most everything else, Rita had excelled in contributing to the community's bylaws and helping things to run smoothly and equitably. Ethel, on the other hand, contributed to the chaos that sometimes erupted. Which was why she'd had to resort to bullying some of the residents to vote for her.

"Doesn't your home phone still work? And why are we having this conversation outside? Is there someone inside you don't want me to see?" Ethel asked with a disapproving tone.

Intrusive, nosy, and oftentimes rude. That was a perfect description for Rita's longtime neighbor and biggest pain in the butt.

"Come on in," Rita said, her tone cordial, with no hint of the reluctance she felt. After their last meeting, Rita hadn't talked to Ethel personally, only via the numerous emails she sent to the board members weekly.

Ethel brushed past her without another word, going straight to the living room, where she took a seat in the armchair.

"I wanted to let you know that I've contacted the police department again," Ethel began before Rita could take a seat. "It's only fair that since you're the current vice president that you know what's going on even though you made it quite clear at the meeting that the theft didn't concern you."

"I made it clear that I didn't like being accused of stealing a flowerpot, or of knowing the person who would steal a flowerpot," Rita countered as she sat.

Ethel pursed her lips, giving the impression that she still believed her assumption was right, and Rita had to resist the urge to cuss her and toss her out of her house.

"Sometimes we're the last to know," Ethel said with a slow nod.

Rita clenched her fists but kept her hands otherwise still in her lap.

"Now, I've been in touch with an Officer Phillips. You might remember him; he was here the morning of your, uh, mishap." Ethel glanced around the living room as if she thought she might spy another pile of burning clothes somewhere. "He's agreed to come out to an emergency meeting this Friday evening where he'll go over some things we can all look out for and some precautionary measures for keeping us safe. We're not accustomed to crime here in Willow Grove, and we'd like to get ahead of this. Find the thief and get them safely behind bars."

With all that Rita had going on in the past couple of weeks, the last thing to cross her mind was somebody stealing a flowerpot. It just wasn't high on her list of priorities.

"I'm going out of town Friday," she stated.

"With Nate? I haven't seen his car in the driveway for over a week. I figured he was already out of town. Will you be joining him somewhere?"

Right. While her family and the church knew about the divorce, Rita hadn't spoken to anyone else about it. Most especially not Ethel, who was, from the way she'd raised her brows in anticipation of an answer, already thinking something was wrong.

"No, I won't be joining Nate, and you're right, his car hasn't been in the driveway." She didn't owe Ethel any explanation and wasn't about to give it to her just because she asked her personally instead of going around to every one of their neighbors looking for an answer instead. "And I won't be at the meeting on Friday. But please, do keep me posted. If we do have a problem with theft, we should certainly take care of it."

Rita wasn't so sure there was a problem. Janice's flowerpot was expensive, not to mention heavy, as she'd already filled it with some tropical plant that Rita had been certain would die as soon as winter hit. There was no way somebody came into the development, picked up that pot, and walked away without being seen. And why would they in the first place? Sure, it was expensive, but last time Rita checked—with Tariq, who was famous for hustling all types of items—flowerpots weren't being sold on the streets for quick cash.

"Are we sure Janice just didn't return the pot? She's been known to go on shopping sprees and then return half the stuff a week later." Thanks to her third divorce and second phenomenal financial settlement due to said divorce, Janice had more money than she knew what to do with and generally spent it on any- and everything she saw. Her one goal in life seemed to be to flaunt every ridiculous purchase to the community in her effort to prove she was better than everyone else who lived here.

"Are you accusing her of making a false accusation?"

"I'm asking a question," Rita replied. "Making an accusation would be standing in front of a roomful of people and pointing the finger at someone without a shred of evidence."

Ethel huffed. "Really, Rita, I'm doing what's best for Willow Grove. I would think as the one to succeed me should I decide not to run for president again next year, that you'd take this more seriously."

Two weeks ago, Rita had been itching to campaign for Ethel's position on the board if for no other reason than to shut the woman's loud and very often wrong mouth. Today, with all the other things going on in her life, she could care less what title Ethel held on to and was more concerned with keeping her hands from going around the annoying woman's neck.

She stood. "As this meeting is a last-minute thing, I'm sure the rest of the board will understand my absence. I'll send an email to everyone to let them know I won't be there." Because she was certain Ethel would tell them something other than what Rita had said. "And I'll read the minutes of the meeting as soon as I return home Sunday night."

Rita waited for Ethel to stand.

"Well, I guess we all have our priorities," Ethel huffed.

"We certainly do," Rita replied and extended an arm signaling that Ethel should walk toward the front door.

She was being as polite as she'd been raised to be when all she really wanted to do was push the overbearing woman out of her house and bolt the door against her ever stepping foot in here again.

"There's also the problem of that awful black spot on your driveway," Ethel said as she walked. "As you well know, we have strict rules about property appearance. Perhaps you need to call Jack's brother-in-law and have him provide an estimate on getting a new driveway poured."

Rita took a deep breath and didn't bother expelling it slowly. "I'm not getting a new driveway just because there're some burn marks. But I will call my cousin to see if he has some power-washing tools that can remove the stain."

She opened the door and waited for Ethel to step through.

"More of your family in Willow Grove?" Ethel crossed her arms over her ample bosom and once again frowned. "Are you sure that's appropriate considering our current situation?"

Having taken as much of this nonsense as she planned to for the moment, Rita placed a hand on her hip and stared at Ethel. "As long as my name's on the deed to this house, I say who comes here and who goes. You nor the HOA have any control over my guests. Now, you have a nice evening."

Ethel didn't hide her displeasure as she flounced out the door and down Rita's front steps. And despite the overwhelming urge, Rita didn't slam the door behind her. Instead, she closed the door and leaned against it. Letting her head fall back, she closed her eyes and wondered how her world had managed to turn so completely upside down in such a short span of time.

Chapter 15

Look, but don't touch.

He was fine. Then again, she'd already come to that conclusion.

Sharae watched Desmond walk across the food court to where she stood in front of the Great Cookie shop. She'd had a good ten minutes to stare at him before he'd turned and noticed her. Cursing now because instead of ogling him she should've taken that time to make a quick exit, she shifted her purse strap on her shoulder and moved the bag with the cute flip-flops in it and the cookies she'd just bought from one hand to the other. Not that she was nervous about seeing him approaching. That would be ridiculous. He was sort of her attorney, after all—her very tall and slightly bowlegged attorney with the alluring bedroom eyes, strong jaw, and lips that appeared very kissable.

Dressed in slim-fit gray slacks and a button-front white shirt with the sleeves rolled up to his elbows, he seemed just as at home in this crowded mall as he would be if he'd been dressed in an impeccable suit moving throughout the courthouse hallways. And as comfortable as he'd been sitting at her dining room table, although she'd been trying her best to forget that night and the weird emotions it'd made her feel.

"Hey," he said in a tone that was as casual as if they were dating.

That thought threw her even more off-kilter, and Sharae stood up straighter. She wished she were still wearing the pantsuit she wore to work instead of the white shorts and purple tank top she'd changed into after her shift. Not only did her pantsuits look good—and cost a pretty penny—but they served as a sort of armor between her and the world. It was much easier for her to interrogate a suspect or stare down a colleague when she felt like she looked as if she should be taken seriously. It was seven thirty at night, and she was in the mall wearing sandals with her toes out and buying chocolate-chip cookies. At least this time she was wearing a bra when she faced him. A few seconds passed before she found her professional voice and managed a quick hello.

He nodded down to her bag. "Shopping?"

"Yes. For a trip. I'm going away tomorrow." Not that he needed to know any of that. "Are you shopping too?" Because really, he just looked like he was walking around the mall sharing his good looks with the masses.

"Yeah, need a couple new things for work."

"The fact that we're standing in the food court definitely says something about our shopping habits."

He laughed and surprised her again. When he was at her apartment, he'd given her only glimpses of his dangerously sexy smile. And the sound of his laughter was genuine, like he enjoyed laughing and did so often. That shouldn't seem so foreign to her considering the only thing she really knew about him was that he hadn't been to church in a while.

Reminding herself that all she needed to know was that he was just her lawyer, she continued. "Anyway, when can we expect the estate documents to be finalized? I've already talked to a real estate guy who can get the houses listed ASAP."

The quick rise of his brow as the laughter abruptly stopped said he wasn't prepared for the topic shift. She didn't care.

"Uh, it usually takes a couple weeks. I'll give you a call and send you copies as soon I receive the final paperwork." He cleared his throat. "The investments might be a little trickier to handle."

She nodded. "Yeah, that's fine. I've got that covered too."

"Oh really? You know another guy in finance?"

He sounded skeptical.

"As a matter of fact, I do." She was thinking of her cousin Ivan but didn't feel like she needed to tell him that.

"Cool. Cool." He reached up to scratch behind his head. "What kind of cookies do you have?"

She stared at the bucket—not a bag, because that wouldn't have been enough cookies for her—that she held in the same hand as the bag with the shoes. "Chocolate chip. And don't ask me if I share." The way he'd eaten half her cold-cut sub last week still had her trippin'.

He didn't laugh again or give her that sexy smile. Instead, he kept a serious look that she suspected meant he was about to lie. "I was gonna tell you they're my favorite."

Now it was her turn to give him a skeptical look. "Really?"

He nodded. "Yeah. Really." This time he *did* smile, and Sharae had to admit she was uncomfortable.

"I guess that look means you want one."

"Or two."

She waited a beat before stepping aside and saying, "Go ahead, the line's right there."

She couldn't help but laugh at the way shock mixed with what he probably thought was clever charm played across his face. It didn't stop him from being sexy as hell, though. *Dammit.*

"Here," she said, opening the bucket. "Take three. We'll call it a tip for good attorney services. I mean, you did track me down while I was at work when you could've just sent a letter to my house."

He took the three cookies, lifting them to his mouth to take a bite out of one. "That's not normally how I like to tell someone their father passed."

She shrugged. "It would've been fine with me."

"Because you didn't like your father?"

"Because my father was an asshole who didn't deserve anyone liking him." That sounded harsh even to her, but she didn't take it back. And now she was feeling uncomfortable for a totally different reason. This guy really did bring out the worst in her. "Anyway, I should be going." They'd covered all the topics they had in common.

"I'll walk you to your car," he said, taking a step toward her.

"Um, I don't need an escort, and I'm not leaving the mall yet. I still have to find a bathing suit." And she probably could've kept that part to herself because the look he was giving her now was definitely not one a lawyer or even a casual acquaintance should be giving.

In what seemed like a lifetime but was probably only about ten seconds, his gaze had gone from her face to her breasts, over her hips, down her legs, and stopped at her toes, which of their own accord wiggled as if to say "Hey!" Her cheeks warmed as mortification mixed with annoyance.

"Would I be stepping over the line if I asked to join you in that quest?" He asked the question with such a straight face and serious tone that she almost believed he had no idea what effect he was having on her.

Hell, she didn't believe this shit herself. She didn't fall for charming guys, and she damn sure didn't let looks pull her in the way his seemed to be doing. And why, in all that was right with the world, was this happening right here and right now? She'd met Desmond two weeks ago and not one time—okay, well, yeah, once or twice—had she given any thought to how attractive he was. She was more focused on hating him for bringing Sanford back into her life.

"That's probably unethical. You are my lawyer, remember?"

He chuckled. "I'm talkin' about accompanying you to a store, not ripping your clothes off and making love to you."

The way her pussy just jumped at his words was all the way ridiculous. "You're kidding, right?" *Please, oh my damn, be kidding.*

Now this grin he was giving her was definitely a sexy-and-I-know-it smile. If she weren't who she was, she might've swooned. Instead, she smirked.

"Just come on before the mall closes," she told him and started walking. "And for the record, yes, this is unethical as hell."

And she wasn't talking about him just mentioning making love to her—his client. No, she was more entrenched in the instant picture of them tearing each other's clothes off and going at it like they were coming off a ten-year celibacy stint.

At ten minutes after nine, Sharae stood at the end of her bed, staring down at the three bathing suits with tags still attached. She'd always preferred a one-piece suit, and the white one at the end was that—of course, it also had a couple of peekaboo cutouts on the left side. One that would show the navel piercing she'd gotten for her thirtieth birthday, and another that may or may not display a bit of side boobage if she wasn't careful. Her breasts tended to have a mind of their own when she wore anything other than her favored button-down shirts, and even then, depending on what time of the month it was, there could be some straining against the buttons.

Switching her attention to the next suit, she marveled at the color: black. It would always be her favorite color for any clothing item. But it was a two-piece—a high-waist bikini that would cover her piercing but expose every inch of her cleavage and possibly a shadow of nipple, which was the part that made her most nervous.

The final one was a push-up plunge bikini in a brilliant cobalt blue. It was by far the most risqué choice for her because it would definitely require another shave. She didn't have time for a waxing appointment tomorrow—she was getting her hair braided in the morning, and that would take the majority of her day. Then, because she'd been severely distracted at the mall, she hadn't gotten the gift for Wendy like she was supposed to and would thus have to go back to the store again.

Jemel was driving, which meant they might have a slight margin of not leaving at precisely four o'clock as they'd planned, but not much. Traffic on the Bay Bridge on a Friday afternoon in the summer was gonna be horrendous, and the later they left, the worse it was going to be. Which was why she'd planned to do all her shopping tonight.

Desmond had thrown a big ole sexy-ass monkey wrench in that plan.

"This color will look great with your complexion," he'd said as he'd held the hanger with the blue bathing suit attached.

The strings of the bikini were tied neatly to the hanger to make a nice presentation, but there was so little material to it, the store had used a dozen of those clear thingies to keep it from falling off. She hated those things because she never failed to leave one attached, and it would scratch against her skin the entire time she wore the new garment.

"There's not much to this one," she'd replied, already over the way his eyes were devouring her body each time either one of them picked up a bathing suit to peruse.

"There's enough," he'd countered.

And then she'd done something she rarely ever did. She flirted.

"Enough for what?" Her tone had lowered slightly, and the sexual buzz that she'd been trying to ignore sizzled around them.

"Enough to show off the woman behind the badge," was his reply.

For the next seconds they'd stood in that store as if they were the only ones there. Their gazes had locked, and an entire silent conversation had ensued. A conversation that they both knew shouldn't be happening.

She'd grabbed all three bathing suits and made her way to the register at that point. From there it'd been limited conversation as he insisted on walking her to her car. He muttered a quick "I'll call you when I have the final paperwork" seconds before she closed the door and drove off.

And now he was on her mind again.

She was horny.

With a nod, she snatched the tags off the bathing suits and then tucked them into the huge duffel bag she was packing. Her body hummed with arousal, her breasts felt full, pussy throbbing with every recollection of his big hands holding those clear plastic hangers, his smoldering eyes staring down at the barely there material, then easing over her body.

It was hot as hell in here too.

She'd kicked off her sandals as soon as she walked into the bedroom and now moved on bare feet across the carpeted floor. Going to her closet, she took out the three dresses she'd planned to pack. Two maxi dresses with flowing material from the bottom of the tight bodices, and a knee-length halter one in her favorite shade of—yes—black, again. She put them in the bag, then went back to the closet determined, telling herself that if she hurried to get the packing done, she could also take care of the incessant aching between her legs that had followed her home from the mall.

But on her next trip to the closet, when she bent down to hunt through the stacks of shoeboxes to find the ones she needed to go with the dresses and the four shorts sets she'd already packed, everything stopped.

Her fingers brushed over the cool cashmere-gray marble tower urn. Last week after she'd picked it up from the funeral home, she'd come straight home and tucked it against the back wall of her closet. Tonight, she stared at her fingers as they moved of their own accord over the surface. It looked like any ordinary chunk of stone. Nobody would ever guess there was a compartment opening on the bottom where the ashes were stored.

Rita had agreed with Medwin III that this one had a bold, modern appearance. Jemel had felt squeamish about the whole cremating idea. And Sharae hadn't cared one way or the other. Except right at this moment, she wanted to look at it.

Pulling it out, she sat with her legs tucked under her butt on the floor. It had weight to it as she held it in both hands. The light swirls of gray throughout the white created a fantastical look. But it was the undeniable emotion emanating from the chunk of marble circling around her that had her gasping. In the next seconds, a pain unlike anything Sharae had ever known gripped her chest, and she pitched forward, closing her eyes against the assault.

There'd been so much blood. More than her thirteen-year-old eyes had ever seen. And the smell, it had been acidic and made her stomach roil in complaint. She'd never known what had awakened her that long-ago summer night, but she'd sat up in her bed for a few moments, trying to determine whether to turn over and go back to sleep or get up and find herself a snack. Her throat was dry, so she'd decided on some juice or iced tea. Mama had made iced tea, and there was a two-liter of lemonade that she could mix with it for a cool beverage. She'd eased out of bed and walked out of her room in a way she'd done so many times before. They lived in a two-story town house, and she walked down the hallway to the stairs. It was dark, as it should've been at that time of night, but she'd lived in that house all her life, so she didn't need the light to know where she was going. There was a light on in the kitchen. She noticed that the second she stepped into the living room. Maybe Mama and Daddy were up getting a snack or a drink too. But if they were, they were being awfully quiet about it.

She moved through the space, passed the small laundry-room area on the left, and then she felt the coolness. The carpet floor had ended and was replaced by white tile that had been cracked in some places.

Her toes had wiggled at the chill, then her nostrils burned, and her eyes had seen all the red. Justine had been sitting up against the refrigerator, her face swollen, blood matting her hair.

Sharae had her mother's thick, coarse hair. Justine had kept hers permed because she said it was easier to manage that way. Sharae kept hers natural because her mother had never put any chemicals in her only child's hair.

She didn't know when she'd begun to rock. Probably when the memories first forced themselves to the forefront, but Sharae sat on the floor, rocking forward and backward, clutching the urn as tears streamed quietly down her face.

Her mother was gone, and now the man who'd taken her away was gone too. She didn't know how she was supposed to feel about all that or what she was supposed to do. All she knew was that the grief that thirteen-year-old girl had tucked into the back of her heart was breaking free, and the woman had no idea if she could survive it. That thought scared Sharae in a way she'd never been afraid before, and she cried harder. The pain spread faster. Her loss seemed deeper.

Chapter 16

DRINKS... AND OTHER THINGS IN HAND.

Rita swallowed another gulp of her second mojito as the lyrics to a hip-hop song purred over a thumpin' beat. There were at least fifty women tucked into one of the hotel's meeting rooms with a wall of windows facing the ocean. Highboy tables were spread around the space, and stools and a few lounge chairs as well. The overhead lights had been dimmed so that the smoky-white uplighting cast the space in deep shadows, everywhere except the center of the floor, where a bright spotlight shone on the stripper pole. On the pole a scantily clad woman did some sort of sexual acrobatics while a couple of feet away from her, a bare-chested man sat in a chair, legs spread, hands gripping what Rita suspected was a thick erection through his jeans.

The first of Wendy's three bridal celebrations had started off with a bang at ten Friday night.

It was almost eleven now, and Rita felt sticky in the pale-pink maxi dress she wore. Sharae was seated at the table to her left. Her drink of choice was whiskey, straight. Every time Rita watched her take a drink, it made her throat burn. Sharae wore a dress tonight too—a floral-print black, white, and pink one. Jemel, whose idea it'd been for all of them to wear dresses instead of shorts and T-shirts—they'd thank her for that later since nobody in the room was wearing shorts and T-shirts—wore a shorter wrap dress in a vibrant yellow color that matched the large earrings and bracelets she also had on. Her drink—the third one in the short time they'd been here—was a margarita, which always made her grin at Rita knowingly when she ordered.

"How long are we staying down here?" Rita asked when her glass was just about empty. She looked at her watch for, like, the hundredth time.

"Till it's over or the bar closes," Jemel added. She was bopping to the beat of the music, clearly enchanted by the show still going on in the center of the room.

"Or until he yanks her off that pole and starts bangin' her right there on the dance floor," Sharae added with a shrug. She didn't look like she was enjoying the show half as much as Jemel, and for the second time tonight, Rita wondered at her mood.

She'd been uncharacteristically quiet on the ride down. And that was after she'd elected to sit in the back instead of arguing with Rita over riding shotgun. While Jemel and Rita had chatted about their upcoming event, Rita had peeked back at Sharae a couple of times. She'd been staring out the window as if she'd never seen the view from the Bay Bridge before. When they'd arrived at the hotel and checked in to their room, both she and Jemel had asked Sharae what was wrong, and she'd shrugged then too, saying she was working on a difficult case and needed this break to clear her mind. Neither Rita nor Jemel had believed that for one minute.

Still, they'd showered, dressed, and ordered room service before coming down here. Rita hated depending on the place where she was going to feed her. She'd never been at this hotel, so she wasn't sure what was on their banquet menus, or what Wendy's budget allowed her to order. So they'd eaten in their room, which turned out to be a good thing because there were only finger foods down here and an open bar.

"He's not gonna do that right here, is he?" she asked when she followed their gaze to the middle of the room once more.

The guy was standing now, undoing the button on his jeans and pushing them slowly down his legs.

"He might," Jemel said and slapped a hand to her leg. "I can't believe this shit! Can you? Like who would've ever thought to have a guy and a girl at their shower?"

Sharae took another gulp from her glass and shook her head this time. "I heard one of the girls at the bar saying Wendy wanted to make all her friends comfortable, and since there were women here of different sexual orientations, she figured this was the best way to go about it."

"Speaking strictly as someone who's planned a lot of events, that was a good idea," Rita admitted. "It's not an idea I would've come up with, or that I probably would've approved. But it's inclusive and definitely interesting."

"It's making me horny," Jemel admitted.

"I was already horny," Sharae added.

They both looked at Rita. She picked up her glass and mumbled, "No comment," before taking another sip.

Half an hour and another round of drinks later, the couple had been replaced by two male strippers who'd already taken it all off and were now dancing their way from one table to the next, waiting expectantly for the dollars to flow. Jemel already had her ones and fives out, but Sharae and Rita were holding out.

"I don't know how he looks close up. I gotta see it and touch it for myself before I put out any of my money. You know, to make sure it's real." Sharae spoke like she was talking about buying a car, not touching a man's dick.

Rita frowned. She wasn't touching anybody.

The guy was at the table next to theirs, and Jemel jumped down off her stool, money in hand. She was shaking her body as if she couldn't wait until he came closer. Rita couldn't help but laugh at her. Jemel had always been the party cousin. Once she'd been old enough to get into clubs on her own, she'd spent more time in them than Rita and Sharae combined. And during the first five years after she'd graduated from high school, all she'd ever done was hair during the day and partying at night. It drove Aunt Ceil nuts and had the Aunts as a collective both praying hard for her salvation and wanting to smack some sense into her.

"You really gonna be an old church biddy all night?" Jemel yelled over to her as if she could hear Rita's thoughts.

Rita crossed one leg over the other. "What I'm not gonna be is some stripper groupie like you. And aren't you and Marc together? What would he say if he saw you acting like this?"

"Don't know. Don't care. He's not here. Get a life, Rita." Jemel was sashaying her way over to the guy clad in just a G-string.

Sharae jumped down off her stool and pushed Jemel to the side, cupping the guy's erection without hesitation or comment. Rita sucked in a breath because she was certain that was some form of sexual assault, and Sharae was a cop. But the guy only grinned before leaning in and whispering something in Sharae's ear.

Sharae afforded him the barest grin, before stepping back and releasing him. "Not bad," she said and then reached down into the top of her dress to pull out a twenty-dollar bill. The guy put his hands on his hips, standing so that his dick escaped the G-string and now jutted forward in expectation. Sharae tucked the bill into the G-string and ran her finger along his length one more time. When she sat on her stool again, she looked over to Rita and said, "It's real."

Rita laughed for a good ten minutes after that. Shock mixed with mojitos was having a strange effect on her. When the entertainment was over and the music played even louder for those who jumped on and off the floor to dance, Rita started to yawn, and Sharae ordered another round of drinks for her and Jemel.

"So when are we going upstairs?" she asked.

"That's like the fifth time you've asked that question, Grandma," Jemel said. "You really gonna act this dry all weekend? I mean, damn, you're about to be a single woman. You can let your hair down and do some dirt for a change."

Jemel motioned to Rita's hair, pulled up in a messy bun because it was hotter than Hades outside tonight and she'd been sweating like she'd been running miles on the treadmill. Which reminded her she wanted to check out the hotel gym before she went upstairs for the night. She needed to know if it was worth her coming down early tomorrow morning to get a little workout in.

"My marital status has nothing to do with me not caring for this type of setting. And before you say it"—she paused and held up a hand to stop Jemel's next comment—"I know Wendy's only twenty-seven and that this is really her crowd. That's fine. We're here to represent Ivan's side of the family, and I'm not in my twenties anymore."

"You're not in your sixties, either, Rita," Sharae said and once again hopped down off the stool. "Come on, let's go to the hotel bar. It'll be quieter out there and less booty thumpin'."

"You mean boring," Jemel said and climbed down too.

Rita didn't say another word, just followed them out of the room. If she'd known part one of the celebration was just going to be a party, she might've avoided going altogether. As a teen, getting into clubs and going to house parties had been something she, Jemel, and Sharae had done on the regular. But after she was married, the appeal of being in dimly lit places with strange men dancing too close and looking for someone they could take home for the night had lost its appeal. There was a luncheon on the beach tomorrow and then another party in the evening. She'd have to look on that little itinerary they'd sent via text in the morning to see which one they had to bring their gifts to. And she prayed this was the last stripper event.

She was so busy turning over all those things in her mind that she'd walked into the bar and nearly bumped into Sharae and Jemel, who'd suddenly stopped walking.

"What in the world—" Whatever else she was about to say stalled as her gaze followed theirs to a table across from the bar.

A table where Nate sat smiling at a girl who didn't look much older than Taryn.

"This bastard," Jemel whispered. She took a step toward the table, and Rita grabbed her by the arm.

"No," she said, the word scratchy in her throat.

"You've been separated what? Three whole weeks? And he's already out in public with his side chick?" Sharae asked, her voice just a little louder than Rita thought was prudent.

"She's not a side chick if we're no longer together," she said.

"Until the ink is dry on the divorce papers, she's a side chick," Jemel clarified. "And I told you we should've run up on her ass before now."

Rita's head suddenly hurt, and her stomach didn't feel much better. She hadn't seen or spoken to Nate since the day she'd been in his office and eventually stood him up for dinner. He'd texted her quite a few times since then, but she'd ignored and deleted every message. They'd been scheduled for a conference call with their lawyers, but at the last minute she'd opted out of it and told Sharon to handle it for her. At the time she'd known it was cowardly, but she hadn't cared. She wasn't ready to face him again then.

Was she ready now?

The answer to that obviously didn't matter because Sharae had circled around her and Jemel and was already on her way over to the table.

"Dang it, Sharae," she muttered and released Jemel's arm so she could follow her.

Jemel was more than happy to be on the move as she caught up with Sharae so that they both came to a stop at Nate's table simultaneously.

Rita stood a couple of steps back from them, staring into the face of the young woman, who'd looked up immediately.

She was darker than Rita, her hair in long, thin braids almost similar to Sharae's. She wore a blue dress, low cut in the front, a silver choker at her neck.

"Hey," Nate said and cleared his throat.

Rita snatched her gaze away from the woman to look at him. Still fine, still a bastard. He was, as always, neatly groomed, from the beige polo he wore to the khaki pants she could see from her side view of the table. He had a fresh haircut and shave. She could tell because he always got a little line at his shape-up right near his ear when he'd just been to the barbershop.

"Excuse me a minute," he told the woman he was with and stood. Then he nodded to Sharae and Jemel. "Let's take this over here."

For an instant Rita's stomach clenched because she wasn't convinced her cousins weren't going to create a scene. Jemel loved drama, and Sharae, even though she was a cop, was still from the streets just like the rest of the Johnson family and could get out of hand as well. Thankfully they started walking behind Nate, and Rita followed them.

She felt like she was having an out-of-body experience. Like maybe she was really back in the hotel room, imagining all this was happening. The second they were outside, standing in front of the hotel, she knew that wasn't true. The balmy ocean air hit her skin with a jolt, as it was in stark contrast to the chilly air-conditioned breeze she'd been feeling inside the hotel all night.

"Before you get started, I know she told you she put me out," Nate said the moment they were standing to the side of the hotel's front doors. "Not to mention the fact that she stood me up for dinner when we were supposed to discuss reconciliation."

"Yeah, 'cause you can't keep it in your pants," Jemel shot back. "I see you're still flauntin' your shit to any taker."

"You ain't lost enough yet?" Sharae asked him. "She's the best thing that ever happened to you. She gave you everything, and you just stupidly tossed it aside."

"What part of '*she* put *me* out' didn't you understand?" Nate countered.

Rita shook her head. This just couldn't be happening.

Damn. Hadn't she been thinking that for the past few weeks? But really, hadn't she already decided how she was going to move on with her life? Wasn't she happy about being able to officially start her own business, something she hadn't even considered when she was with Nate?

Well, regardless, this *was* happening. Right here and right now, her cousins were confronting her cheating soon-to-be ex-husband, and she was just standing there like a stranger on the street.

"Stop it," she said finally. "This isn't necessary."

"Right! Tell 'em. You wanted this divorce, not me," he said.

"You're not fighting it," she said without thinking. It was probably better just to walk away from this simple man. Arguing had never been Rita's strong suit because that only led to her being even more irritated by a situation. Something she'd only proven to herself that day in his office. Tonight, she could feel the air buzzing with tension waiting to be released.

He locked his gaze on hers, and for an instant she felt the familiar warmth of being the only woman on Nate's radar. Of course, that turned out to be a temporary situation since the moment he wasn't staring at her, he was obviously finding another woman to stare at, touch, sleep with . . . She took a deep breath and stepped closer so that she now stood only a few feet away from him, instead of behind her cousins.

"How would you know if I was fighting it or not? You won't talk to me," he said, his tone noticeably calmer, but still full of exasperation. "You've embarrassed me at my office, torched thousands of dollars' worth of my clothes and shoes, and now you're refusing to have a simple conversation."

Well, she certainly wasn't apologizing for doing any of those things. He deserved that and so much more. "You're right." She folded her arms across her chest. "I haven't wanted to talk to you."

"And you certainly can't talk now since you've got a date waiting for you inside," Jemel added.

Not that Rita needed a reminder.

"We can still talk about this, Rita. Maybe work something out." He had the nerve to look imploringly at her. Raising his brows, putting that compassionate look in his big brown eyes, making his voice sound more agreeable than confrontational. But he hadn't tried to touch her again, not like he had that day in his office.

She almost laughed.

"Nate, we can't work anything out. And not just because you're actually on a date with another woman right now, but because there's nothing left." That familiar warmth she'd felt a few moments ago had only lasted about 5.6 seconds. Then, the chilly emptiness returned. That was the feeling she'd been sleeping with every night since she learned he'd emptied those accounts, and she suspected it'd be around a little longer. But she could live with that. She could reside in the big house they'd bought together and live half the life she'd created just fine, as long as she didn't have to remain legally entangled with him.

He sighed. "What am I supposed to do? Eat alone?"

"Or die alone, we're not picky," Sharae snapped.

"I don't care what you do," Rita said while Nate frowned over her shoulder at her cousins.

"Don't perform for them, Rita. You know we're better together. Our lives are together, not apart. We can work this out."

She was shaking her head before he finished that last ridiculous sentence.

"Oh, I see," he continued. "The Three Stooges strike again."

He'd always called them that whenever they got together to push back on something somebody said or did. It wasn't often that he was their target because Rita had claimed any personal issues with her husband off-limits between her and her cousins. As close as they were, whatever Rita chose to share with them, it was with the caveat that they never go back to him and repeat it or interfere in any way. She hadn't really had to say all that to them; they were blood, they knew how to be there without noticeably being there.

"Only because the asshole is determined to show just how shitty he can be," was Jemel's quick retort.

"We're done," Rita said, raising her voice and then immediately regretting it. "The marriage is over, and we'll work out all the other details. You can return to your date. We're leaving." She turned away from him then because she couldn't stand the sight of him.

Not after all the years she'd given him, all the intimacy they'd shared. He'd been her first and her only and now . . . fuck him! The words seemed so loud in her mind that she trembled but kept on walking.

Chapter 17

ACT LIKE A LADY, AND KEEP A BLADE ON HAND.

"What the hell are you doing?" Rita yelled as Jemel walked through the hotel parking lot.

"Looking for his car. What do you think I'm doing?"

"Why are you looking for his car?" Rita was so confused. After the scene that had just played out with Nate and Sharae holding some strange man's dick in her hand a little while before that, combined with the mojitos, her mind was shot.

"So I can tear that shit up!"

Rita stopped, but Jemel kept right on walking.

"That bastard's fanatical about his car," Jemel said as she walked. "Whichever one he's driving at the time. He flaunts every vehicle he leases, just like he flaunts his business, his house, that big-ass gold pinkie ring he wears like he's part of the Black mafia." She stumbled and then leaned over to look closer at a car.

Shaking her head, Rita tried to clear it. She hoped when she stopped, all this would've been a very bad dream. Including the phone call that had started all this drama.

"Can you believe he actually stood there telling Rita they could work out their marriage when he had another woman sitting not even a few yards away waiting for his return." Jemel was yelling at Sharae now, and Rita turned to see where she was.

She'd just come to stand next to Rita and was staring ahead at Jemel as well.

"He's so fuckin' foul!" Jemel yelled. "But that's okay. My pet-ty-o-meter is on full blast tonight!"

"Went straight back in there to that child like it wasn't nothing, the flat-foot bastard!" Sharae added and put an arm around Rita's shoulders.

"It doesn't matter," Rita said. And it didn't. She'd never let anything Nate said or did matter to her again.

Jemel continued moving, looking over her shoulder once to see if they were with her.

"If you're about to do what I think you're about to do, I'm out," Sharae yelled to her from their distance of about seven or eight cars away. "I share your fury, but I'm a cop, remember?"

"Noooooooooo." Rita gasped after exaggerating that word in what definitely sounded like a tipsy accent.

Gracious, she hoped she wasn't drunk. But Jemel probably was, and if she was thinking of doing what Rita suspected Sharae thought she was gonna do, then they were all in a world of trouble. She left Sharae's side and started toward Jemel because she couldn't let this happen.

"Well, yeah," Jemel said as her legs wobbled and she reached into her purse. "You turn around and close your eyes. You can't stop what you don't see," she said to Sharae.

"You can't do this, Jem." Rita was up on her now, tugging at her arm so hard, Jemel's hand popped out of her purse.

Jemel frowned and jerked away so hard she stumbled back a couple of steps. Then she pitched forward, holding her arms out like she was an airplane, in an effort to steady herself and keep from meeting the concrete in an embarrassing splatter. "You can close your eyes and turn around too," she said and then hiccupped so loud and hard her entire body vibrated.

In the next seconds, Jemel was running down the parking lot, stopping so fast that Rita really did think her butt was gonna meet the asphalt. That was when Rita realized Jemel was standing right next to Nate's gold Lexus. He'd pulled into the spot headfirst, so she'd probably spotted the license-plate frame with the McCall Motors logo on it. She pumped her fists in the air and did a victory dance like she'd just scored the winning touchdown, instead of standing in a dark parking lot about to break the law.

"Jemel Nikkita Coleridge, you get yourself over here . . . right . . . now!" Rita hush-yelled like she thought they were in church and then looked around to make sure nobody else was in the parking lot to hear her.

Jemel waved her away and crouched down low so Rita could no longer see her. "Jemel," she hush-whispered this time. "Dang it!" She stomped and then turned again to confirm that she hadn't seen anybody in the parking lot. Not even Sharae.

She should run down there and find her, pull her drunk behind up, and drag her back into the hotel. But when she took the first step, those mojitos really hit, and the entire parking lot swayed like a broken TV screen.

"Run for it!" she heard and then felt a swoosh of air in the next seconds as Jemel ran past her.

Taking off behind Jemel, Rita wanted to curse and scream before they were side by side at the hotel's secondary entrance.

"Stop looking guilty," she hissed, yanking Jemel's hand away from the door handle. "Catch your breath so we can walk back in there normally."

"I gotta pee," Jemel whined and then held up her pocketknife. "But I slashed the hell outta his tires!"

"Shhh!" Rita pushed down the hand holding the knife. "It figures you scared the piss outta yourself with that stupid stunt."

Jemel rolled her eyes. "Only you could still manage to chastise when you're drunk and just caught your husband cheating . . . again!"

Rita didn't respond to that. Instead, she pushed the button to call for the elevator while Jemel focused on standing upright. Her face had gone ashen, and she looked like she was struggling to fight both pissing on herself and losing her dinner all over the tiled floor. Their room was on the fifth floor, and they made it inside in just enough time for Jemel to jet to the bathroom.

Tired, irritated that Nate could still hurt her, and now extremely sleepy, Rita fell facedown on the bed closest to the door. Sharae had been lying on the other bed.

"She did it, didn't she?" Sharae asked.

"You knew she would," Rita said. "You should've helped me drag her irrational behind up here instead of leaving."

"Nah, the last thing I need is to be at the scene of another family-involved crime."

That comment had Rita turning so that she could look at Sharae. "I'm sorry."

Sharae quickly held up a hand to stop anything else Rita was going to say. "Stop. I told you that's over. And to be clear, I'd do it again. So just drop it."

But there was something bothering Sharae, and if it wasn't her job, Rita couldn't figure out what else it could be. Rita could barely figure out her own life right now, let alone attempt to decipher what was going on in someone else's.

When Jemel finally came out of the bathroom, she held a wet cloth to her forehead.

"Feel better?" Rita asked as she stood and fished out a bottled water from her duffel bag. She gave the water to Jemel.

Jemel accepted it with a half nod. "Li'l bit," she said and opened the water to take a very slow sip.

Sharae grinned and shook her head. Jemel sat on the bed beside her, and Sharae wrapped an arm around Jemel's shoulder.

"I can't believe you did that," Rita said, her face smashed against the floral bedspread. She was either tipsy or just too damn stressed to care about the yuck factor of her face touching the hotel spread she'd yet to spray down with Lysol.

"I can't believe you didn't help me," Jemel replied and reached behind her to find a pillow. She pounded the flat pillow and then cupped it between her arm and her head as she lay gingerly on her side.

"I can't believe I had to leave the two of you down there so I didn't witness any more law breaking this month," Sharae added.

She sat at the end of the bed where Jemel was lying and reached down to take off her sandals.

"I should've busted his windows too," Jemel added and then groaned because she was obviously feeling nauseated again.

"And what good was that gonna do?" Rita raised herself up on her elbows and stared over at Jemel. "He went right back to sitting with her at that table. They probably have a room here. Taryn said he was staying at a hotel."

"Not at this hotel, Rita," Sharae added. "This is three hours away from the dealership and the girls. Why would he stay down here?"

Rita shrugged. "Maybe she lives down here."

"She's a child," Jemel said. "Did you see her? She's maybe twenty-two, twenty-five tops. What the hell is he thinking?"

"That he wanted someone younger to fuck," Rita said.

Jemel met and mimicked Sharae's shocked stare.

"Did you just cuss?" Sharae asked when she turned her gaze to Rita.

Rita rolled over and flopped onto her back. She brought her hands up to cross over her stomach and thought for an eerie moment that she must look like she was lying in a casket instead of on the bed in a mundane hotel. "I'm so tired, y'all," she admitted.

Sharae leaned over to rest her elbows on her knees. "We know. But you can let go now. It's just us, the way it's always been. You don't have to be strong tonight."

Jemel's voice was low and surprisingly steady. "He never deserved you."

"She's right," Sharae added. "He wanted a trophy wife, and you gave him so much more. You're so smart and organized. You built that business. You gave him two beautiful daughters, kept an immaculate house, sat in church beside him when you knew he was disrespecting you and your vows."

Sharae stopped abruptly as if she thought she'd said too much. Rita had known all this time that they didn't like Nate, and now she hated that she'd made them feel they couldn't talk to her about their feelings for him. It'd been the only way she thought to keep the people she loved most in the world from killing each other, and from making the hardest decision of her life.

"I did everything I was supposed to," she said, staring up at the ceiling now. She used the inside of her arm to wipe at the tears. "Don't give away the milk before he buys the cow." She gave a wry chuckle. "That's what the Aunts always said. And Mama insisted I learn to cook and take care of a house. Benny didn't have to do anything but go to school and get good grades. I did all the cleaning. I was washing my own clothes when I was ten. Sunday school, Bible study, choir, ushering—I did it all so I'd learn what it meant to be a godly wife." She slammed her hands down on the bed. "I did everything right, dammit! And he still betrayed me! He still treated me like crap!"

Jemel got up from the bed and walked over to the other one. She sat beside where Rita lay and took her hand. Sharae did the same, going to the other side of Rita to sit there.

"It's his loss, not yours," Jemel said. "I wish I had better words. Something that would take your pain away, but it's just that simple, Rita. You're better off without him."

Through her own hurt, Rita could hear the commiseration in Jemel's tone. Her cousin knew how it felt to have her heart broken; her first breakup with Marc had been devastating. But Jemel had been quick to pick up the pieces. Rita was struggling with that right now. While one minute she felt like she was bold and confident, making decisions for her new life, ten minutes later she could be curled into a fetal position on her bed praying for the pain to subside.

"There were things he was supposed to do too, Rita. Having a great marriage wasn't all on you," Sharae said.

Nodding, Jemel added, "She's right. He took the same vows you did, sat in church, and read those same scriptures. He owed you so much more than he gave you."

Rita gave a wry chuckle. "Well, at least he didn't give me something I needed to be treated for." When she noticed Sharae and Jemel's quizzical silence, she continued. "I went to the doc to get checked for STDs. Got my negative results this morning." A heavy sigh followed. "What am I gonna do now? This is what I was taught to do—be a wife, a partner, a mother."

"You already know what you're going to do. You're gonna open that catering business and be the real you. The one who's a fuckin' boss!" Jemel said, and Rita loved her just a little bit more.

"She's right. The girls are grown—at least they like to think they are. Let them be adults, Rita. Stop entertaining Taryn's tantrums about her father and focus on what will make you happy. This business you're building is your happy. Grasp it and hold on tight. You deserve it," Sharae said.

Rita shook her head. "I don't even think I know what happy is anymore." And that was the truth. While the business sparked a new energy in her, she hadn't ventured to say she was happy. Not just yet.

"Chocolate-chip ice cream and *Grease 2*," Jemel said. "That's what used to make you happy when we were young."

Rita turned her head to look up at Jemel, who broke into a goofy smile.

"That did make me happy," she admitted. "Remember we used to act like we were part of the cast?"

Sharae groaned. "I remember the two of you actin' like that old-ass corny movie was a new release. We watched it so many times when there were plenty of other movies to watch."

"It's the best worst musical ever." That was always Rita's defense.

"Because you're the perfect alto," Sharae said and nodded. "You never let us forget that."

Rita sat up then, dropping their hands and belting the first lines of "Cool Rider," one of the songs from the movie.

"Nooooooo," Sharae said, echoing Rita's word from the parking lot, but with a hint of laughter in her tone.

Jemel was game. She ran to the dresser and grabbed one of the brushes she'd unpacked from her bag. Picking up the next line of the song, she joined in with Rita. Climbing off the bed, Rita went to the dresser to grab a brush too. They sang until Sharae couldn't resist. Shaking her head in dismay, she crawled off the bed last and added the little rap verse she'd made up to go with the song.

Now, if ever there was something corny, it was Sharae tryin' to rap. But they kept the song going, even bustin' into the dance moves they'd made up for the song. By the time the song ended, they were all laughing and clapping like they'd just recorded a hit single.

Exhausted from the effort, they fell back on the one bed, each of them touching the other because it was only a double bed. It didn't matter. This was how they'd slept whenever they spent the night together. Sharae and Rita had bunk beds. The bottom one was a full-size, and the top—the one where Sharae slept—was a twin. But whenever Jemel came over, they all slept on the full together.

Rita took their hands, holding them the way she used to when they'd lie in bed at night talking about their hopes and dreams.

"I'm gonna be okay," she said, squeezing their hands in hers. "I'll figure all this out, and I'm gonna be just fine."

The fight that had always been in Rita would never die. She knew that. Vi hadn't raised a quitter, and thanks to Benny, she was a damn good fighter too. So no matter how much she hurt now, Rita knew joy would come in the morning. It was something they'd all learned. No matter what was thrown at them, they battled through. Their mothers had done it, especially Aunt Ceil, who'd fought Jemel's father vigorously over child-support payments. Their grandparents and ancestors before them had all persevered through difficult and oftentimes devastating circumstances. So yeah, Rita would prevail. It was in her blood.

Jemel lifted her arm, bringing the back of Rita's hand up so she could kiss it. "We know you will. And we'll be right here to help in those moments that you're not okay."

"She's right," Sharae said, again mimicking Jemel's motions. "We'll get through this together. Just like we always do."

Rita nodded. "Yeah, we will. I love y'all, and I'm so blessed to have you with me."

Jemel rolled over first, wrapping her arm around Rita. "We love you too, Margaritaville!"

Sharae followed suit. "We sure do!"

They fell asleep just like that, or at least Jemel did first. A few minutes after she'd felt the heaviness of Jemel's head against her shoulder, she heard Sharae's soft snore. Rita lay awake a long time after the two of them were asleep, thinking about all that her life had been and all that she wanted it to be in the future. She'd known happy once, and if it was the last thing she did, she was going to find it again. She had to, otherwise Nate won, and she'd be damned if she let that happen.

Chapter 18

DATING STATUS.

"I don't date," Sharae replied and clapped the files she'd been carrying close to her chest.

Three days had passed since she'd last seen Desmond, and now here he was, standing in the middle of the first floor of the precinct, asking her out on a date. She'd just come from downstairs in the records department searching for a case file that linked one of her suspects in her current case to a homicide from last summer. Her mind was focused on a botched carjacking when she'd seen him coming straight toward her—confidence, briefcase, and sex appeal in hand.

"And I'm starting to think you're stalking me," she continued when the silence between them seemed to stretch. There was plenty of other news around on a Monday afternoon with cops, other department staff, and some civilians—namely, Desmond—in the building.

She supposed she should've expected his nonresponsiveness, considering she'd just turned him down. But his silence was a different reaction from what she'd experienced with other guys she'd refused to go out with. There was usually some sort of back-and-forth with them trying to convince her why they were such good catches and her standing firm in her resolve to not get involved with dating and all the crap that went with that. The last date she'd had was with Meadows, almost nine months ago, and while she didn't regret that—the sex had ended up being pretty decent—she wasn't in the mood to do it again. Especially not since her physical response to Desmond was already beyond anything she knew she could've ever expected with Meadows.

"I'm not stalking you," he said with a half grin. "I came in with a client to make a statement and just so happened to run into you."

"Criminal and probate law—you're just a jack-of-all-trades, huh?" And delicious looking, to boot. That and everything about Desmond was in conflict with the memory of watching the ultimate demise of her parents' relationship. It had been the first glimpse she'd had of what love between a man and a woman should look like and had tainted her forever.

"My degree isn't for only one area of law." Why was his tone so even? So regular when she knew there was nothing regular about him.

Regular guys could never manage to intrigue and entice her simultaneously.

"I know that," she replied with a little edge to her tone.

With his legs spread, he brought his briefcase forward until he was holding it in front of him with both hands on the leather handle. It was a semi-aggressive, dominant type of stance that didn't irritate her as much as it probably should. "Then why bother acting surprised that I'd be here on a criminal case?" he asked casually.

"Why stop me while I'm at work to ask me out on a date when you had to know I'd turn you down?" Since he was obviously in the mood to go back and forth with her.

"Because I haven't been able to stop thinking about the way you looked when I mentioned ripping your clothes off."

Oh. Well. Shit.

"That doesn't mean I want to go out on a date with you." And yeah, she knew how ridiculous that sounded. She shifted from one foot to the other, then willed her legs to remain still.

"So you just wanna have sex? 'Cause that can probably be arranged too."

Cocky and courageous, a dangerous combination. She was about to respond when he held up a hand to stop her.

"I'm joking," he said, the smile falling so that now he looked serious.

Like, seriously hot in the plaid chocolate-brown suit, crisp white shirt, and brown tie. The suit was another slim fit, molding against his muscled arms and broad chest. His goatee seemed to have grown in a bit more, and his brow was slightly furrowed.

"Listen, I'm not lying or even saying this as a come-on. It's just the blunt truth. I've been thinking about you all weekend." He shrugged. "Didn't expect to see you here today, but the moment I did, I knew I wanted to ask you out. It's that simple."

She sighed. "It's that complicated."

"Come on, Sharae. We're both adults. Don't toss that unethical bit at me again. We can do whatever the hell we want. If you want to go out with me, cool, let's do it. If not . . ." He let that hang in the air.

She felt like a goofball. He was right. They could go out on a date, and nobody would care. Not that she worried about what others thought anyway. So what was it? Was she really gonna go into why she dated only when she felt like it, and for the shortest amount of time possible? And if not, could she really pull off the lie of saying she didn't want to go out with him? Because she did, or rather she wanted to have sex with him. Of that, she was certain.

"I can't do this. I've got a lot going on right now."

"Fair," he said and reached inside his suit jacket to pull out another one of his business cards. This time, he also slipped a hand into the side pocket of his briefcase and retrieved a pen. He held the case against his arm now and used it to bear down on as he wrote something on the back of the card. "Here's all my personal contact info," he told her and extended the card in her direction. "Let me know when you're ready."

She took the card, looked down at his personal email, cell number—which was the same as the cell number on the front of the card—and his home address. Did he really think she would simply show up at his house one day?

"And you want me to believe you're just gonna be sitting around waiting for me to respond?" Desmond was a great-looking guy who she knew instinctively would have no problem getting a date.

He chuckled. "Nah. I didn't say I'd be sittin' around waiting. Just that you can let me know when you're ready."

Well, that sent a shot of something weird straight through her chest. She was *not* jealous of who he might spend time with while he waited for her to answer him. This guy had been causing all types of confusion in her life since that first moment he sat down beside her.

She smirked. "Yeah. I'll let you know." It wasn't running if she really did have to work, so Sharae turned to walk away from him.

"Sharae."

She stopped at the sound of her name, looking back over her shoulder.

"Don't take too long," he said and then winked.

He walked away before she could respond, but not before her heart had done a ridiculous pitter-patter in her chest.

This Monday wasn't getting off to such a great start.

Her shift ended at six Monday evening, and Sharae pulled into the driveway along the side of Aunt Vi's house at six forty-five. She had no idea why she'd come here straight from work. Just felt like this was the place she needed to be.

The brick-front single-family dwelling had been her home from the time she was thirteen until she'd graduated from the police academy and leased her first apartment. Aunt Rose's house was around the corner.

And Aunt Ceil had rented a house down the block from Aunt Vi's two months after she'd left her husband.

Using her key, Sharae let herself in and stepped through the front door. A blast of cool air-conditioning hit her the moment she was inside. Then, the scent of vanilla, Aunt Vi's favorite, wafted past. Across the room was the wide stone-front fireplace that spoke intrinsically of the seventies, and on the walls on either side of that were thick brown shelves with fat beige-colored candles on each one. Those candles and the plug-ins Aunt Vi had inserted in almost all the electrical sockets throughout the house kept the place smelling sweet and familiar.

For a few minutes, Sharae just stood there in the living room, staring around at a place that meant the world to her.

The sofa, love seat, and recliner were relatively new—maybe about four years old—since Aunt Vi loved to redecorate. That was one of many traits she'd passed down to Rita because that woman changed the look of her house as frequently as Sharae tended to change cars. With a slight shrug, she figured everybody had their vices. Hers just didn't tend to revolve around the domestic things like Rita's did, or the flashy material things like Jemel. Sharae liked nice cars, and since Rita had built a car dealership, she'd always had access to the most up-to-date models for a very reasonable price. Sure, she liked her designer purses and shoes too, but her apartment was just a place where she slept, so not too much effort had gone into her bland gray-and-white decor.

She walked through the living room, past the strips of mirror pieces on the opposite wall—no matter how much Aunt Vi redecorated, her tastes didn't stray far from that retro look. She moved through the dining room and kitchen, opened the back door, and stepped out onto the porch. Looking for her aunt there was an instinct, one that paid off when she saw not just Aunt Vi, but Aunt Ceil and Aunt Rose too.

"Good evening," she said once she was outside again. Going to each woman, she leaned over to give them a brief hug and kiss on their cheek.

"Well, what a nice surprise," Aunt Vi said, holding on to Sharae a little longer and a lot tighter than the other aunts had.

"Mm-hmm, what brings you into the city during the week?" Aunt Rose asked, always with a hint of worry.

"You hungry?" Aunt Ceil asked as Sharae adjusted her crossbody bag so she wouldn't sit on it when lowering herself to the bench across from the Aunts and their color-coordinated chairs.

It had been so funny and not at all as abnormal as it should've been when they'd come over to Aunt Vi's for a Sunday dinner two summers ago and saw the sisters' new chairs. Aunt Vi's was a noble navy-blue color, while Aunt Rose had a brilliant red, and Aunt Ceil had a subtle yellow. The colors couldn't have represented the sisters' personalities more even if they were the only things on the porch that didn't match the muted brown-and-orange rug, bench, and planters.

"I've got leftover oxtails, potatoes, and gravy in there on the stove," Aunt Vi chimed in.

"And there's macaroni salad in the fridge. Chocolate cupcakes on the dining room table," Aunt Rose added.

"Nah," she said with a shake of her head. "I'm good." Well, at least she wasn't hungry, but she wasn't sure she was totally good either. "I've been thinking about my mom."

That was how she'd learned to refer to Justine around the Aunts, because once they'd brought her to live in this house, Aunt Vi had truly become her mother in every sense of the word, and Uncle Hale had filled the space of the father she hadn't wanted to mourn. For Sharae, there was a difference in the title—her mom had given birth to her and for a time had nurtured and cared for her, even if there'd been moments when Sharae had considered her a weak woman. Aunt Vi had been a mother when she needed one the most, giving her love, support, discipline, and purpose. She'd raised Sharae into the woman she was today, and for that she'd be forever grateful.

"Anniversary's coming up," Aunt Rose said with a nod. She wore purple capris with a matching striped shirt and brown sandals on her wide feet. The only one of the Aunts who'd never married, but had kept a slew of boyfriends who'd often contributed to her bills as well as offered her entertainment, this was the sister Sharae was most like in personality and in looks.

"You wanna do something other than the usual gravesite prayer and brunch?" Aunt Ceil asked.

Sharae glanced at this aunt, the one who'd been closest to her mother before Aunt Ceil had gotten married and moved away with her soldier husband. They were the two youngest Johnson girls, and Sharae could remember listening to them talk on the phone. Aunt Ceil would call on Sunday afternoons when it was cheapest, and her mother would sit in the kitchen holding the phone between her ear and her shoulder, smoking a cigarette and laughing. It seemed her mother was always the happiest when her sisters were around, which, with the exception of Aunt Ceil, they always were.

"No," Sharae answered. "We can keep the same ritual." Every new year, Sharae marked the date in August on each of her calendars with a pink rose. There'd been so many pink roses at her mother's funeral. If Sharae closed her eyes and visualized them, the scent would waft freely through her nostrils, and sadness would follow.

She cleared her throat. "I've been thinking about why she stayed with him." Those thoughts had come after she'd sat on the floor in her bedroom, crying her eyes out while holding Sanford's ashes. "He always hit her. Some of my earliest memories are of them yelling and fighting. Well, it was never really a fight since Sanford was the only one ever doing the hitting."

Logically, Sharae knew the answer. There were so many barriers the woman faced in these situations, ones that oftentimes outsiders didn't understand. During her years on the force, Sharae had seen plenty of domestic-abuse cases end in the same way her mother's had, and she'd taken the time to speak to therapists and counselors at the women's shelters in an effort to gain clarity on the situation. So she knew about those barriers and how difficult they were to break through, and with every woman in this situation she'd encountered throughout her career, she'd done everything she could to support and empower them to make the best decisions for themselves. The abuser was the criminal and the one who needed to be held accountable for their behavior. She never lost sight of that, except when she thought about Justine. The realization made her heart ache.

"I wanted her to leave. Every time, I just wanted her to walk away from him and never look back. Like you did, Aunt Ceil." Sharae heard the emotion in her voice, and she felt the pain and confusion she'd held in over the weekend swell in the center of her chest.

"We did too," Aunt Ceil said. "I could hear the sadness and the fear in her voice each time I talked to her."

"I wanted to slice that bastard's throat every time I saw him with that slick ole smile and those evil eyes," Aunt Rose continued.

Aunt Vi shook her head. "It's in the past. We can't go back now, baby girl." She looked at Sharae with nothing but love in her deep brown eyes. "We all loved Justine and thought many a time of what we could've done to make that situation better. To save our sister."

"I would've saved my sister," Sharae said vehemently. But she hadn't, had she? She and Jemel both knew Nate wasn't the right man for Rita, and yet they'd stood at that altar beside her, smiling while she married him. To their credit, they'd tried to talk some sense into her the night before the wedding, but Rita was in love, and she was insistent, and they loved her, so they'd backed off and supported her. Even through the years when they all knew he was cheating. She felt like an ass for doing that now that Rita was going through a divorce.

"Some situations aren't for us to save," Aunt Vi said. "I prayed so hard for Justine."

"And it didn't work!" Sharae leaned forward and dropped her elbows onto her knees. Tears burned her eyes, but she clenched her hands together in an effort to keep them from falling. "Your prayers didn't work! God didn't save her."

"Oh, but he did," Aunt Vi said in that quiet tone she used sometimes. It was her praying tone, the one that said she was about to give a spiritual lesson that wouldn't soon be forgotten. "He gave her peace that this world couldn't give her. As long as she was here, there would've been turmoil and pain and suffering. San was a troubled man, and he wasn't going to change until he got ready to. The Good Lord didn't want Justine to have to wait that long."

Sharae shook her head. She knew that at the root of this, her aunt was right. That didn't make it any easier to swallow, and it didn't stop that pain searing through the center of her chest. "Men ain't shit," she muttered.

Aunt Rose laughed so loud and hard, Sharae's head shot up as she stared at her. After another couple of seconds, Aunt Ceil joined in the laughter while Aunt Vi gave Sharae a scolding glare.

"You still got that potty mouth. Remember all the bars of soap my mama used to wash your mouth out? Guess it didn't work." Aunt Vi shook her head, but there was light in her eyes now.

"Sorry," Sharae said quietly.

"Whew, chile," Aunt Rose said between the breaths she had to take or her raucous laughter would surely cause her to go into a coughing fit. "I remember saying those same words so many times."

"Don't encourage her, Rose," Aunt Vi told her sister.

Aunt Rose shook her head. "What?" She waved a hand at Aunt Vi and continued to chuckle. "It's the truth. They ain't shit, and the Good Lord knew it too; that's why he created woman."

"She got a point there," Aunt Ceil added. "I mean, I found out the hard way, but once I did, I got a clue and learned how to proceed accordingly."

"By never getting married again?" Sharae asked.

Aunt Ceil nodded. "That's what worked for me. I had my hands full taking care of Jemel anyway, so getting another husband wasn't on the agenda. But even when I started dating again, I knew there'd never be another ring on this finger."

And she'd been happy. Or at least Aunt Ceil had always seemed happy.

"I ain't nevah want no ring on my finger," Aunt Rose said. "I learned early that men were only good for two things, and sometimes they fell flat on that."

Sharae wasn't about to ask her sixty-three-year-old aunt what those two things were. But Aunt Rose, with her candid self, told her anyway.

"Sex and money," she said, counting off the two on her fingers. "And like I said, sometimes you don't even get that in a good way. But in all my life I knew that's all I was ever tryin' to get from any of them. I didn't want none living with me or tryin' to tell me what to do. Had my own everything—house, car, job, bank accounts. They couldn't tell me nothin', evah."

Exactly. While Sharae had never asked a man to pay any of her bills or give her money to buy anything, she felt the same way Aunt Rose did. She just didn't need the hassle. So why had Desmond's business card been burning a hole in her pocket since she'd stuck it there earlier this afternoon?

An hour and a plate of oxtails and macaroni salad later, Sharae sat in her car across the street from the address Desmond had written on the back of his business card.

She dropped her keys in her purse and stepped out of the car, refusing to think on this another minute. Her long legs carried her across the street with purpose, and she jogged up the five cement steps that led to his front door. Clearing her throat, she pressed the button and listened as a bell chimed. It occurred to her then that the bell was actually one of those doorbell-camera things, and that he was probably staring at her right now. Should she fix her hair, hurry to pull out the compact in her purse to check her teeth for remnants of the fantastic dinner the Aunts had fed her?

Time didn't permit her to do either of those things—not that she was really going to do them anyway. Desmond opened the door.

"Hey. Ready so soon?" The corner of his mouth tilted into that smile, and it was really all Sharae needed.

She took a step forward, wrapped an arm around his neck to pull him down closer, and touched her lips to his. Desmond caught on fast. He tilted his head slightly and parted his lips to join in on the kiss. Their tongues had only just met when he backwalked them farther into his house and slammed the door closed.

Sharae felt herself being pressed against that door in the next seconds, and she wrapped her other arm around his neck. Now the kiss was a scrape of teeth, a duel of tongues, and a few guttural moans tossed in for good measure. He lifted one of her legs, locking it back behind his waist, and rubbed what she surmised would soon be an impressive erection against her center.

Dragging his mouth away from hers, Desmond kissed down the line of her neck. Sharae let her head fall back to hit the door with a light thunk, and he chuckled.

"This isn't the date I had in mind," he said before tracing his tongue in teasing little circles on her neck.

He wore a black T-shirt that she grabbed and pulled up his back until her fingers felt the warmth of his bare skin. "I told you I don't date."

Leaning back, he yanked the shirt up in the front and pulled it over his head. She'd kept her leg tucked around his waist, and now her hands were on his picture-perfect pecs instantly, her tongue sliding slowly over her bottom lip as she stared at him.

With a finger to her chin, he tilted her head up until they were gazing into each other's eyes. "Then what are we doing, exactly?"

"In about five minutes I expect to have my clothes ripped off—well, not ripped, per se, but you know what I mean." He grinned, and her pussy throbbed. "And then I think you can imagine the rest."

There was a brief moment when she thought he was going to turn her down. She would've been monumentally pissed off in that instance. But that was not what he said.

"I can imagine a lot of things."

"Good," she said, cupping her hand to the back of his head and pulling his mouth close to hers again. "You've got an hour. My next shift starts at six, and I need to go home and get some rest."

He surprised her then by lifting her other leg and pushing it behind his waist. His hands cupped her ass, and he turned, walking her toward the stairs, she assumed. "Then you should've packed an overnight bag because I'm gonna need more time than that."

She shook her head as he took the first step. "That's all the time you get."

Desmond took her mouth in a hungry kiss. His hands moved up and down her back, over her ass to squeeze each mound, up her back again to riffle through her hair, and then finally back to cup her ass. When he pulled his mouth away from hers this time, they were both out of breath. "Wanna bet," he whispered and then carried her up the stairs.

Chapter 19

PLANNING A NERVOUS BREAKDOWN.

Stress could lead to high blood pressure. High blood pressure could lead to heart disease. Heart disease could lead to a cardiovascular event and death.

Rita rubbed her temples and willed herself to calm down. This had been a long Wednesday morning, and she still had a couple more errands to run before she could go home and take a soothing hot bath. She'd been working on her breathing techniques, and knowing now that it really did start with settling her mind first and foremost, she let her arms fall to her sides and tried to do just that.

Taryn and Necole were coming over tonight for dinner, but they'd insisted on ordering from Rita's favorite Italian restaurant and bringing the food to her. She'd been touched by the thought and had immediately accepted their offer. So that was something nice to look forward to.

Breathe in. Breathe out. Slow and steady breaths that focused on pushing out the bad and filling herself up with the good, the refreshing, the regenerating.

Nate had sent a moving truck to the house yesterday to pick up more of his things. After seeing him in Ocean City, she'd been more determined than ever to rid her house of any semblance of him. He'd thankfully not given her any pushback when she'd sent him a text message about getting the rest of the things she'd found and whatever else he wanted out of the house as soon as possible. She'd sat in the dining room nursing a cup of coffee while the movers took all the designated items away.

Breathe in. Breathe out. Her shoulders trembled a bit, but she kept on going.

Her mother had called last night to remind her of today's meetings at the church. The Women's-Ministry Anniversary was in September, and they were having a banquet as their yearly fundraiser. Rita was catering the banquet, but Vi was micromanaging on the sidelines.

Breathe in. Breathe out.

"So, do you think baked and barbeque chicken, ham, and salmon are going to be enough meats?" Florence Bakersfield asked. It was her ten-thousandth question of the morning, and Rita wanted to scream with the annoyance of it all.

"We've gone over this menu a dozen times, Florence," Maddie Hemp replied with a deep southern accent. She was from Kentucky but had moved to Baltimore fifteen years ago to be with her new husband and his two daughters.

"There'll be more than enough food," Rita assured Florence and the other three women who'd taken Florence's side on this committee.

There were always sides to one committee—those who planned, those who planned and executed, and those who talked—that is, complained.

"Lollie is in charge of ticket sales. That money needs to be turned in no later than August twentieth, so I'll have more than enough time to finish getting all the food and decorations. We've organized a setup and cleanup crew. The honorariums have been approved, and gifts for them were ordered. The pastor is looking over the preliminary program, and we're working on securing a gospel group to perform. We're in a very good planning position heading into July, which works out well since

Vacation Bible School will be starting in a couple of weeks, and most of us will be teaching, so that'll take up our attention."

Thank the Lord she'd opted out of teaching this year, but she was still in charge of the daily brown-bag meals they planned to serve, so all the pressure wasn't completely off her shoulders.

Florence—a staunch member of the "those who talked" group—rolled her eyes. She sat back in her chair with her signature burgundy lipstick slathered over her full lips and continued to grumble. "I'm just wondering if we shouldn't have hired a professional caterer. Or even rented one of those banquet halls. Why have it here at the church, putting more work on us?"

Rita knew full well this wasn't about Florence having more or less work to do; the woman simply didn't do anything but run her mouth on whichever committee she chose to be on. That had always been the case, so Rita was neither surprised nor particularly irritated by this behavior. She was, however, physically and mentally tired and wanted this meeting over with as soon as possible.

"I've been catering events at this church for the last fifteen years," Rita told her.

Florence didn't bother to look at her directly. "That's because your daddy's the pastor."

It wasn't the first time that had been thrown in her face, but it did hit kinda different today. Rita tried for a steadying breath, but it came out shaky, and she cleared her throat. "That's not news either. But this event is meant to be a fundraiser, and to that end, the trustees decided we would clear a higher profit if it was held here at the church. We have enough space in our large fellowship hall to accommodate seven hundred and fifty guests, which is considerably higher than a lot of the banquet halls in the city."

"They're professionals. You don't have any professional training," Florence continued.

"That don't stop you from eating everything she cooks at the Sunday-afternoon fellowships. Or from taking plates of that same food home to your family for the rest of the week," Maddie added.

Rita had to remember to buy her a thank-you gift when this was all said and done. She also imagined the look on Florence's face when she found out Rita was opening her own *professional* catering company.

"Look, I'm not only catering the event, I'm also the chairperson of this committee," Rita said, her voice much steadier now. "We've discussed this issue ad nauseum, and I don't intend to keep taking up everyone's time going over the same points. The banquet will be held in our fellowship hall, and I'll be catering it. If that bothers you or it's not in line with your vision, you can take it up with the trustees and/or the pastor."

Closing her event book, Rita stuck her pen in her bag and looked to Lollie. "Can you close us out in prayer?"

Florence needed as much Jesus as she could get at this moment, and Rita just didn't have it in her to be any nicer to the woman. She knew people saw her differently because of who her parents were. She'd grown up with that cloud hanging over her head. But she'd proven herself and her commitment to this church years ago. She wasn't about to sit here and do it all over again. Not with all the other things going on in her life.

After the meeting was over, she sat at the table in the small meeting room a little longer just staring at the walls. They'd been painted a subtle blue, and framed scriptures were evenly spaced. On the floor was the same dark-brown carpet that lined every office, Sunday school, and meeting room on this level of the church. She drummed her fingers on the table and thought about all the other things she needed to do before she could make it back to her house.

For weeks she'd sat in her safe haven. While she'd gotten up every day and gone about her schedule as if nothing had changed, it was always with the thought that she could hurry and get back home. To be behind the doors of the house that she owned, the space that offered her more comfort than any other. Today was no different. She was ready to go home.

"Hey, Rita. You okay in here?"

Turning completely around in her chair, she glanced toward the doorway to see a tall, not-so-dark, and extremely handsome guy standing there. "Oh, hey, Vance." A member of their church who did a lot of handy work around the building, Vance Graham was someone she'd known for a couple of years now. "I'm good. Just needed a minute to gather my thoughts."

He chuckled. "Had one of those meetings, huh? That's why I steer clear of committees and stuff here. Just come to church on Sunday morning and mind my business the rest of the time."

She couldn't tell him how many times she'd considered doing the same thing. Her upbringing and the massive guilt trip she'd take herself through if she did put a stop to that dream.

"It's okay. I don't mind using the gifts I've been blessed with." Regret circled in her gut the minute she saw his brow furrow. "I'm not accusing you of not using your gifts," she hurriedly said.

"It's cool. I'm not upset." He stepped inside, and she noted his worn jeans, super-tightly fit dark-gray T-shirt, and magnificent arms. If she wasn't mistaken, his full-time job was being a personal trainer. She couldn't pinpoint from whom she'd heard that, but the fact had been floated around via some members of the NVB's congregation a while back.

"But if you need to unwind, you should come down to my gym. We've got some great yoga classes going."

Well, the gossip mill had been partially correct. "Your gym? You're a personal trainer, right?"

Nodding, he came to a stop just a few steps away from her. He smelled like man—woodsy, smoky, maybe some bergamot—what did she know? He smelled really good was all that actually mattered at the moment.

He grinned, a dimple in one cheek appearing. His head was shaved bald, and his thick beard of black hair was long but neatly trimmed. "Yeah, I do some training, but I also own the gym, so I manage all the programs there."

Ohhhhhh, he *owned* the gym.

She managed a small smile. "I apologize. I was just going on what I'd heard around here. So yoga, huh? I've heard that's good for stress relief."

He nodded. "It is, as well as flexibility."

If that word was supposed to send spikes of desire shooting through her like fireworks, it succeeded. But no, this wasn't happening. She was not looking for a man or any type of entanglement with a man. And she was certain that sounded cliché—the new divorcée not looking for a relationship—but she was dead serious about that. She didn't want a man in her life. Going from her parents to Nate had seemed like a natural transition at the time, but in the past weeks that she'd been alone, she'd started to like keeping her own company.

"Why don't you stop by when you have time," he said and reached into his back pocket to retrieve his wallet.

She waited for him to pull the business card free and hand it to her.

"It's a simple process to get you signed up for some classes. But," he said and raised his brows when she opened her mouth to say something, "if you're not ready to make a commitment to a specific regimen, I could offer you some complimentary classes just to get an idea of what might work for you."

"Massages," she said, staring down at the card so he wouldn't see the flush of embarrassment she was certain still stained her cheeks after the flexibility remark. "I've never heard of a gym offering massages."

"It's new." He shrugged. "I'm always interested in learning new things, seeing how VGFitness can be set apart from the other gyms. So I took some masseur classes and got certified. Still toying with a real schedule and when or if I'll bring on more massage therapists. I guess that all depends on customer interest."

"I'm interested." The two words just fell from her lips before she'd had a chance to consider how it might sound or if she really wanted this type of connection with him.

Rita had always tried to keep her church relationships in church. Being in her position, it'd been hard to ever really trust members of the congregation. Did they really want to be friends with her, or did they just want to be closer to the pastor and first lady? That question had always circled in her mind, and she'd learned that keeping her distance on a personal level worked best.

"In a massage," she said, hoping the pause in her response hadn't given him the wrong idea.

He nodded. "I knew what you meant." But he had raised a brow initially, so she still wondered what he was actually thinking about her at this moment.

Not that it mattered. Well, she refused to let it matter.

"Anyway, I'll give you a call to set up an appointment." She was tucking the card into her purse when he spoke again.

"I've got time this afternoon."

She looked up at him. "Oh."

"Around three. Is that good for you?"

"I was going home after I run a few errands. To take a ba . . . I mean, I was just going home."

He'd pushed his hands into the front pockets of his jeans. "I can come by your place when I'm finished here. I've got my table and oils in the truck. But I need to check out the bathrooms on the lower level first. Trustee Fornsby reported a leak and a blockage last week, so I need to take care of that before Sunday."

She'd stopped listening to what he was saying after he'd said he could come by her house. Did she want him coming to her house? Her private safe haven? The place where no other man besides Nate and her relatives had ever been? This wasn't a date. The reminder blared through her mind, and she stood, smoothing down the flared top she wore over denim capris.

"If you're sure it's not an inconvenience," she said, her voice sounding way more confident than she was feeling. "I don't require any special treatment just because of who my parents are and your relationship with the church."

He frowned. "That's not how I operate. But I can see how you'd think that. Anyway, no, it's no problem. I understand you're busy, and if this is an opportunity to win a new customer to the gym, then I'm a businessman—I'm not gonna pass that up."

With a tilt of her head, she really looked at him. He hadn't made any moves on her. Ever. Not in the years she'd known him and not today. For a few moments she'd ridiculously entertained a notion . . . but then, no, she had no clue what it would feel like to actually have a man flirt with her. It'd been so long since she'd experienced it. And anyway, all of this was pointless. He said he was a businessman, and she believed him. It did make sense to try to win a new customer whenever possible.

Today, she was his possibility.

Not that she was going to make the mistake of saying that out loud.

"Fine." She slipped her book into her purse and eased it onto her shoulder. "Three is fine with me. Let me give you my address."

He pulled his phone from his pocket, swiped over it, and then handed it to her. "Put all your contact info in here. I'll text before I come. That way, if anything has come up, you can just let me know, and we'll reschedule."

"No problem," she said and typed in all her information. "And thanks, Vance. These past few weeks have been really difficult, so maybe a massage will help."

He nodded. "It will, but you know it's only a temporary fix. If stress is your issue, you have to work on that from the inside out. But I'm no therapist," he joked.

Rita smiled. "I get it," she said. "And thanks for that too."

Chapter 20

RUB MY BACK, AND I'LL RUB YOURS.

At ten minutes after two, Rita's cell phone rang, and she answered the moment she saw the caller's name on the screen.

"Hey, stranger," she said and settled back in the chair across from her bed.

"Margarita," he replied.

"Don't play."

Benny laughed, a sound Rita hadn't heard in far too long. Her older brother was currently living in Virginia, where he was attending seminary. Having already held both the trustee and deacon position at NVB, becoming a minister was the next natural step. Their parents had been bursting with pride the night Benny had preached his trial sermon, but it was when he announced he was going to seminary to complete his biblical studies there and become ordained that their father's chest had puffed out, and he'd begun planning Benny's takeover of the church. Rita had been more than happy to escape that type of attention from their parents.

"How've you been? And when are you coming home for a visit?"

"I'll be there next weekend, don't worry. Mama's already called me a dozen times reminding me of the cookout y'all are throwing."

"It's summertime," she said. "We're always having a cookout."

"That's the truth," he replied with more laughter.

It was so good to hear from him. She missed him much more than she'd allowed herself to believe.

"So what's going on? I heard about you and Nate."

One thing about having a big family—secrets were never kept for very long, at least not the ones a person wanted to remain a secret. "Who told you? Mama?"

"Nah, Ivan called me. Said he was worried about you and Sharae."

Ivan, Tariq, and Benny were older than Sharae, Rita, and Jemel, but only in the three-to-five-year range, so the six of them were the closest of all the Johnson cousins. Of course, the guys had always been protective over the girls, and as was the norm, the girls hated them for that overprotection—while secretly appreciating it when they deemed it was warranted. Rita had thought about calling Benny when things hit the fan with Nate, but she'd quickly dismissed that because she didn't want her brother coming home to handle her problems.

"You should've told me," he continued. "And you should've said something sooner than just a few weeks ago."

She rolled her eyes because she knew there was no one here to see her do it. "What did Ivan tell you?"

"That some woman called to tell you she's carrying Nate's baby."

"Okay, well, there was nothing to tell you sooner than that," she said.

"Don't try to lie to me, Rita. You know you were never good at it."

He was right. Of the six of them, Rita had been the worst at lying. After her was Ivan and then Benny. The other three could lie their way into a government position if they chose to.

She sighed. "What was I supposed to do? Report all my suspicions to you? Then what? You were gonna hunt my husband down and threaten him."

"I would never threaten Nate," Benny said. "I'd promise to beat his ass if he hurt my sister. As a matter of fact, I did make him that promise the day he married you. So he's got it comin'."

"Stop it," she said, hating the serious tone of her brother's voice. "It's not that big a deal."

"Oh yeah, it is, and I told Ivan and Tariq it was too. They wanted to handle him, but I told them no. You're *my* sister."

"And you're a minister, Benny."

"I'm a man first. A brother second."

She sighed again. "I shouldn't have been surprised." And yet she had been. Never in all that Nate had done to her had she thought he would be stupid enough to get another woman pregnant.

"You shouldn't have had to accept that as the norm. If he's been cheating for years, you should've told me."

"It's *my* marriage, Benny. I didn't owe anybody any explanations about it. What I decided to accept was my business." And she'd carry those decisions with her for the rest of her life. They weren't regrets, she couldn't afford regrets, not when her time with Nate had produced her beautiful daughters.

"Well, I'll be home next week, and I'll deal with him then."

"There's nothing to deal with. We're getting divorced. We have another meeting with our attorneys next week, and then this will be done. You don't have to approach him at all." Rita wasn't afraid that Benny would do something to physically harm Nate. Her brother had been in more than his share of fights growing up on the streets of Baltimore City, but he'd matured during his time in the marines, and when he'd come home, he'd been a different man. While hearing him talk now was reminiscent of the teenage Benny, she also had faith in his growth in the church as well as in the world, that he wouldn't resort to such basic measures. Tariq, on the other hand, could be a loose cannon, even at forty-five years old.

"Now I'm gonna tell you to stop it. You can't tell me not to talk to him because I'm just gonna do it anyway."

That was the truth. "Well, just make it a quick conversation," she told him.

He laughed. "You still so bossy. You can't tell me how to deal with the dude that hurt my sister, Rita. That's off-limits for you. Now we can talk about my nieces. How are they?"

The conversation took on a normal tone for the next thirty minutes, until she received the text that Vance was on his way. Reluctantly ending the call with Benny, she ran to her closet and pulled off the robe she'd put on after her bath. She slipped on sweatpants and an oversize T-shirt, then added a pair of fluffy gray socks with ridiculous green frogs on them. With a shake of her head as she passed the floor-length mirror in the closet, she shrugged. She had no idea how to dress for a massage.

In fact, she'd been wondering why she'd even requested one. Nate had used one of the rooms in the basement as an exercise room, so there was a treadmill and other gym equipment that she used sporadically. She had no need to go to Vance's gym or to ask for a massage, and yet there was a pep in her step as she headed downstairs to wait for him to arrive.

By the time she hit the bottom of the steps, she'd told herself there was nothing wrong with asking for a massage. She could book any type of self-care she wanted and didn't have to answer to anyone—not even her nervous inner thoughts—about it. This was the new Rita, the one who was going to live her life on her own terms. That was what she'd told herself after the run-in with Nate in Ocean City, and it was what she was determined to live by.

When the doorbell rang, she walked calmly to answer it. Vance greeted her with a smile, and she returned the gesture.

"So where would you like to set up? We have a gym down in the basement."

"Wherever you like, or rather, wherever you have enough room for the table." He held up said folded table, and she nodded.

"Yeah, let's go to the basement." She locked the door and started walking through the foyer. "There's a bunch of equipment in the exercise room, but you could set that up in the front of the basement with no problem."

"Good." He followed her down the basement steps and immediately began setting up the table. "I've got towels in that bag over there. You can remove your shirt and wrap the towel around you, and we'll start up top."

Okay, she hadn't thought about being topless, or bottomless, for that matter, but she probably should have. It was a massage, after all. She went to his white duffel bag with the black-and-gold VGFitness logo on the side. Grabbing a towel, she took it into the bathroom and removed her shirt and bra. With the towel wrapped securely around her chest, she returned to the room to find him standing near his table, digging out bottles of oil from his bag.

He was wearing joggers now, not the jeans he'd had on earlier today. The joggers fit him nicely, especially in the front, where just the slightest hint of an outline appeared.

"Are you allergic to nuts?"

She quickly averted her gaze to the bottle of oil in his hands. "Excuse me?"

"Nuts. Do you have any nut allergies?"

"Why? Are we having a snack before the massage?"

He grinned and held up one of the bottles of oil. "It's almond oil. I like it because it allows my hands to glide easily and doesn't usually irritate the skin. It can stain sheets, though, so I use this yoga mat over the cushions on the table instead of a cloth. But if you're allergic, then I have other options."

"No," she said, shaking her head. "I don't have any allergies."

"Okay. Good. Well, whenever you're ready, we can get started."

She was as ready as she was ever going to be. Rita walked over to the table and eased onto it.

"On your stomach," he instructed her.

She did as she was told, and when his hands went to the top of the towel to ease it loose, she struggled with the unfamiliar feeling of another man's hands on her bare skin. All her doctors had always been women. Besides Nate and the two boys she'd allowed to fondle her breasts during her teenage years, there'd never been another man's hands on her. Vance didn't try to cup her breasts like those three had; instead, he eased the towel from around her but left it draped down by her waist.

The moment his hands were on her, Rita forgot everything else. There was no Nate, no other teenage boys, and most of all, no worries. With every stroke of his hands, her mind emptied of more of the distractions that had been running through it rampantly for the past few months. She'd even mastered her doctor's deep-breathing technique with the sound of Vance's extremely soothing voice in the background.

"You could be reciting an X-rated fairy tale, and I don't think I'd mind one bit," she murmured when his hands moved from her shoulders to work down her spine.

He chuckled. "That's part of the training. I can also yell like a ferocious lion, as my son puts it."

"You have a son?" She didn't know why she hadn't considered he might be married with children. Perhaps because there'd been no ring on his finger.

"Yeah. Sons. One's twenty-five, and the youngest is twenty-three." She nodded. "Oh."

"I'm forty-nine, by the way." When she didn't immediately respond, he continued. "Didn't know what the rumor mill at the church might've said about my age."

"Women don't want to talk about their age or anybody else's," she said with a grin. "Unless you're breaking the law."

"I hear that." His fingers were magical, and her mind drifted again. "I'm also single. My wife and I divorced ten years ago, so if you need any advice on how to get through it, I can lend an ear."

Her eyes opened then, and she tried to steal a glimpse of him, but he was leaning into his work, his fingers applying pressure at the base of her spine, drawing a low moan from her.

"So you heard through the rumor mill that I'm getting a divorce?" She should've known.

"Yep. And like I said, I've been there and done that, so I know it's not easy."

"No," she admitted. "It's not."

"Well, if you ever want to talk."

"Does talking lead to sex in your book, because if that's the case . . ." She'd started to rise up off the table at that point, totally forgetting that she was naked from the waist up.

Vance put his hands on her shoulders and moved so that she could now stare into his eyes. "Not sex. Conversation. Relax, Rita. You don't have to worry about every little thing."

Oh, but she did, she'd realized over the years. Because the things she'd decided not to worry about had come back to bite her in the ass.

"I just want to be clear on the boundaries here, that's all."

"I can relate. While I've been through a divorce, I've never been a preacher's daughter. So here's the deal: our sessions are private. I don't talk about my clients to anyone. And if we have a personal conversation, that's private too. I may hear a lot of the gossip that floats around the church, but I don't spread any of it."

First, she felt chastised, and then she felt relief. "That's good to know," she told him. "Sorry if I offended you."

"You didn't," he said and continued working his magic. Now he was lifting an arm and massaging her biceps. "And don't apologize for setting boundaries. They're necessary."

That was the truth and made her think of the boundaries she'd had to set with her mother over the years. Although Vi still thought her word was law with Rita, it had taken a long time for Rita to learn how to push some of Vi's most outlandish comments to the side, and more recently how to steer Vi around even making those comments to her. Now she needed to work on the boundaries between her daughters and her personal life, but she could certainly handle that.

An hour and a half had passed before Rita climbed off the table, her limbs so supple she almost melted into a puddle on the floor. Vance had folded his table and packed up his oils by the time she came out.

"Mind if I use your bathroom to change? I've got a meeting at five thirty. I thought I'd have time to run by the gym to change, but we ran a little over."

"Oh no," she said quickly, now feeling guilty for enjoying her conversation with him almost as much as she'd enjoyed the massage. "That's perfectly fine. In fact, I need to run upstairs and take something out of the freezer. Just come on up when you're done, and I'll walk you out."

She left him there and went upstairs to the kitchen. She'd made chocolate-mousse cake when she came home earlier and had wanted the mousse to set quickly before her dinner with the girls. There were also some flavored waters she wanted to have chilled before the girls arrived, so she stepped into the pantry to get them. It had only taken a few moments, but the second Rita stepped into the kitchen again, she heard the commotion.

"Drop it or I'll shoot!"

What in the world? Rita moved toward the sounds coming from the basement.

"Don't move! I'm calling the police!"

She ran down the stairs, coming to such a quick stop at the sight of Taryn holding a gun on Vance, she almost tripped over her feet.

"Taryn, what are you doing?"

"Intruder!" her daughter yelled, her arms trembling as she held them extended before her, fingers wrapped tightly around the gun.

In the doorway of the bathroom, Vance stood holding the blue joggers he'd been wearing in front of him, but not quite hiding the black boxer briefs or his toned legs completely. His chest was bare too, and Rita had to force herself to look away.

"He's not an intruder, Taryn. Put the gun down." The gun. Her daughter had a gun, and she was acting like she was prepared to use it. Rita would have to wrap her mind around that later.

"Then who the hell is he?" Taryn asked, casting a quick glance in Rita's direction.

"He's my personal trainer," she replied. "*A* personal trainer. Just put the gun down."

Rita stepped toward Taryn, but Taryn turned fast, and now the gun was pointed at Rita.

"Taryn!" Rita yelled.

"For real, Mama? Are you having sex with him? How could you? That's so cliché!"

For one, Rita felt some kind of way about her daughter pointing a gun at her. And two, she definitely didn't like the tone or the questions coming from Taryn either.

"Girl, if you don't put that gun down," Rita warned, but it was too late.

Vance had come up behind Taryn and reached around her to grab her wrists and turn her arms away from Rita's direction. Taryn tried to buck back against him, but she lost her grip on the gun, and it fell to the floor. Rita ran over to kick the gun away.

"What in the world is wrong with you? Why do you even have a gun?"

"Why are you hiding a half-dressed so-called personal trainer in your bathroom?" Taryn yelled.

Then, as if this situation couldn't get any more bizarre, Necole also decided to show up early for dinner. "A fine half-dressed personal trainer," Rita's youngest daughter said while wiggling her brows in Vance's direction.

It only took ten minutes for Rita to order her daughters upstairs and then wait for Vance to come out of the bathroom, fully dressed this time.

"I'm so sorry," she said the moment he shut the bathroom door behind him. "I don't know what got into her."

He was shaking his head. "She was just protecting you."

"With a gun? In my house? No, she's way out of line, and I'll deal with her later. But I wanted to apologize to you."

"It's not necessary. Remember, I told you I know firsthand how tough it is going through a divorce. My sons took it hard when I started dating again too. It's normal."

"She's grown, but not as grown as I am," Rita said as they walked toward the steps. "She doesn't have a say in my dating life. Besides the fact that I'm not even dating."

He grinned. "But you will, at some point. Instead of apologizing to me, make sure you reiterate those boundaries with your daughters. That's something I took too long to do."

Rita took the advice and didn't even glance in the kitchen as they came upstairs and turned straight into the foyer. "I guess she could've really thought you were an intruder."

He nodded. "I can see that. But if she's gonna pull a gun, she might want to actually learn how to use one. She never took the safety off; that's why I moved in on her."

Rita opened the door and sighed heavily. "But that could've ended a lot worse," she said.

"Right." He walked out the door. "Anyway, let me know when you're ready for your next session."

Leaning against the doorjamb, Rita smiled and shook her head. "You sure? I know it's not every day that you have a gun pulled on you by a client's daughter."

"No. It's not. But I'm not upset by it. If you want another massage, all you have to do is call me."

"I will," Rita said as she watched him walk away. "I most definitely will."

Chapter 21

THE SPICY SAUCE.

Rita walked into her kitchen to see Taryn and Necole unpacking the food they'd brought in. Neither of them looked up to see her enter, but the air was thick with tension and filled with the scent of red sauce and oregano.

"For the record, Vance is a personal trainer." She decided to start with that because the presumption that she would lie about it was only one of the things that had her filled with annoyance right now.

"I've seen him at the church," Necole said as she set containers of food on the island.

Taryn moved, carrying the bag she'd finished unpacking with bowls of what Rita knew were extra sauces, Parmesan cheese, and side salads, and put it in the recycle bin near the slider doors across the room. Rita went to the cabinet for the plates.

"Yes, he goes to NVB, so I've known him for a few years." Or at least she knew of him. Until today there hadn't been much more connection between her and Vance than there was a good number of the large congregation.

"How long has he wanted to get his hands on you?" Taryn asked when she returned to the island.

Her arms were folded across her chest, thin lips pursed, eyes blazing with what Rita would call a mixture of anger and hurt. Rita knew that look well because so many times she'd stood in the mirror and watched it staring back at her. For that reason alone, she took a deep, steadying breath and released it slowly before replying. "I honestly don't think that man had given much thought to touching me in any way," she said. "As I'm sure you're aware, there are hundreds of women at NVB."

"There's only one pastor's daughter who owns a car dealership. How do you know he's not just after your title and money?" Taryn wore dark-blue jeans today and a pink halter top. Her hair was pulled back from her face to hang in a low ponytail down her back.

"Can we at least eat first?" Necole asked. "I mean, we came over here to have dinner and talk."

Rita set the plates on the island and stared at her youngest child. She wore a pale-blue maxi dress that fit her slim frame perfectly. There were flat natural-colored sandals on her feet and at least two dozen Alex and Ani charm bracelets on her left wrist. Her hair was held back with a thick paisley band and fell to her shoulders in a riot of curls.

She was trying to keep the peace, and Rita appreciated that. But today, she figured they might as well have the knock-down-drag-out argument that'd been brewing between them for the last week. As much as she hated that the divorce was affecting her daughters in this way, and though she'd never wanted to get into confrontational discussions with her children before, she knew this was the only way they could move forward.

"We can do both," she said. "But first, let's at least have a seat and bless the food."

They moved in silence to continue warming up their food and getting their drinks and any other toppings they wanted from the cabinet. Necole loved a sprinkle of sugar on her spaghetti no matter who made it or which restaurant it came from. It was her favorite pasta, and Rita thought the plate with generous sauce and meatballs looked terrific. The

Italian dish Rita loved most was shrimp marinara, and her daughters had known to order it with extra shrimp and extra sauce. And Taryn's preference was lasagna that she drenched with more sauce and a small mountain of grated Parmesan cheese.

Rita's prayer was not only for the Lord to bless the food they were about to receive, but to also guide their thoughts and words so that the discussion was steeped in love and respect and not anger and discord. When she was finished, her daughters muttered a spirit-filled amen along with her, and Rita felt a moment's peace before they began.

"I want you to know that I'm okay with your decision," Necole said while using her knife and fork to cut her food. "I know you don't really feel like it's me or Taryn's business what goes on between you and Daddy, but you're the two most important people in our lives, and whether you like it or not, that affects us."

Rita could accept that. She carefully cut the tails from her shrimp, then made a second cut because they were too big to eat with one forkful of the pasta. "It's not that I don't expect you to have feelings about the situation, I just need you to understand that I won't be changing my decision based on what you may want or expect me to do."

"I don't like it," Taryn said, the edge still present in her tone.

It was hard to swallow that this might be the new norm between her and her daughter. For so long she'd prided herself on having a better relationship with her children than she'd ever had with her parents. She'd always encouraged them to talk to her about anything and to feel comfortable expressing themselves to her and Nate. There was never really an off-limits subject in her house, whereas in Vi's house there were so many things that Rita had never been "old enough" to discuss. Sex and finances were just a couple.

Taryn continued, her fork and knife hacking away at the square of lasagna. "I don't like walking in here to see some half-naked stranger coming out of the bathroom, and I definitely don't like when I have to find out from my landlord that our rent payment was returned."

"What?" Rita held her fork still as her gaze moved quickly to Taryn and then to Necole.

Necole was chewing, and Taryn let her utensils fall to the plate with a clatter. "I got the call on Friday and tried to call you but got your voice mail."

"I went to Ocean City for the shower last weekend. I texted you both to tell you." She'd actually thought they might come down since Wendy was only a few years older than they were, and Rita figured her guests were more of Taryn and Necole's crowd. But neither of them had showed up.

And she'd been trying desperately not to think about Nate and his petty move of emptying the account while she was away. The rent for the girls' apartment was set up as a direct payment from Nate and Rita's main checking account, which was now empty. "I'm sorry," Rita whispered because she'd been so upset by what Nate had done that she hadn't thought to change all the payments that came out of that account monthly; she'd simply focused on her new account and what she needed to do to get her business off the ground.

"You shouldn't apologize," Necole said, sending a searing glare to her sister. "You're not the one who emptied the account."

Taryn rolled her eyes and sighed. "She's right. Daddy did it. He told me when I called him, but he said you had other money to take care of it."

Her daughters knew that she took care of all the monthly household bills. There'd been many times in the past when they'd seen her at the dining room table with bills, a checkbook, and a laptop. Still, it irritated Rita that they were here releasing all their frustration out on her while seemingly letting Nate off easy.

Keeping her composure and trying to play fair in a situation that wasn't her fault was starting to grate on her nerves. But she kept it together and managed to reply, "There is another joint account. Actually, there are two—a savings account and an account for your tuition. I can set it up so that your rent comes from the savings."

After confronting Nate in his office, she'd decided to use that account to pay things like her mortgage and utilities. Anything she needed personally and all her upcoming business expenses, she was going to take from her own account.

Even with that said, Rita paused and glanced at her daughters. "But things are going to be changing," she continued. "My financial situation, your father's, and ultimately yours. You can get a job to help support yourselves." By the time Rita had been Taryn's age, she didn't have a job, but she did have a husband, a house, and a child to take care of, all while taking evening courses. If she could do it on those terms, then her daughters, who didn't have any of those obligations, could do the same.

"So we have to start paying all our bills ourselves?" Necole sounded like the concept was totally foreign to her, and Rita's gut clenched with regret.

Had she been trying so hard to be everything her mother wasn't that she hadn't properly prepared her children for the real world at all? At least with all Vi's rules and declarations, Rita had always known that if she wasn't a wife and mother, she'd still need to find her own way and take care of herself once she turned eighteen. Her parents weren't a fan of taking care of children beyond that point. And truth be told, Rita had spent so much time anticipating turning eighteen so she could be free from living under her parents' thumbs that she'd often planned for what her adult future would look like.

"That's what adults do," she told her. "It's what the two of you will have to learn to do. Now, I'll call the bank in the morning and get this month's rent situated."

Taryn shook her head. "Daddy came over yesterday and gave us some cash."

"But he told us to come to you and get the rest straightened out," Necole added.

"Oh." Rita said the one word with finality. "So you didn't just want to have dinner with me tonight? You needed to come over here and find out how your bills were gonna continue getting paid?"

Necole hurriedly shook her head. "I wanted to come over and talk last week, but when we texted, you said you had a lot of running around to do."

She had. The previous week had been full of meetings, but that wasn't any different from her schedule any other time. Truthfully, Rita hadn't wanted to focus on anything other than her new business plan last week. And she decided in that moment that she wasn't going to feel guilty for taking that time for herself.

"I don't mind getting a job," Taryn said, surprising both Rita and Necole. "Daddy was acting so weird when he was talking about money and the effect the divorce was having on him that I just don't even want to need him like that anymore. I guess it's expensive taking care of a young girlfriend and an upcoming baby."

And there was that sound of hurt again. This time it was also tinged with disappointment, and Rita couldn't resist reaching a hand out to grab Taryn's and squeeze. "I know this is hard for you, baby. And I really wish we could've shielded the two of you from our messiness." But Rita understood now that it wasn't possible. Her daughters had been right in telling her that this divorce affected them as much as it did her and Nate. Everybody's lives would be different now because of the choices Nate had made.

When Taryn looked up at Rita again, it was with a sheen of tears in her eyes. "I'm sorry I've been such a brat," she said, and Rita's heart broke into a million pieces. "I just don't know how to be without you two together. It's all I've ever known."

Rita eased from her seat and stood next to where her daughter sat, pulling her in for a tight hug. "I know. And none of this is your fault.

Not yours or your sister's. I'm sorry if I didn't understand what you were going through before."

Necole, who'd always been her most affectionate child, came around the island to join in the hug, a deep sob coming the moment Rita dragged a hand down the side of her head. What had they done? How had this wonderful family unit she and Nate had worked so hard to construct come tumbling down, leaving such pain and destruction in its wake?

"We're going to get through this," she whispered to them. "The Lord will see us through."

How many times had her father said that to her while she was growing up? Rita hadn't always known what was going on, because she was expected to stay in a child's place. But as a young girl, she'd heard things like when money was tight and her mother had to get a part-time job at the department store. Or after Aunt Justine had died and Sharae wouldn't eat in the days that followed. Her parents had never talked about what happened with Aunt Justine and Uncle San—Sharae had told her during many of their middle-of-the-night conversations. But every night as she and Sharae had said their prayers that first year, Rita's father had come into the bedroom to say their prayers with them. And he'd always hugged and kissed them both afterward, saying, "The Lord will see us through."

And He had, so Rita believed unconditionally that this time would be no different from all the tough times before.

When the tears and hugs were over, Necole declared, "All right, I'm hungry, and my food's getting cold."

Taryn chuckled, and Rita grinned as they all went back to their seats. For a few moments they were silent as they each took bites of their food. Taryn spoke first again. "So can we talk about why there was a naked personal trainer in your bathroom now?"

Across the island, Necole moaned and said, "Ooooh, spicy."

Rita and Taryn stared at her quizzically.

"The sauce," she said, pointing her fork down at her plate. "The sauce is spicy."

As Taryn laughed, Rita felt comfortable enough to do the same. Apparently, she and her daughters were going to have a discussion about sexy men and the massage table whether she wanted to or not. And really, Rita wanted to. Sure, Vance had said it was important to set boundaries with her children, and she knew he was right to an extent, but tonight, she wanted to enjoy her daughters. She wanted them to start acting like adults and learn to take care of themselves, so it made sense that she treat them like adults and answer the questions she felt they had a right to know.

"Well, I never had a massage before," she began. "But I liked it, and I'm going to have another one just as soon as I find the time to schedule it."

"Oookay," Taryn said as she chewed. "I see you, Mama. If I found a masseur that fine, I'd be all up in his appointment book too!"

Necole nodded and high-fived her sister across the island. "You ain't lyin'!"

Rita laughed, enjoying the sound and feeling of this moment. "But no more guns, young lady. At least not until you learn to properly use one." She was still the parent, after all, and she needed to get that warning in there.

"You're right," Taryn said with a nod. "I was scared to death holding that thing."

Necole shook her head. "Told you we needed to take the classes before we started carrying."

"So you both have one?" Rita asked after taking a bite of her food.

"Yup. It's for protection, Mama," Necole said. "We're going back and forth on campus at night, and then when we go out, it's rough out there, and Uncle Tariq said it was a good idea."

"Well, I want to see the proper permits, and I want you to take those classes right away," Rita said. What she really wanted was for her daughters not to feel the need to carry guns in the first place, but she couldn't change the world.

Instead, she sighed. She should've known Tariq had his big mouth all up in this. She'd deal with him later. For now, she settled in to enjoy her meal and her children.

When Hale Henderson woke up before dawn on a Saturday morning and returned hours later with two bushels of live Maryland Blue crabs, the Aunts invited their girls over for a mini crab feast.

It had started to rain just as Rita got out of her car to go into her mother's house at a little after three in the afternoon on Saturday. It'd been cloudy when her mother had called her a couple of hours ago, so she already knew they'd be setting up inside the house instead of in the backyard where they normally ate crabs.

"Hey, Mama," Taryn said when she came into the house a few minutes after Rita. "Whatchu need me to do?"

They all knew the drill. The Aunts were moving around Vi's galley-style kitchen while Rita and Jemel were already in the dining room getting things set up.

"Get the extra folding chairs from the basement, and then start lining the table with that paper over there," Rita told her.

"Y'all gettin' along better?" Jemel asked when Taryn left the room.

"Yeah." Rita was happy to report that news. It'd only been a couple of days since they'd had dinner, but she'd spoken to both her girls on the phone during that time. "We've been good since we got everything out in the open the other day. Necole even surprised me by stopping by last night, just to chill, she said." Rita smiled at the memory.

"They think you're going to be lonely," Jemel said.

"Probably." Rita could've told them all she was enjoying her alone time. "But it gave me a chance to talk to her about working on the graphic design for the event."

"Oh, so you told them about opening the catering business too?"

"Yeah, I told them that when they were over for dinner on Wednesday. Figured since we were clearing the air, I might as well tell them that too. They're not going to say anything to anyone else in the family, though." Especially not Nate. While it wasn't what Rita wanted, her daughters seemed more than a little agitated with their father at the moment. She'd decided not to advise them how to feel about him either way. They were grown enough to make their own decisions about the relationship they would have with their father from this point on.

"I still can't believe Taryn actually pulled a gun on that poor trainer," Jemel said. She was on the other side of the room, lining up the Sterno racks and trays.

In addition to the crabs, they would have corn on the cob, the country smoked sausage Rita had brought over, and the pasta salad that Aunt Ceil was in the kitchen making now.

"Girl, I can't wait till I see Tariq so I can let him know how I feel about him arming my children." Rita was still hot about that. But Tariq and their other cousins wouldn't be at the house today. When her mother called this morning, she'd said "my girls" only, and that meant Rita, Jemel, Sharae, Taryn, and Necole. Every now and then the Aunts loved to sit in a room and marvel at how the generations of Johnson women continued. Of course, her father would be here, but he was used to being surrounded by the women.

Aunt Rose came into the dining room then. "Y'all in here chitchatting. There's stuff in the kitchen that needs to be brought out."

"I'll get it," Rita said, grinning behind her aunt's back as Jemel scowled.

"Don't put too much water in those pans, Jemel. It'll spill over when we put the top tray inside," Aunt Rose scolded, and Jemel rolled her eyes at Rita.

Laughing, Rita went into the kitchen and transferred the corn from the huge pot on the stove to an aluminum tray. After she reached into the refrigerator to grab the butter dish, she turned to see her mother sprinkling Old Bay over the corn in the tray. When Rita had put the corn into the pot, she'd seasoned the water with Old Bay and butter, but Vi always had to do things her way too. The Aunts always wanted things their way, even though they'd brag about how well they'd taught their girls everything they knew. It appeared they just didn't all the way trust their girls to do it. The thought made Rita smile because it was something that would never change. And to be honest, if it did, she'd think one of the Aunts was terminally ill because that was probably the only thing that would stop them from being who they were.

Sharae and Necole came in just as they were sitting down to eat. Vi blessed the food, and Hale came up from the basement carrying a bucket of hot crabs that he dumped in the center of the table. Her father had a steamer in the backyard. He'd put a canopy over it and gotten to work right after he'd come home and showered. Hale used a variety of seasonings to flavor his crabs, and he wasn't telling anybody what those other seasonings were. "Y'all don't like to talk about anything other than Old Bay anyway, so no need for me to give you the details," he always joked.

But it was the truth.

Taryn didn't like too much seasoning on her crabs, so she'd brought a bucket of water to sit beside her on the floor. She dipped her first crab inside before bringing it to the table to crack open. Necole loved hers heavily seasoned while Rita preferred to get a little food in her stomach first before feasting on the crabs. They never filled her up, so she always felt she needed a meal to go along with them. She fixed her plate, cutting a sausage and adding a piece of corn. Aunt Ceil's pasta salad wasn't her favorite because she used a brand of Italian dressing that Rita couldn't stand. Plus, Rita added a little more to her pasta salad, like cubes of Genoa salami, mozzarella balls, and yellow, red, and orange peppers for even more flavor.

"You okay?" Rita asked Sharae after she'd watched her cousin take the longest time to eat just one crab.

Sharae called herself a crab aficionado and could usually eat as many as fourteen in one sitting. Especially when Tariq and Benny were there to challenge her. Today she didn't seem at all interested in the taste or the art of cleaning a crab quickly.

She sat back and sighed heavily. "I might as well tell y'all 'cause Aunt Margaret's probably gonna be calling to ask for money sometime today."

Aunt Rose looked up from the other side of the table where she was busy working on her third crab. "To ask who for money?" Aunt Rose could never be considered the generous Johnson sister. She made her own money, and she kept it until she decided to give it to someone else, which wasn't very often.

"Why does she need money?" Hale asked. "She's been getting a healthy pension check from the steelyard since Raymond died. I know because I sat with her filling out all the paperwork."

Rita's father had worked at Bethlehem Steel, along with a good number of his close friends, for twenty years before he left to become a full-time pastor when Rita was ten years old.

"What's going on?" Vi asked.

"It's for Tariq."

"Tariq? I've been calling and texting him for the last couple of days, but he's probably ducking me." Rita didn't want the Aunts, or her father, for that matter, to know why she was looking for Tariq. But her daughters knew, and they wisely kept their heads down and continued eating.

Sharae shook her head. "He's not ducking you; he got locked up."

Everybody at the table stopped eating at that announcement.

"What?" Rita asked.

"When?" was Aunt Ceil's follow-up.

"Back child-support payments," Sharae said with another shake of her head. "It just happened yesterday. He called Aunt Margaret, and she called her brother like she always does when she needs something. So Uncle Jimmy called me last night just as I was getting off my shift. I went down to central booking to see him, and he looked good. Pissed, but he's good."

"I thought he was still with Kaelin, and Jasmine's only a year old. How far behind could he be on payments?" Rita asked.

"The payments weren't for Kaelin's baby," Sharae told them.

"What?" That question was spoken simultaneously by Aunt Ceil and Aunt Rose.

Taryn looked over to Rita, who felt the same uncomfortable tug she figured her daughter was feeling at this moment. Anybody having babies outside of a relationship they were supposed to be in was probably going to be a sore spot for them for a while.

"When I showed him the charging documents I was able to get from a buddy at BPD, he said it was some woman he'd met at a club a couple years back. Said she never told him she was pregnant."

"Then how'd she get his address and other info to file for child support? They can't just walk in and say 'Tariq's the daddy.' This ain't *Maury*." Jemel frowned. Child support and men or even women who didn't want to pay to support the children they created would always be a sensitive topic for her.

With that in mind, Rita glanced at Aunt Ceil, who was hastily wiping her hands on a napkin. She was probably ready to grab the phone, thinking she could call Tariq and yell some sense into him for shirking his parental duties.

Sharae shrugged. "He thinks she might've known somebody he worked with at the landscaping company. I don't know. It's like thirty thousand that he owes, and he said he had no idea. And by the time they arrested him yesterday, it was too late to see a commissioner, so he's gonna be there until Monday."

"Oh my gracious," Aunt Rose whispered. "He's too old for this mess. He gotta get himself together."

"Well, if he didn't know about the child, he couldn't be expected to pay the support," Sharae added.

"How does a man not know he's gotten a woman pregnant?" Rita asked, irritation clear in her tone.

"Easy, the same way he forgets to pay his daughters' rent because he's too busy focusing on the side chick carrying his child," Taryn snapped, and all eyes immediately fell on her.

"Say what now?" The look Vi was giving her granddaughter had Rita shook.

She swallowed and tried to speak up. "It was just a misunderstanding," she said, but Vi held up a finger to silence her.

"Your father forgot to pay your rent?" Vi asked Taryn.

Now, Rita knew her mother's opinions on her and Nate paying for the girls to have their own place. Vi felt like the only people who had their own place were those who could afford it. Rita didn't disagree with that, but she and Nate had been trying to help their daughters get situated. She knew now they were probably doing too much, but that situation wasn't just going to change overnight. Still, if there was one thing Vi wasn't going to tolerate, it was somebody messin' with her grandbabies.

Taryn looked at Necole, who stared at Rita. Then Taryn cleared her throat. "Um, no, ma'am. Not exactly."

"Then what happened, exactly?" Hale asked, his tone as icy as the cubes dancing around in Rita's cup of ginger ale.

Sending an apologetic look to Rita, Taryn shrugged. "He took all the money out of the bank accounts so when the landlord tried to process the rent payment, it was returned."

"What the holy hell?" Aunt Rose yelled, drawing a stern look from Hale that she properly ignored.

"It's okay," Rita said again. "I've taken care of it. They're going to be fine."

"Yes, ma'am, we are. I just scheduled an interview for an internship at the hospital," Taryn said.

"Oh, that's wonderful, baby." Rita hadn't known about that, but she was proud that Taryn had taken their talk the other day seriously.

"And I'm going to have a freelance project coming up that I'll be getting paid for," Necole added. She glanced at Rita with a look she hoped conveyed that she, at least, wasn't telling their secrets. Rita smiled at her in return.

"I don't like this," Vi said, shaking her head. "Not one bit."

"It's okay, Vi. Let it go," Hale told her. It was said in the tone he used to end all discussions, and Vi opened her mouth to speak again, but closed it quickly.

She continued to shake her head, and now her leg was going too. That meant she was really pissed.

"I'm sorry. We shouldn't be talking about Tariq's situation when I know what you're going through," Sharae said.

But Rita had asked her what was wrong, so she waved her hand. "No, it's okay. We're family. If Tariq needs help, then we're the ones to give it to him."

"That's right," Vi said. "So what does he need?"

"Probably ten percent down to get him out on bail," Hale said. "Sharae, you and I'll go down there on Monday to get things squared away."

"Yes, sir," Sharae replied.

And just like that both those topics of conversation were officially closed. Her father was most likely going to put up the money to get Tariq out of jail. Either that or he was going to appeal to the commissioner for Tariq to be released on his own recognizance. He'd tell him that Tariq had been working part-time at the church as a sexton, and he was actively involved in his daughter's life. If Tariq didn't know about this baby, it wasn't fair to punish him for not taking care of the child. But Hale was almost certainly going to tell Tariq to get a DNA test so he could do right by the child if it was his.

It just made Rita think of what her mother had said when they'd been at lunch about women not always telling the truth. Rita knew that it was plausible that Tariq's newest baby mama and the one Nate was shacking up with were lying to get what they wanted. But she also knew there was just as good a chance that they weren't, and while she didn't give a damn how Nate's situation turned out, she whispered a silent prayer that Tariq got things straightened out as soon as possible.

Glancing into the living room forty minutes later, nobody would've known the two bombshells had been dropped during this impromptu crab feast. After they'd all eaten their fill, Necole had gone into the living room and turned on the stereo her grandparents still had. She'd figured out a way to plug her phone into the dated system and had started playing current music. She, Taryn, and Jemel had been in the middle of the floor dancing and singing along for too many songs to count while Rita and Sharae helped the Aunts clean up their mess.

"Oh wait, c'mon, Vi, that's your song, baby," Hale called into the kitchen.

Rita watched as her mother came out just the way she'd expected, with her hands already up in the air, fingers snapping as she sang the first few lyrics to the "Booty Call" line dance song.

"Yeaaahhh." Aunt Rose came out right behind her. "Big girls, let me back it up," she sang, and Rita and Sharae shared grinning faces.

"Here they go," Sharae said. "They love this song."

"Yes, they do," Rita added when Aunt Ceil came out of the kitchen too.

In the next moments, the Aunts were in one row, and Taryn, Necole, and Jemel were in another, each of them doing the moves to the song. Aunt Rose especially loved the part when they had to back it up, tossing her behind around with as much gusto as a twenty-year-old.

"That's why she always has a man," Sharae said.

"You ain't lyin'," Rita added.

"C'mon, y'all two. Stop acting like old maids," Aunt Ceil yelled to them.

With a shrug, Rita stepped up first. "They're just gonna keep trash talkin' if we don't."

Sharae agreed, and they joined in on the dance, laughing and joking when somebody missed a step. Hale had pulled out his phone to record them. He did that from time to time, saying it was good to preserve these moments with family, to have something to share with future generations. Rita let all her cares go and danced for she didn't even know how long with her most favorite women in the world. It was just what she needed after the couple of weeks she'd had—just what they all needed.

Chapter 22

TAKIN' OUT THE TRASH.

On Monday at exactly two o'clock in the afternoon, Rita pulled out a chair and sat across the conference-room table from Nate.

They were at Sharon's office. The dark-oak table had a glass top installed and could seat eight on both sides, two at the ends. Nate's attorney, Chris Rebonowitz, was a man Rita knew well. He'd been to dinner at their house and to both Taryn's and Necole's dedications at the church. At one point she'd considered him a family friend, in addition to being their attorney. Now, when she glanced over at him, she gave him the same cordial nod she'd given Sharon's assistant when she walked in.

"Do we want to put this all on the record?" Chris asked when Sharon sat in the seat next to Rita.

"The record will be reflected in our final settlement agreement. But for posterity purposes, we can record this meeting." As if she'd known this would be an issue, Sharon opened a folder and pulled out a stack of papers.

Passing one to Nate and his attorney, and then another to Rita, she said, "If everyone will sign saying they agree to the meeting being recorded, we can begin."

Rita signed her name, staring down at the "McCall" portion. Did she want to change her name? She hadn't considered that until this very moment but suspected that before this meeting was over it would probably come up.

She'd been Mrs. McCall for twenty-three years. And before that she'd been Miss Henderson. Who was she going to be when this was all over?

"Okay, with that out of the way, we can get started," Sharon said.

Her lawyer had another thicker file that she opened. Rita opened her book and turned to the page where she'd taken notes on her previous conversations with Sharon. She'd rewritten the notes twice so that the three pages were a neat outline of all the points of discussion in the marriage. Again, she found herself staring down at the page. Had this all boiled down to a series of bullet points on a paper? All the love, devotion, time, and energy she put into this marriage. The union that she'd thought would be forever.

"Rita, are you okay?"

She jumped at the touch of Sharon's hand on hers. Looking from Sharon across the table to where Nate sat, she held his gaze.

"Are you okay?" he repeated her lawyer's question. "We can stop and go someplace to talk if you want."

Was that what she should do? She hadn't before. Not in the four weeks since they'd been separated. Did the talks in his office and in Ocean City even count? They hadn't resolved anything on either occasion. And truthfully, what could he say that was going to change the situation? The fact that he'd cheated on her and then had the audacity to take the money they shared.

"No," she told him quietly. Glancing over at Sharon, she nodded. "I'm fine."

The talking began. Sharon went first, then Chris. For what seemed like forever, the two attorneys went back and forth, negotiating one point after another.

All the joint bank accounts would be divided equally, using the balances from last month's bank statements—prior to Nate's withdrawals—to come up with the totals. And then each account would be closed. A couple of days ago she'd realized there was twenty-five thousand in cash in the house. Both Rita's grandmother and Nate's grandfather had the same aversion to banks and had instilled in them the need to have some ready cash just in case. She hadn't touched the lockbox they kept in the bedroom closet where the money, their life insurance policies, birth certificates, and marriage license were stored. That money would be split too.

"I'm going to update my will," she blurted out.

"All life insurance policies and personal wills will be updated, I suspect," Sharon added.

Chris nodded. "Absolutely."

"The girls should remain primary beneficiaries. We always planned to leave everything to them. That shouldn't change." What Rita was really saying was that she didn't want her daughters to be cut out of their inheritance because he was out here creating more kids. And yeah, that probably sounded harsh, but she didn't care. Let that other woman worry about and protect her child's well-being.

"I wouldn't change that," Nate said. He was looking at her as if he couldn't believe she would even say that.

Rita still couldn't believe she was here in this place discussing the dissolution of her marriage.

"I sent you a copy of our valuator's report for McCall Motors last week," Sharon said, obviously ready to move on to the next point.

Chris shuffled some papers around until he found the ones she mentioned. "Yes. Nate and I had a chance to look them over. We also had our own report created. You should've received that as well."

Sharon flipped to that page. "There's no significant difference."

"There's an eighty-five-hundred-dollar difference and some investments that were made through the company that I'm not sure should fall into the same pot for distribution," Chris said.

"She gets half," Nate said, and Rita stared at him in shock.

In the days since she'd known this meeting was scheduled, the one thing she'd been prepared to fight about was the business. While she and her lawyer intended to ask for half, she'd been ready for Nate to offer some lowball settlement, especially after the stunt he'd pulled with the bank accounts.

"Fifty percent of McCall Motors and all the investments outlined on our valuation report? Is that what you're agreeing to?" Sharon asked him.

Chris lifted a hand toward Nate to stop him from replying. "We have to hash out which of the investments should be excluded. If it's something Nate did on his own, without her knowing, she might not be entitled to half."

Rita frowned at being referenced as "she." She'd fed this man, and she'd set him up on a date with her cousin Chanel in Virginia, because that was where Chris lived as well.

"Whatever is in the business name falls under the business. If your client wished for these investments to be separate and apart from same, he should've made them solely in his name. In which case we probably still would've asserted a claim," Sharon told him.

"Give her half," Nate said, raising his voice slightly. "Of everything. And the house, she can have the house in Willow Grove and her car."

"Nate," Chris said, rubbing over his face, "we should talk about this a little more. Let's take a break."

Nate shook his head. "No. Give it to her."

"Along with the monetary settlement of three hundred and fifty thousand that we requested?" Sharon asked him directly.

Nate nodded. "Yeah. And alimony," he said. "I didn't see that on these papers."

"I don't want it," Rita replied. She'd been speechless for the past few minutes, listening to the exchange, but her gaze had never wavered from Nate's.

He was watching her just as intently, like the vows they'd spoken were still creating some type of connection that neither one of them was letting go of until the very last moment. No, that wasn't an emotional connection; she wasn't entertaining any thoughts of taking him back. That ship had long since sailed. But she did love this man. She'd loved him all of her adult life, loved the part of him that lived in both their daughters, and now, at the moment she expected to hate him the most, she didn't. She would probably always love him to some extent.

"I can take care of myself," she said, knowing that alimony meant so much more than that. She just didn't want it. This was a clean break, and she was already on her way to starting her own business and building a new life for herself. One that didn't hinge on anything Nate would continue to do for her. "Give me my half of McCall Motors and the lump sum. We can have your name removed from the financial documents and the deed of the house and my car, and then we'll be done." She paused and then added, "I'm also keeping my name. It's my daughters' name too."

Nate nodded slowly. "Yeah. We'll be done."

Sharon was beside her, busy scribbling something down on her notepad, and Chris was shaking his head like he thought Nate had just signed his death sentence. But he'd do what Nate said in the end. Chris had always been Nate's yes-man. Today wouldn't be any different.

"I'll continue paying for the girls' cars, and I'll move them over to my insurance," Nate added.

Rita nodded. "What about their tuition? The 529 college savings accounts have our names as well as the girls' names on them. We don't have to liquidate those, do we?"

"No," Nate said. "Leave those intact."

"We can have Rita's name removed from the accounts," Chris stated evenly.

"That's fine with me," she said.

"No." It was becoming Nate's favorite word today. "She's their mother. Her name stays on the account in case something happens to me."

Why was he doing this? Why was he being so generous, giving in to her when the last two times she'd seen him, he'd been set on arguing this split between them?

"Well, that takes care of everything," Sharon said. She picked up her papers and made a clacking sound against the table as she eased them into a neat pile. "My assistant will get this all typed up, and we'll have a settlement agreement to you to review and sign by the end of the week."

"We'll need some time to review it and to make sure this is what we want to do," Chris said, trying to salvage some room for Nate to change his mind.

Nate stood. He wore a dusky-gray suit with faint teal stripes. His shirt was a very light blue, his tie dark gray with blue polka dots. He straightened the knot of his tie and then smoothed his hand down its length. How many times had she watched him do that with different ties? It didn't stop her from watching him at this moment.

"Can I talk to you outside for a minute, Rita?"

This man was her husband—he'd never had to ask to talk to her in this way before. After today, this was how it would be. He'd have to request her attention, and it was up to her whether she wanted to give it to him.

"Sure," she said and closed her book. Picking it up and then grabbing her purse, she looked over to Sharon. "I'll call you tomorrow."

Sharon nodded. "Great."

Rita walked away from the table without saying a word to Chris. Nate arrived at the door before her, and he opened it, stepped aside, and held it while she walked through. Once they were in the narrow walkway that would lead to the reception area of Sharon's offices, he turned to face her.

"I owe you an apology," he said.

She wanted to stop him because an apology wasn't going to take away all the pain she'd endured. But something about the way he was looking at her imploringly kept her quiet.

"That day I came home and you were putting all my stuff out, you said I didn't even have the decency to deny the accusations. Instead, I jumped on you about believing everything you heard." He shrugged. "You were right."

Rita released a breath she hadn't been aware she was holding.

"Each time you confronted me about what I was doing, you were right." He dragged both hands down his face and rolled his shoulders as if he were getting ready to do or say something big.

She gripped the handle of her purse and tried to steady her breathing, because for whatever reason, her heart had begun pounding in her chest.

"I'm not gonna stand here and offer you some excuse for why I did what . . . why I was doing all that I did." He shook his head again. "I thought about it last night, and I had all these words to say to you. All these scenarios that I was gonna apologize for, others I was going to provide explanations for. I was gonna say there were times when I wasn't sure you were in love with me or in love with the idea of being married. But I realized, sitting across that table from you just now, that all this is my fault. If there was ever a time I felt insecure in our marriage or discontent, I should've been man enough to come to you."

"I wish you would've," she said honestly. "I thought we were fine." Well, there'd been times when she knew that wasn't true, and she probably should've said something then. Now it was too late.

"I know this was all on me. I'll apologize again, but I accept that it might never ever be enough to heal the pain I've inflicted." He clasped his hands together and did that thing where he pressed his lips together tightly because the words he wanted to say were overwhelming him emotionally.

At another time, in another life, she would've gone to him and touched her hand to his cheek. She would've assured him that everything was going to be fine, meaning that whatever was bringing him to the brink of emotion wasn't necessary to express because she knew and she'd stand by him. Today she didn't move.

"You burned my clothes. And I'm guessing Jemel slashed my tires with her ride-or-die self. I probably deserved both." He smiled and shook his head. "I talked to the girls," he added. "Apologized about the rent mix-up and told them all the things I've done over the years and asked for their forgiveness too."

She nodded, feeling emotion welling up inside her as well. "Thank you for doing that. Taryn needed to hear it." There were witnesses to her burning his clothes, but she wasn't admitting anything about those tires.

"I'm not her favorite person right now, and you know that's hard for me to swallow. I'm used to being her everything, and Necole's too." He waited a beat. "And yours too."

Oh boy, she was gonna cry, and she so didn't want to cry in front of this man. She didn't want to give him one more tear, not ever again.

"I've always wanted you to have the best, and I'm sorry that couldn't be me." He stepped closer then, and Rita was still stuck in her emotional trance, so she didn't move in time.

His arms went around her, and before she could blink, the first tear slipped down her cheek. The next thing she knew, her arms were going around his waist. They stood there for she didn't know how long simply holding on to each other, like they were both afraid to let go but knew that it was inevitable.

Chapter 23

The hired help.

Sharae almost sliced her finger off thinking about the fight she and Desmond had last night. She'd gone to his house again, the fourth time since that first evening the week before last. They'd had a great dinner ordered from her favorite steakhouse where they always prepared her very well-done filet just right, with tender baked potatoes and creamed spinach, which had been Desmond's selection that she'd refused to eat. She'd hated spinach since she was little, and having a sexy guy hold it in some creamed concoction on a fork, inches away from her face, wasn't changing her stance on that.

Not long after the delicious—sans spinach—dinner, they'd had phenomenal sex. That seemed to be their ritual. She'd go to his place after work, he'd think of something for dinner, they'd eat, have sex, and she'd get up and go home. Until last night.

"Why don't you stay?"

"Because this is your place, not mine," she'd tossed back at him just before pulling her shirt over her head.

He'd been lying on his bed, the beige sheets twisted so that they only covered his groin. His dark, muscled legs and bare, toned chest were still on full and perfect display. But she really did need to leave. It was late, and she'd stayed much longer than she'd planned. She'd told Rita she'd be at her house by eight, which was barely a few hours away.

"I think we've already proven we can both fit in this bed," he told her.

"You're correct, we have fit in this bed a good number of times." And when she stood to push her legs into her pants, she let herself recall all the times and all the things they'd done in this bed. Her skin tingled with arousal, and she really considered climbing back into that bed. But she couldn't spend the night with him. That wasn't what she did.

"But you won't sleep here," he said, folding his arms behind his head.

"No." She shook her head just in case he hadn't heard her response.

He'd heard it just fine; he just wanted to have this conversation. Again. It was the same as the conversation about them going out on a date. Sharae didn't want to talk about either. She grabbed her suit jacket off the chair and hunted down her shoes before slipping them on.

"I have to be at my cousin's by eight to help her get set up for our family cookout."

"Oh, your family's having a Fourth of July cookout."

She'd frowned. "It's just a cookout. We don't do any of those red, white, and blue decorations. It's another day for us to gather and celebrate each other with good food, music, and just old-fashioned family fun."

"My family's all in Atlanta," he'd said.

Finding her bag was a little more difficult, and she'd walked back and forth across his room until she saw it on the edge of his dresser.

"So, you're just not gonna invite me. Even after I dropped that big hint."

She turned to face him then and thought about what he'd just said. "You want to come to my family cookout?"

He shrugged. "I like good food and family fun. What y'all playin', Tunk or Spades?"

She'd tilted her head and recalled the last time she'd played cards. "We have card nights, but sometimes somebody'll start up a game at the cookouts too. The younger kids have games and . . ." And what he was asking her was much bigger than eating grilled food or playing cards. "You're trying to make this a dating thing, aren't you?"

"You're trying to keep this a secret thing, aren't you?" he asked, and she frowned.

"You're not funny."

He sat up then, swinging his legs over the side of the bed before standing. The sheet fell to the floor, and her gaze fell to his semi-erect dick. She swallowed, the desire switch he seemed to have taken possession of clicking to on and igniting the flames inside her. But she didn't move. She had to think.

"I told you I don't date."

He came closer, touching his hands to her arms. She tried to focus, to keep her gaze on his eyes, not his . . . other parts. When he'd eased her to the side and then went to open the top drawer of his dresser instead of pulling her to him for a kiss or wrapping her hands around his length like he'd done just a little while ago, she'd realized just how much trouble she was in.

"Are you angry about that? Because I made myself perfectly clear," she said.

"You did," he'd replied and pulled out a pair of shorts that he then stepped into. "I guess I've just been trying to figure out why you're so stuck on that rule."

She put some space between them, going over to look out one of the narrow windows in his bedroom. The street he lived on was one-way, and at this time of morning it was pretty quiet. Her car was parked right behind his like they were really a couple. The thought sent a chill down her spine, and she turned back to face him. "It's just my thing. I'm focused on other stuff."

He leaned back against the wall, hands behind him. "Considering taking the lieutenant's exam? Or maybe coming off the force and doing some private security work?"

"Not really, but work is a priority."

"And you can't possibly date and work at the same time. I mean, 'cause you've been coming here kind of regular for the past two weeks. I thought we were getting into a groove."

"A physical one," she clarified. "If that's a problem, say so now, and it'll stop."

"That's what you want me to say. Then you'll be justified in walking out because I'm being unreasonable. Right?"

Wrong. She wanted to scream but felt like that would be playing right into his hands. "I know what I want, and this . . . It was never meant to even get this far. I didn't even like you at first, bringing me that unwanted news."

Her chest clenched at the thought of the ashes she'd tucked back into her closet and the upcoming anniversary of her mother's death.

He walked to her then, but before he could get too close, she stepped back, her fists clenching at her sides. She hadn't realized her breathing had quickened, and she must have had a strange look on her face, because Desmond stopped a breath away from her and folded his arms over his chest.

"Not all men hit," he said softly. "They all don't mentally berate women or tear them down in whatever way they can."

She willed herself to calm down. "I didn't say they did."

"You didn't have to," he told her and then reached down to ease her fingers apart. "Everything you do is a message that screams loud and clear. You're protecting yourself, and now that I know what happened between your parents, I can see why."

"How do you know?"

He arched a brow. "You think I didn't check up on the charges against Sanford that got him life in prison? I read his entire criminal file. I know what he did to your mother, and I'm really sorry you had to go through that."

She looked away from him. "I don't need your sympathy."

He laced his fingers through hers. "I know. But I'm offering it anyway. Just like I'm offering to take things slow with you."

"I don't want . . ."

Putting one finger to her lips, he silenced her. "I'm not telling you what you should want. I'm telling you what I'm going to do."

Turning her face slowly away from his finger, she cleared her throat. "If you think you can wear me down or change my mind, it's not going to work."

He nodded. "That's cool. But what I'm really thinking about now is the food your family's probably gonna have tomorrow and how hungry I'm gonna be just sitting in this house alone."

Her lips pursed as she stared at him, watching as a smile slowly crept across his face. "You think you're so slick. I'm not inviting you to my cousin's house as a date, Desmond. We're not even going there."

He released her other hand and turned so that he was beside her. Draping an arm over her shoulder, he walked her to the door. "I'm not coming as your man. I'm coming as a guy whose stomach is surely going to be growling all day until . . . What time should I be there?"

They'd made it out to the hallway when she glanced over at him. "Four, and erase that triumphant smirk from your face. I'm not looking for a man."

He turned her then, cupping her face in his hands and easing her closer to his. "Sometimes good things find you, Sharae. Shhhh," he continued when she would've replied. "Just relax and see what happens. You might like it."

"I won't," she'd whispered seconds before he kissed her.

"Girl, give me that knife. We don't want no blood or fingers in our food!"

Rita's words and the way she plucked the knife out of Sharae's hand snapped Sharae out of her reverie, and she cursed. Looking down at the cucumbers she was supposed to be cutting, she breathed a sigh of relief that she hadn't done serious bodily harm.

"You over there deep in thought," Jemel said. "What's going on? And don't even think about saying *nothin'*."

Sharae turned around and leaned against the counter. The three of them were in Rita's kitchen, and it was barely ten o'clock on Sunday morning. Jemel was at the island cutting strawberries and watermelon— her favorite fruit—for the fruit salad. She wore sage-colored sweatpants that hung low on her waist and a white T-shirt she had tied in a knot at her back. Rita hadn't only taken the knife from Sharae, but she'd also taken the rest of the onion, vinegar, and dill that needed to go in the cucumber salad too. She had on old, faded jean shorts and a gray tank top. They were all going to change into better outfits this afternoon, but while they cooked, it didn't matter how they looked. Which was why Sharae had pulled on yoga pants and a wrinkled Morgan State T-shirt when she'd rolled out of bed after barely getting any sleep this morning.

"Nope, this I definitely need to talk about because it's new territory for me," she said. Thoughts of Desmond rolled nonstop through her mind as she'd lain in her bed after arriving at her apartment in the early-morning hours. And considering how she'd just been so distracted by the same thoughts, she figured it was best to simply get it all out.

"Uh-oh." Rita came over to reach behind Sharae and grab the glass bowl she'd been putting her cucumber slices in. "This sounds serious."

Sharae nodded. "It is. I slept with Desmond again."

Jemel looked up and popped a slice of strawberry into her mouth. "Okay, twice. That must mean he's good. Give us all the deets."

"Are we really going to have detailed sex talks?" Rita asked and crinkled her nose as if the mere thought offended her. "I mean, we're not teenagers anymore."

"If I'm not mistaken, you didn't have much input on those conversations when we were teenagers," Sharae said and raised a hand to stop Rita's reply. "But anyway, yes, he's good. I mean, like real, real good."

"Oooooh yes! Sharae's finally gettin' that good-good sex. Girl, I'm happy for you," Jemel added.

"It can't be too good if it leaves you lookin' like you look." Rita got her dig in anyway, and Sharae let her have it without qualms. There were just too many other things on her mind.

She rubbed a hand to the back of her neck. "I've been to his house five times. Each time we had lots of sex. We ate and talked too, but there's been lots of sex."

"Wait, you just tellin' us this. I thought you'd only been there once and then last night. That's a lot of visits and a lot of sex for you. But okay, tell us more." Jemel looked pleased as punch to be helping with an actual dish—albeit fruit salad so it didn't require any cooking skills—and to be listening to Sharae talk about sex, which she didn't do often because normally there wasn't much to talk about.

To be fair, most of her silence on the subject of sex over these past years had just been because Jemel and Rita were having so much of it with their live-in dicks, and she was mostly partaking in the self-induced pleasure options.

"Last night I was there until five . . . in the morning. He wanted me to stay, but I don't do that." Hearing herself now, she knew what was coming, but the words hit the air.

"I've got news for you, baby girl. If you left at five this morning, you did stay," Rita replied with a bland look on her face.

Dropping her head back, Sharae moaned. "I know."

"Where's the problem?" Jemel asked. "'Cause I know you've been manufacturing one. That's what you do when it comes to men."

Sharae's head snapped up. "I do not."

"Yeah, you do." Rita nodded. She'd resumed slicing the cucumbers.

It didn't really bother Sharae that she'd taken over that task because she hated slicing onions, which were up next, and Rita always fussed that she wasn't slicing them thin enough.

"I need to do something with my hands," she said, because she was harboring a lot of nervous energy. This thing with Desmond was really freaking her out. "I'll make the hamburgers."

She went to the refrigerator and grabbed the plastic-covered bowl with ground beef.

"Get the ground turkey too. We're having a few healthier options today," Rita told her.

After a brief hunt for the second bowl of lighter-tinted meat, Sharae grabbed that one too and closed the refrigerator.

"Talk while you work," Jemel said, her cheeks full of whatever fruit she'd just stuck into her mouth this time.

"Like you're eating while you work," Rita said.

Jemel shrugged and snapped a grape from its stalk. "You've got enough fruit here to feed a cruise ship full of people, so I can have my share now."

Sharae had gathered the other ingredients to mix into the meat and stood at the other end of the island ready to get started. "He wants to date me."

"Instead of just fuck you?" Jemel asked.

"Language!" Rita huffed.

Jemel rolled her eyes. "A'ight, Grandma."

Rita smirked, and Sharae enjoyed seeing that the light had returned to her eyes. They'd talked on Thursday about the meeting with Nate and made more plans for the event and her new business that they were finally going to announce tonight. She was really happy to see Rita coming through this divorce situation. "Look, that's all I'm used to," she continued. "I'm not the boyfriend-husband-live-in-relationship type like the two of you are. I just like to do my thing on my own."

"You've been doing that a long time. You ain't gettin' no younger," Jemel said.

"Well, we're not all lined up for that marriage-and-family train like you and Marc seem to be," Sharae said and then wished she hadn't because she knew Aunt Ceil pressured Jemel enough about when she was getting married and giving her grandchildren.

"Girl, he hasn't said anything about marriage, and neither have I. We're just ridin' this good wave while we can." There was a moment of bleakness in Jemel's tone, but when Sharae looked to Rita to see if she'd noticed it too, Rita was slicing those onions in perfect paper-thin slices. Sharae frowned, not only at the smell, but how effortless the task seemed for Rita.

"I mean, I'm content having my own space. Not depending on no man to make me happy," she told them.

"That part right there," Rita said, lifting her head up. "What I've had to come to terms with in these past weeks is that only *I* can make me happy. I can't afford to trust that to anybody else."

"Humph." Jemel glanced at Rita, then back to Sharae. "From the way you talked about that massage from Vance, I kind of thought his hands and all that oil made you pretty damn happy."

"You so nasty," Rita said with a shake of her head. "But I do have another appointment with him next week."

Sharae grinned at the way Rita's grown ass continued to blush.

"Listen," Rita said to Sharae. "You have to get out of your head. Every time you meet a guy, you think about your father."

Sharae froze. Jemel smacked Rita's arm and gave her a warning gaze.

"What?" Rita asked. "It's the truth, and she knows it. She also knows we don't sugarcoat stuff when it's just us."

Sharae and Jemel shared a glance, but Rita didn't notice it.

"You remember those first days after you came to live with us?" Rita continued.

Nodding, Sharae cracked two eggs and mixed them in a small bowl. She poured that mixture over the ground beef and then added the hamburger seasoning Rita had already mixed and put into a small plastic bag.

"You wouldn't even cry. Mama kept coming into my bedroom to check on you, but all you did was sit in the window seat and stare outside. That's when I believe you locked away all your feelings. Not for or from us or any of the rest of the family, but for any type of relationship with someone who wasn't related by blood."

Both her hands were immersed in the chilly meat now, and Sharae did her best to focus on that instead of the pricks of pain Rita's words were causing. *The truth hurts.* Aunt Rose said that all the time, and Sharae had said it a time or two in her interrogations. Most of her suspects were long past the point of having feelings about anything they did or the repercussions, but there'd been a few who'd completely broken down after confessing to their crimes. So she knew the saying had merit, and she hated how much it seemed to fit what she was experiencing right now.

"I don't need a man." Defense was a reflex.

"No." Rita's voice softened. "I don't think you do. I don't believe any of us do, for that matter. But it's still okay to want one."

"Whew, that's a word right there," Jemel added. "I fought that for so long. Like I always wanted to be with a guy, but not really for keeps. Mama had been through enough, and I swear I would kill any man that put me through the type of grief my father put her through."

"Yeah, but Aunt Ceil walked away from him," Sharae added. "She stood up to him. My mother . . ." Her voice trailed off, and she had to take a deep breath to push back the emotion.

"She did the best she could, Sharae. In the end, that's really all any of us can do." Rita finished with the onions and measured vinegar in a cup before pouring that on top of them and the cucumbers. "The important thing is, we can't stop living. We can't let the pitfalls hold us down."

Sharae thought about those words as they continued to work in the kitchen for the next couple of hours. Rita was starting her life over. She'd given herself to a man who'd never deserved her, but she was pulling herself up and moving forward with a new business and a possible hot trainer guy on the side. And Jemel, even in the midst of the back-and-forth between her and Marc, had managed to build the life she wanted for herself. So why couldn't Sharae do the same? Why couldn't she have her dream job and a nice, easygoing, good-looking, semipermanent lover—because she still wasn't talking marriage. But maybe, just maybe, there could be something more with Desmond.

"Stop being afraid. If you like him, let him like you back. He's not Sanford, and you're not Aunt Jus," Rita whispered to her just before she went upstairs to get dressed.

Sharae knew that was the part she needed to reconcile and wondered if she could really do it this time.

Chapter 24

FAMILY IS EVERYTHING.

Rita smiled when it seemed Sharae had taken her advice from this morning. They'd finally gotten everything all prepared; then they'd each taken showers and changed their clothes.

Jemel, after complaining how badly she needed a nap, had put on faded jean shorts that barely covered her butt, but showed off her magnificently toned legs. Her top was a frothy white halter with a ruffled bottom that floated around her waist. Wearing wedge sandals and her hair up in a high-top tail, she looked like a teenager again. Rita had opted for a comfortable mint-and-fuchsia floral-print maxi skirt and white crop top, with her natural-colored flat sandals for comfort.

But it was Sharae whose bright-yellow romper accented her rich skin tone and offset the brilliant smile she had when she introduced them to Desmond just a little while ago. Now she was standing near the bar that Uncle Jimmy was working proudly with his self-taught expertise, and laughing at something Ivan and Desmond said.

"She looks so happy," Vi said when she came to stand next to Rita.

"Yes," Rita replied. "She does."

"She deserves some light in her life, and so does Jemel. When do you think her and Marc are gonna settle down and get married? Ceil's 'bout to have a conniption waiting for grandchildren."

"I don't think Aunt Ceil should keep pressuring Jemel about having babies. People can make their own timetables," she said. She knew firsthand how much pressure mothers could apply to their daughters and the lives they wanted them to lead. She didn't wish that on anyone, but she also knew the Johnson sisters and their strong will.

"Nobody's pressuring her. But she's not gettin' any younger either."

Rita walked away after that comment, remembering that Jemel had said something similar to Sharae this morning. She spotted Jemel sitting at a table with Marc and Omar and Jason from down the street. Omar and Jason had also brought their dog, Trixter. Rita had meant to give the dog a special treat after hearing he'd chased Ethel down the street the other day because she'd been snooping around in Omar and Jason's yard. Rita had already prepared her letter of resignation from the board, deciding that it was one of the things she just wanted to release from her life. Besides, once the announcement was out about her catering company, she knew things were going to take off and much of her time would be devoted to seeing that come into fruition.

"Hey, Ma. Aunt Rose wants to know if there's another bowl of seafood salad. Cedric and his greedy kids have already wrapped up four plates." Necole shook her head as she talked, her golden curls moving with the motion.

Rita was so happy to see both her daughters here today. Taryn had even brought a friend with her. Glancing across the yard, she saw them sitting in two chairs. Taryn had no doubt purposely moved away from the tables where the rest of the family were seated. Since the incident with Vance, she and her girls had grown closer. Rita knew that Nate had spoken to them, but neither of the girls had mentioned it, nor did they talk much about the divorce anymore.

"Yeah, I knew that would go quick, so I made three pans of it last night." She looked down at her watch. "Let's see, it's almost six now. You can go ahead and get the second pan out of the refrigerator. By the time they go through that, things'll be winding down, and it'll really be time for people to get their to-go plates. We'll use the third pan for that." Rita knew her family and their eating habits well. That was why she never made one pan of anything when they were all gathered together.

Two of Cedric's children ran past squirting water guns at each other, and Necole yelled something about them being rug rats before heading into the house.

"There she is," Hale said, coming up to wrap his arm around Rita's shoulder. "My baby girl. You've prepared a good spread once again."

Her father rubbed his protruding belly with his free hand and chuckled. This man right here had been Rita's first love. Six feet two inches, with a burly frame and the same amber eyes Rita stared at in the mirror each morning, he'd been her first glimpse of what a man should be. She'd never witnessed him yelling at or disrespecting her mother in any way, and even though there were lots of rules in their house, there was never a day that she or Benny doubted their father's love for them. Not even in the times when he put the church before them. They'd been taught to understand the sacrifice of sharing their father with his congregation.

"Thanks, Daddy," she replied and then frowned when Benny reached out to tweak her nose.

"It's a'ight," he said and grinned the same smile their father had.

When he pulled her away from Hale to fold her into a hug, Rita went willingly and held on tight. "Missed you so much," she murmured.

"Missed you too, Margarita." He was grinning when they pulled apart.

"Tell her the good news," Hale insisted.

"What news?" Rita asked. She was hoping that she, Jemel, and Sharae would have the only announcement tonight. They'd planned to do it at around six thirty or seven, but it seemed Benny was going to beat her to the punch with his news.

"Yeah, it's not really news just yet," her brother said, the look on his face conveying how he wished his father had kept his mouth shut.

Now she was eager to know what was going on. "You can tell me now, and I'll still act like it's a surprise when the time comes for you to share with everyone else," she said.

Benny, who was just a couple of inches shorter than their father and wore his hair in a low afro, shrugged. "Sure you will." They both laughed. "I'm comin' home after I graduate. I'll be ordained at NVB."

That wasn't really news, but still Rita smiled. "I can't wait."

"There's more," Hale said.

"Yeah, that's the part we haven't really ironed out yet," Benny said. "I'm not sure I wanna come into NVB and go straight to the top. You've got other preachers there now, Dad. If you're about to name a new assistant pastor, it should be one of them. I can wait my turn."

"Nonsense," Hale interjected. "You're my son."

And NVB was Hale's church. Nobody said that part, but Rita knew that each of them was thinking it. She also knew that Benny wasn't going to win this argument. He would become the assistant pastor at NVB because that was what Hale wanted. She wouldn't allow herself to get into the politics of that decision. As long as Benny was back home, she'd let them hash out the details of his pastoral career.

"Well, it's about time for me to make an announcement of my own," she said and tried to ease away from them.

"Hold on," Benny said, grabbing her arm. "You don't get away that easily. What announcement?"

She only smiled at him. "You'll see."

Minutes later she had an arm locked with Jemel's as they went to where Sharae was now sitting with Desmond and Ivan.

"What?" Sharae asked when she looked up to see the two of them.

"We're doing it now because she's too excited to wait," Jemel said. She was smiling with barely restrained enthusiasm herself, so Rita ignored that playful jab at her eagerness.

"Oh." Sharae looked down at her watch and then back up to them. "Well, I guess it's close enough to six thirty."

"Even if it wasn't, we're doing this now." Rita didn't want to chance someone else having an announcement that would come before theirs.

Even though Benny's announcement had been a private one, she was just ready to share the news. For weeks, she'd been working on the details of her business with her attorney and accountant. And she, Jemel, and Sharae had spent hours hammering out plans for Jemel's first fundraiser and how best to make that an event nobody would ever forget. With her cousins on either side of her, she walked to what was almost the center point of her backyard.

There were six tents and twelve tables spread out in the space. A few feet away from the tables, Uncle Jimmy had his bar, and on the other side of the yard, there were four long tables loaded with food. The gas grill was on the deck, where another two tables were positioned. Going on the tips of her toes, she waved her arms to get Uncle Jimmy's attention. After a few seconds, during which time she thought she might have to just run over to his table, Uncle Jimmy finally saw her and turned down the music.

"Good evening, everyone," Rita said. Then, because her family preferred to focus on food and fun above all else, she had to yell the greeting again to finally get their attention.

"Hey. Hi," she said when they were all looking at her as if she'd just said there was no more food left. "Um, we just had something that we want to tell y'all real quick."

"Real quick, Rita! I'm 'bout to beat these jokas over here!" That was Tariq, who'd brought Kaelin and Jasmine to the cookout and insisted he didn't want to talk about the other girl and the baby he wasn't sure was his. He'd found his nirvana as always at the card table.

She chuckled. "Okay, Tariq. Calm down." Beside her Jemel and Sharae laughed along with a few others, and Rita felt totally relaxed being surrounded by family. Sure, it was the first cookout where she and Nate were officially separated, but nobody said a word about his absence, and for that alone she'd love them forever.

"So, as you all probably know by now, I'm making some changes in my life. The change that I'm most proud of is something I guess I've been heading toward for a very long time. For that, I'd like to thank the Johnson sisters—Mama, Aunt Rose, and Aunt Ceil—for teaching me everything that Great-Grandma Fannie and Grandma Patty taught them about the solace of good homecooked food." Her voice cracked on that last word, and she paused to get herself together. This was a happy time, and she didn't want to cry, even if they would be tears of joy.

Sharae took her right hand, holding it tight and smiling when Rita glanced over at her. Jemel did the same with her left hand, a symbol that they were with her and they had her back, as always. Rita cleared her throat and continued, "I'm pleased to announce that I'll be opening Johnson's Joy Catering Company. I've already hired a contractor to convert some of my space here into an office, and I'm super proud to announce that JJC's first official client will be the Black Butterfly Florist's first annual community fundraiser scheduled for January fifth."

Applause sounded, and she felt warmth spread through her.

"Y'all know how much I love Rita. We all do." Jemel spoke loudly over the clapping. "I couldn't be prouder of her for taking this step, and I'm so excited to work with her on this fundraiser."

"And as y'all already know, whatever is going on, the three of us are always stuck together like glue, so we're equally pleased that Sharae's lending her police training to provide security for this event and all other events we plan together," Rita said before holding both their hands up.

Many members of the family stood and continued clapping at that point. But Taryn and Necole both came running over to give Rita big tight hugs.

"So proud of you, Mama!" Taryn whispered in her ear.

"Love you so much! Can't wait to get to work," Necole added when she wrapped her arms around Rita.

"Oh my goodness! This is so lit! You're gonna be the best caterer in Maryland!" Wendy said the moment she was able to hug Rita. They now had what seemed like a receiving line going as family lined up to hug and congratulate her, Jemel, and Sharae.

"I can't wait to start pumping you up on my IG and TikTok," Necole said. "This is gonna be huge!"

Benny was next to come and congratulate her, and then her father, who hugged her long and hard again. "Proud of you, babygirl. I told Nate you'd be fine without him, and now you're all set to show him that's the truth."

"Thanks, Daddy," she whispered and wondered when he'd talked to Nate again. Had it been before their meeting on Monday? Was that why Nate had seemed to turn over a new, more amenable leaf?

She didn't have time to ask her father those questions because her mother was embracing her next. But Rita figured it probably didn't matter anyway. Things were over between her and Nate.

"We've got lots to talk about, young lady," Vi had said, and Rita just nodded because that was code for *I'm 'bout to tell you how to run this business.*

She knew her mother well, and she also knew how to put her in her place, nice and politely. But not tonight.

Uncle Jimmy brought Rita a mojito, and she sipped on it while watching Desmond pull Sharae into a hug. Sharae didn't go easily. Rita saw the moment's hesitation as Desmond took her hand and eased her toward him. Her heart ached for the pain her cousin still carried with her, and she said a silent prayer that the Lord would remove it so Sharae could finally live fully.

Marc had found Jemel once everyone else was finished congratu-lating her, and the two were cuddled, smiling and whispering to each other. A mild brush of sadness swept over Rita, and she turned away to find a seat just as the DJ began playing the "Cha Cha Slide." This was a joyous occasion, she reminded herself as she sat down. Her family equaled joy, which was how she'd come up with the name for her com-pany. Now, she only had to remind herself of that every day moving forward. In a few months, she'd legally be a single woman, and she'd have to get used to seeing others in love.

"It'll get easier," she said and took another sip of her drink.

Rita nursed that drink for another two songs before she figured it was time to get up and play hostess again. Standing, she glanced around to see that Desmond had taken a seat at the card table. She shook her head, hoping he'd survive Tariq's trash talkin' and the intense question-ing he was about to undergo about his intentions toward Sharae by just a handful of their male cousins. Marc was now, as usual, wherever the music was—he stood next to the DJ he'd booked at Rita's request.

She wondered where Sharae and Jemel had gone as she headed toward the house. It had been pretty warm today, so she knew a few family members had gone inside to sit in the air-conditioning. She knew that was where the Aunts were hanging out. During a quick stop at the food tables to see what, if anything, needed to be refilled, she grabbed discarded pieces of foil and picked up a napkin to wipe around the edges of the pans where food had spilled when it had been scooped out. Humming along with Whitney Houston's "My Love Is Your Love," which the DJ was mixing with a house music beat, she continued on toward the house. She stepped onto the deck and passed more cousins sitting at the table, eating and chatting. Walking through the patio doors, she entered her sunroom and noticed three of the younger children lounging in chairs while watching some movie on the wall-mounted television. Continuing, she was just about to enter the kitchen when a familiar voice stopped her.

"You've got to be fuckin' kiddin' me," Sharae said. "You're the one?"

"I thought your cousin would've told you that I called her." This woman's voice was vaguely familiar, but Rita couldn't immediately place it.

Rather, a deep foreboding had come over her, and she'd not only remained totally still, but her heart had begun to thump wildly.

"She didn't say it was you," Sharae replied. "I'm pretty sure she didn't know it was you. And what the hell are you doing here?"

"Ms. Rose told me to come over and pick up a cake she baked for my mother," the other woman said.

Sharae cursed. "I really can't believe this shit. When I saw you with him last year, I told both of you to end this! And since I just saw his trifling ass in Ocean City with another chick, I thought you had."

The sound of teeth sucking was loud and clear. "In case you didn't notice, we're both adults. Besides, Nate hasn't been happy in that marriage for a long time. This was bound to happen sooner or later."

"No, this was not!" Sharae yelled. "You getting pregnant by my cousin's husband wasn't bound to happen. You're triflin' as hell, waltzing around that church, knowing you were sleeping with her husband and smiling in her face."

Rita moved at that moment. She'd heard more than enough, and her heart thumped so wildly now it was a wonder it remained intact. She entered the kitchen, rage boiling in every crevice of her soul. Their gazes locked instantly.

Amy Edmonds. Her mother was on the missionary ministry with Aunt Rose. Amy sang on one of the other choirs at NVB, and she was one of the adults who led the dance ministry. She was also in her late twenties, something Rita knew because they'd planned to have presentations by women in different age groups at the women's ministry banquet. She'd seen Amy's name and age on the list just last week.

"You." The word came out in a hoarse whisper.

Sharae turned to Rita. "Let's just walk away," she said and reached out to touch Rita's arm.

Rita yanked away. "I'll deal with you in a minute," she said, her body vibrating with anger. Sharae's eyes widened, but she didn't respond.

If she didn't know what to expect from Rita, that was just fine, because Rita would've never expected this from her.

In the meantime, she stepped closer to Amy. The woman was slim but for the slight bump of stomach protruding through the very fitted tangerine-colored dress she wore. Her french-manicured nails were long, and she ran them through wavy auburn hair that fell to her waist. A wig, of course, but a pricey one.

"You have the audacity to step foot in my house." There were so many words Rita wanted to say. Questions. Thoughts. Curses.

She could only shake her head.

"How fuckin' dare you be here in my house!" Her arms shook as she took the step that would close the distance between them.

"Rita," Sharae called from behind her.

"Shut up, Sharae! You had your chance to tell me you knew this bitch, but you didn't!"

Amy frowned. "You know me too, Margarita. We see each other in church every Sunday."

Rita could hear other voices. Somebody else had come into the room, but she didn't care. Right now, it was just the two of them.

"I want you out of my house, and don't you ever set foot in here again."

Amy didn't look at all bothered by Rita's statement. "That's fine. I just need to pick up this cake, and then I can go." She tilted her head then and gave Rita a half smile. "Nate's buying a bigger house for us and the baby."

All the words that had been in Rita's mind drifted away as her palm connected to Amy's cheek with a smack that echoed throughout the room.

Chapter 25

Disaster.

When Sharae went to grab Rita to stop her from hitting Amy again, Rita turned and pushed her back. She fell into the island, and Jemel and Aunt Ceil stepped in, pulling a yelling and raging Rita back.

Amy was spouting profanities as Aunt Rose approached her, and Sharae quickly eased around her aunt to step between her and the pregnant heffa. "You need to go!" Sharae said. "Now!"

"Not without my mother's cake." This girl really was out of her mind. "Oh, and I'm pressing charges against you, bitch! See if your daddy can pray you out of that."

"You're gonna need somebody to pick your ass up off this floor if you don't get the hell out of here!" Sharae was in her face, waiting for her to act like she was gonna swing on her the way she'd tried to swing back on Rita.

But even that effort had been fake. Amy didn't want this. She was stuck in the middle of it right now, but Sharae was convinced this child didn't come here expecting to get her ass beat down at this cookout. And yeah, she knew the girl was pregnant, but she was also way out of line, so all rules were out the window.

"What in the hell is goin' on?" Aunt Rose asked from behind.

"Y'all told her to come to my house while she's pregnant with Nate's baby, that's what's goin' on!"

Sharae heard the hitch in Rita's voice and knew she was about to cry. She grabbed Amy by the shoulders and began pushing her toward the breakfast room. The patio door was the quickest way out.

"Get off me! I came here to get something for my mother, and that jealous wench put her hands on me!" She barely struggled as Sharae continued to push her out of the room. "Where's my phone?" she continued. "I'm callin' the police!"

It took less than ten seconds for the entire cookout to stop once Sharae pushed Amy out onto the deck. The girl stumbled and turned back to look at Sharae like she was gonna jump.

"Please, do. Please," Sharae said.

Desmond was by her side in the next second. Tariq, Ivan, and Cedric came up to stand between her and Amy.

"What's goin' on?" Desmond asked.

"She needs to go," Sharae said and then looked at him. "Disrespectful bitch!"

"I'm not the one who's disrespectful. It's all y'all dumbasses believing whatever lies she tells y'all just 'cause she's a PK or y'all family. She wasn't treatin' Nate right, and that's why he came to me." Amy just didn't know when to shut up or go home. Hadn't that been what Sharae had been trying to get her to do?

"Hold up! Wait," Tariq said. "This is the one who messed up Rita's marriage?"

"You the bitch my father got pregnant?" Necole asked.

"Rita messed up her own marriage," Amy spat and rolled her eyes in Necole's direction.

Wendy was right there next to Amy now. "Oh, you need your chin checked, ho."

"Where's my bag?" Sharae heard Taryn yell, but so many people had crowded onto the deck that she couldn't see her. "Where's my damn bag?"

Oh, this was going to get bad really quick. She knew what was in Taryn's bag, and if Taryn was carryin', then Tariq definitely was too. Sharae's second gun was locked in the glove compartment of her car. Her first personal weapon was in a lockbox under her bed. Unless she was on duty, she never wore her gun at family functions. For reasons just like this, it was too easy for stuff to pop off, and shit could get serious.

"You still here?" Rita was outside now, pushing through people to get to Amy.

Aunt Vi, Aunt Ceil, and Jemel were right behind her.

Sharae turned to Desmond. "Get her out of here. Now!"

He nodded and moved past her to grab Amy by the arm. Amy continued to run her mouth, but Desmond, with Ivan, Tariq, and Cedric right behind him, managed to get her out of the yard. And not a moment too soon.

The second Sharae turned back around, Rita was right there in her face.

"You knew?" She shook her head, tears already streaming down her cheeks. "You said you saw them last year. You knew he was cheating on me, and you didn't tell me."

"Rita," Sharae began, "let's go back inside."

"No!" Rita yelled. "I'm not going back in the house so you can figure out how to lie to my face again. You're supposed to be my cousin, my best friend . . . my sister."

Guilt swarmed through Sharae's chest like a hurricane, and she began to shake her head, trying to figure out what to say. "You don't understand."

Rita nodded. "Oh yes, I do. You knew, and you what? Laughed behind my back? Oh, Rita thinks she's got it all—a husband, kids, business, and a big fancy house. But Nate's running around behind her back."

"Come on, Rita, let's go back in the house and talk about this," Jemel said. She'd been standing next to Rita, looking as if she were torn between going after Amy herself and staying there to support Rita.

"That's not how it was," Sharae told her, because Rita needed to understand how this happened.

"Who else knew?" Rita asked. "How many of you knew he was cheatin' and didn't say anything?"

Nobody answered, and Aunt Vi came up to Rita, putting a hand on her arm. "You don't do this here. Not like this. You know better."

The air crackled with the rage Sharae could see building in Rita's face. "Don't tell me I know better!" Rita said. "Not when I'm the one who's done all the right things but still keeps getting crapped on by everybody who's supposed to love me!"

"I'm telling you not to do this here," Aunt Vi continued. "It's rude and disrespectful to your father."

"What did you want us to say, Rita?" Sharae interjected. Aunt Vi was only angering Rita more, and Sharae couldn't stand it. Rita wanted an explanation, so she was going to get it. "When Jem and I tried to talk to you before you married him, you basically told us you were the oldest and so you knew what you were doing. Benny asked you if you were sure, and you damn near bit his head off defending your choice." Rita looked taken aback by her words, but Sharae was on a roll now. "Then when he started takin' all those business trips and spending more and more time at the dealerships, we tried to tell you again. When the three of us went to the Poconos that time for Jem's birthday, we tried to bring it up, tried to tell you something wasn't right."

Rita shook her head. "You didn't have any proof. How was I supposed to believe you?"

"Because you knew something wasn't right, Rita. You knew, but you didn't want to say anything. You didn't want to admit that your life wasn't perfect."

"I never claimed to be perfect!" Using the back of her hands, Rita wiped tears from her face. Her breathing was coming so fast her chest heaved, her eyes were wild, fingers shaking with her anger.

Sharae wanted to hug her, but more important, she wanted her to understand her part in this. It pained her to admit it, but Rita's continued denial had contributed to this current situation. "You didn't have to claim it; you acted it out every damn day, and we all just stood by and watched."

"You stood by and watched my husband cheat on me with a woman at my church! Damn, Sharae! How could you not tell me that?"

Rita was hurting, but Sharae was too. After she and Jemel had tried to talk to her about Nate that last time, they'd decided not to bring the subject up again. Rita had been hurt that they'd accused him of something they couldn't prove, and it'd almost broken their hearts to watch her so upset. So she was never going to tell her she'd seen Nate and Amy coming out of a hotel where one of her suspects was under surveillance. She'd confronted them and told Nate if he didn't end the affair, she was going to bust his ass. He'd assured her it was nothing and that he'd take care of it. No surprise that he'd lied. Or maybe he had at the time and this just started up again. She didn't know, and, dammit, she didn't care.

What worried her now was the look of betrayal on Rita's face as she gazed at her. Sharae was just about to say something else . . . what, she had no clue, but she had to try and make this better.

"You got my purse?" Sharae heard Taryn yell. "We're goin' now!"

"I'm goin' with you," Necole said, and Wendy stepped off the deck to follow them.

"Stop it right there! Ready to run out of here and start more foolishness like you ain't been taught better. Each one of you stop and don't move another muscle," Aunt Vi yelled.

This wasn't gonna be good, but Sharae knew it was too late to stop it now.

"She's right, nobody's going anywhere," Aunt Rose said. "Now, Rita, you go on back in the house. Sharae and Jemel, you might as well come along too. We're gonna get to the bottom of this."

Aunt Vi nodded, agreeing with her sister's proclamation, but when she pulled on Rita's arm to guide her into the house, Rita pulled away.

"Don't talk to my daughters that way," Rita said, her tone deadly quiet. "You and your sisters are always so busy telling us how to act, what to say, what not to do, you never stop to listen to anybody else. I'm pissed the hell off, Mama! And so are my daughters." Rita sighed heavily and shook her head. "Nate betrayed them the same way he betrayed me. So if they feel like slapping that little conniving wench silly, then why shouldn't they do it?"

This wasn't good. Rita didn't do this. She didn't yell, and she most assuredly didn't disrespect her mother or the Aunts. Jemel came to stand beside Sharae, and they both exchanged a knowing look.

"Sharae lied to me for years, and I'm hurt and angry about that," Rita continued. "Why can't I yell and scream, telling her so? This is my house, dammit!" She pushed past Aunt Rose and Aunt Ceil and stomped into the house.

For a few seconds nobody dared to move. Rita had never spoken like that to her mother before. Nor had she ever told Necole and Taryn it was fine to slap somebody. To their credit, Necole and Taryn realized just how tenuous this situation had turned and hadn't moved since Aunt Vi halted them.

Jemel grabbed Sharae's hand and walked her into the house. The Aunts followed behind them. Rita was already in the living room grabbing her purse from the sofa table where she kept it.

"Where are you going?" Jemel asked when Rita pulled her keys out of her purse and continued toward the front door.

"I'm leaving," Rita snapped. "Is that okay, or do you want to tell me why I shouldn't do that too?"

"Whoa," Jemel said, raising both hands. "Hold up. I'm not your mother, Rita."

"No," Rita said, shaking her head. "You're supposed to be my closest friend, just like her. But I bet you knew about this too. You knew he was screwing around with that young girl, and you didn't tell me either."

"No," Sharae said, stepping between Rita and Jemel. "She didn't know because I didn't tell her either. When I saw Nate with Amy, I told them to end it. He said he would handle it, and I let it be." She sighed. "Should I have called you right away and told you? Maybe. But I didn't, and we can't go back and change that."

"No, we can't." Rita shook her head. "But I don't have to lie down and get run over anymore, Sharae. Not by you, and not by anybody else."

"Where do you think you're going?" Aunt Vi asked when Rita yanked the door open.

"Out!" Rita shouted. "And I don't want any of you here when I get back."

Again, a hush came over that house like Sharae had never heard before as they all watched Rita walk outside and down the driveway and get into her car.

Rita knocked on the door, willing her fingers not to shake as she released them and let her arm fall to her side.

Her head hurt so bad she'd felt a little dizzy when she'd stepped off the elevator, but she hadn't turned back. She couldn't. Anger pumped through every vein in her body. It had pushed her feet down on the gas as she'd broken every speed limit to get here. Only the grace of God had kept her from getting pulled over or worse, ending up in an accident.

She could hear the buzzing of her phone. It was in the purse that she'd crossed over her chest. In the car she'd put it on vibrate because she hadn't wanted to be alerted to the text messages and calls she knew were coming from her family. She had no words for them right now. Every thought, every movement of her body, was all for Nate at this point. She should've turned the phone off completely, but that nagging responsible part of her couldn't manage that, just in case there was an emergency.

"Hey, Rita. What're you doing here?" Nate asked when he opened the door.

He looked like he hadn't a care in the world. Wearing brown basketball shorts and a beige T-shirt, he stood in only his socks, and watched her curiously.

"Your baby mama was at my house tonight." That was all she said before pushing past him and walking into the room.

It was a standard hotel room. Well, no, it was a suite, which she should've figured he'd reserve for himself. Before she'd left her lawyer's office on Monday, he'd given her the name and room number of the hotel where he was staying, just in case she needed to find him. Rita had taken the information, believing she'd never have a reason to visit him here. Oh, how wrong and misguided she'd been.

She heard the door close behind her and turned with her back facing the minimal sitting area of the suite. Nate's expression had gone from casually questioning to impending dread as he came to stand a few feet away from her.

"What do you mean she was at your house?"

If hearing him say *your house* sounded foreign, she ignored it and folded her arms over her chest.

"She brought her bright dress and pregnant self into my house to pick up a cake for her mother," she snapped. "You know, the woman who also goes to my church." Yeah, it was easy now to claim that church as hers because she prayed Nate would never show his face in there again. "How the hell could you sleep with a woman at my church? At my father's church? Have you no shame? No scruples? Or do you really just think with your dick?"

Nate used both hands to rub down his face; then he let his head fall back and groaned.

"Yeah, there's no point in you trying to come up with an explanation, because there is none. You're just as dirty and deceitful as she is!" Her heart thumped in her chest, fingers going into fists at her sides. She wanted to hit him, to punch every good-looking part of him so that he'd never be attractive to another woman again.

She wanted to stomp on his chest so that it felt like it was going to implode with pain the same way hers did.

"I thought we were gonna do this amicably," she said and then shook her head. "But I can't. I can't do this with you. Not anymore."

"Rita, listen," he started, "I don't have an excuse. I can't begin to—"

"No! You don't and you absolutely can't explain!"

"I wasn't going to say *explain*. I was gonna say I can't begin to try and figure out how to make this up to you."

She held a hand up to stop him. "You can't! And I don't want you to." Again, bringing her fingers into fists, she had to close her eyes this time to remind herself why striking him wasn't a good idea.

The memory of slapping Amy was still fresh in her mind, and while she didn't regret that, she knew it wasn't her best moment. None of the moments since that child had called her house had been Rita's best. But damn if she was going to let what Amy and Nate did continue to make her sacrifice her character.

She pointed a finger at him now. "I don't want you or that . . ." All the names she shouldn't call that girl flowed through her mind, and Rita struggled to find the grace and class she'd been raised to project. "You nor that bitch bet not evah show your face at my church again. Do you hear me, Nathaniel? I don't want to see you or her."

Now her entire body vibrated with anger. "She better not look at my daughters cross-eyed, or that smack I gave her today will only be the preamble to the ass-beatin' she'll be signed up for. And you better make sure our children have everything they need until they get on their feet, or so help me, Nate, I'll gladly let Benny and Tariq handle your sorry ass."

He took a step toward her because, damn, he was as foolish as she'd started to believe he was. "Rita, listen. Let's just talk about this calmly."

She shook her head, and the moment he was close enough, she used both her palms to push at his chest until he stumbled back.

"Rita," he started again, but she didn't want to hear a word he had to say.

Instead, she went to him and pushed him again. Then she balled her fists and slammed them into his chest. Nate only stood there, letting her hit him as tears streamed down her face. "Don't say my name! Don't whisper it or think it! I hate you for doing this to me, and I'll never forgive you. Never!"

He finally grabbed her wrists, holding them tight as he lowered his head. "I know," he said. "I know."

It seemed like an eternity that she stood there crying, him holding her wrists and whispering his apologies. It was too long, and she pulled away from him, hating herself for even coming here. She moved around him and started for the door.

"I'll make sure she doesn't bother you again," he said.

Rita didn't even turn to look at him. She opened the door and walked out.

Chapter 26

SAFE.

The cars were gone. That was the first thing Rita noticed as she drove down her block. Well, good. She'd told all of her family she didn't want them here when she returned, and she'd meant that.

She'd also meant what she'd told herself as she'd walked out of that hotel two hours ago—that was the last time she would cry over Nate and their marriage. For a few minutes she'd sat in the driver's seat, hands in her lap, gaze focused forward, and told herself all the things she was no longer going to do. Crying over crap that wasn't her fault and commiserating over the years she couldn't get back or change were on the top of her list.

The long drive afterward was meant to clear her mind and refocus her energy on herself and her future. It was alone time she'd desperately needed to work through everything that had happened in the past month.

Her cousin had betrayed her. Even letting those words play in her mind sounded wrong. Impossible. Sharae would never do anything to hurt her. Ever.

But Sharae had known Nate was sleeping with Amy. She'd known Amy was a member of their church, which wouldn't be such a big deal because the cheating was the focal point, but yeah, it *was* a big damn deal. Sharae knew that next to Rita's marriage, children, and family, NVB was a big part of Rita's life. She gave that church and the congregation so much of her time and her heart, it was one of the few places she felt safe some of the time. And no, Rita had never fooled herself into believing that every member of NVB loved, respected, and cared for her just because she was the pastor's daughter. She knew that there were some who talked negatively about her, her children, and who knew whatever else. Still, learning that one of those members was sleeping with her husband was a deep invasion of her personal space that she couldn't easily let go. Sharae would've known that.

Which was probably why she hadn't told her.

Even that long drive hadn't cleared that issue from her mind, but she was tired. The headache that had made a painful appearance after she'd left the hotel had tamped down to a dull ache. It coexisted with the exhaustion that hit each night after she'd had a big event. Pressing the garage-door opener, she pulled her car alongside Necole's. So everybody hadn't left her house after all.

The garage door rumbled to a close as she stepped out of her car and made her way to the door leading into the house. Once inside, she checked the knob to make sure she'd locked the door, then walked into the kitchen. A spotless kitchen, she noticed with a soft gasp. There were no dishes in the sink, no leftover food containers on the island. The Sternos and racks that had been outside weren't piled in a corner, and when she crossed the room to peek through the patio-door blinds, she saw that all the tables and chairs had been removed from the yard as well.

"We knew you'd only fuss more if you had to come home and clean up."

Rita spun around to see Necole and Taryn easing into the room. They were both in their bare feet, their hair pulled into messy tails as they stood next to each other in a way that reminded Rita of when they were little girls.

Her smile was genuine but small, as she really did feel like she'd been depleted of all her energy. "I'm used to handling the cleanup."

Necole stepped forward first, coming to put an arm around Rita's shoulder. "And we're used to helping with the cleanup. So tonight we just spearheaded the effort."

"Yeah," Taryn said when she walked up to Rita and took her hand. "We learned how to lead the team from the best."

Looking from one of her beautiful daughters to the next, Rita couldn't help but be thankful. The last two decades had brought these two into her life, and she would never regret that. "Thanks," she said. "Now, you two better be on your way. It's late. You know I don't like you out driving at night as it is."

"That's why we're spending the night with you," Necole said.

Rita had started leading them out of the kitchen. Taryn turned the light off and added, "Well, we really decided to stay because we didn't want you to be alone."

She could've told them to leave. That she was a grown woman and could certainly take care of herself after such a tumultuous evening. But she didn't. "Thanks," she said instead. "That means a lot to me."

And it had. They locked up downstairs, and Rita went to her room to wrap her hair and change into her pajamas. She thought about just how good it felt to have her daughters down the hall in their bedrooms and went into the bathroom to brush her teeth. It didn't mean that she wanted them to move back home, although they knew the door was always open. But just knowing they were there if she needed anything made her feel good. In fact, it made her feel just a tad old. Her daughters were here to provide comfort for her when Rita was used to being the one comforting them.

She rinsed her mouth and shook her head while picking up one of the many hand towels she kept in a neat stack on the double vanity.

Wiping her hands and face, she dropped the towel and walked back into her bedroom, only to stop and stare in disbelief.

"What are you doing in here?" she asked the girls, who'd also changed into nightshirts that Rita hadn't seen in years, and were now sitting on her bed.

Well, Necole was already under the covers, on the side of the bed Nate used to occupy. Taryn was sitting cross-legged at the end of the bed, TV remote in hand while she channel-surfed.

"We told you we were staying with you tonight," Necole said and patted the spot next to her on the bed. "C'mon, it'll be just like old times."

Old times when Nate was out of town and the girls joined her in bed to keep her company. The smile that spread this time was huge, as that memory traveled like warmth and comfort throughout her soul.

"During old times, one or both of you were afraid of some horror movie you'd watched and called yourself coming in here to comfort me, when you were the ones who really needed the comfort." She chuckled and walked to her side of the bed and got in.

Taryn turned and pointed her finger at Necole. "That one right there! *Candyman* had her scared for a whole year after she watched it."

Necole pulled the covers up to her neck, shaking her head. "Don't say that name, girl."

"See, she's still scared." Taryn laughed and Rita joined her. Necole had been terrified for a long time after seeing that movie. And Nate had seemed to be gone a lot that year, so she'd been in this bed with Rita.

"Here, this isn't scary," Taryn said and crawled to the top of the bed to settle under the covers. She took the end of the bed, so Necole scooted over to the middle.

"Oh yuck, *Law and Order* reruns," Necole said.

"Yep, we'll all be asleep in no time." Taryn's giggles made Rita smile.

"Not me, I love *Law and Order*," she said and turned to fluff one of her pillows.

"That's right, well, we can watch one episode," Taryn said. "And then if I'm still awake after that, I'll find something else to take your mind off things."

It was that last part that had Rita going still. "You know that's not how I deal with issues," she said solemnly.

Taryn sighed. "No. You keep them all bottled up inside until you explode like you did tonight."

"Or you bury them in scriptures and prayer and hope that'll be enough to make things better," Necole said softly before easing her hand over to cover Rita's.

They were right. That was exactly how she'd handled any difficulties that had ever been thrown her way. "Not this time," she told them and laced her fingers through Necole's. "This time I'm confronting all the nonsense head-on and then pushing it right outta my way."

"Ooookay, that's what I'm talkin' 'bout." Taryn sat up and held her hand in the air for a high five.

Rita released Necole's hand and obliged Taryn. It was past time she took control of this situation and her life. If that meant cutting Nate and his drama completely out, then that was exactly what she planned to do. As for Sharae, well, Rita settled back down in the bed and tried to focus on whatever case Jack McCoy needed to win in court this time. She still didn't know how she felt about what Sharae had done. Hurt, dismayed, conflicted—all those words came to mind.

What also occurred to her was that Sharae was probably lying in bed wondering how she was going to deal with Rita the next time they saw each other too. They were family, so there was no doubting that they'd see each other again, and most likely soon, but how would that first meeting go? Would there be apologies, forgiveness, tears, or more arguing? Rita didn't know, and for tonight at least, she didn't want to think about it anymore.

"What are you thinking about over there?" Desmond asked Sharae.

They'd been at her apartment for an hour now, and she was still sitting on the couch, fully dressed and just as somber as she'd been when she'd finally left Rita's house.

"I let her down," Sharae replied. Her hands were in her lap, and she didn't have a clue how long she'd been staring down at them.

She wasn't totally comfortable with Desmond being here. No, it wasn't the first time he'd ever been in her apartment, but it was the first time since they'd started sleeping together. That would explain why this time, him being in her private space felt different. It could also be that a few hours ago, he'd witnessed her cousin have a complete meltdown and some of her family members—herself included—come dangerously close to beating down a pregnant woman. The part she played in Rita's implosion was what rested so heavily on her shoulders at this moment.

"By trying to protect her?" he asked from where he sat at the other end of the couch.

"We don't lie to each other, and we don't hold back," she continued. "That's always been an unspoken truth between the three of us. We share everything, no matter how painful, embarrassing, or uncomfortable."

"That's a pretty strenuous rule."

She shrugged.

"Rita was nineteen when she married Nate. The night before the wedding, we were in the bedroom at Aunt Vi's where we all practically grew up." She could see it as clear as if it had been yesterday.

Rita was sitting on the top bunk bed, her legs dangling down and barely missing Sharae's face as she lay on her side, propped up on her shoulder. Jemel was sitting on the floor, weighing whether it was worth it to risk Aunt Vi's wrath by lighting a cigarette in the house.

"We asked her if she was sure," Sharae continued. "She had this dreamy look in her eyes, and she said yes in this breathy voice. How could we argue with that?"

They couldn't, and so they hadn't even tried.

"Did you really know he was a bad guy that soon?"

Sharae nodded. "I found out about his reputation before Rita did. About five minutes after he swept her off her feet and she introduced us to him, I was at a party with some girls in my class, and some frat guys showed up. We were in high school, so everybody wanted a college guy. And the college guys wanted some fresh meat." Even now the thought made her sick. "Nate was in the group. But when he saw me, he backed down, sticking to the sidelines, acting like he wasn't interested in anyone there. But I knew. From the way he'd walked in casing the joint like he was on the prowl, I just knew."

She laced her fingers together, then pulled them apart, huffing because she couldn't figure out what to do with them. Or what to do with the emotions welling up inside her.

"Jemel's younger than us," she continued. "But once we got her that fake ID and she could slip in and out of certain clubs, she tended to party much more than Rita and I did. She saw Nate a few times, and he wasn't actin' like he had a girlfriend at home that was madly in love with him. So yeah, we knew pretty early on."

He moved over so that now their legs almost touched. "And did you tell her all you knew then?"

He'd worn black cargo shorts to the cookout; a T-shirt with a black, orange, and white silhouette of Eddie Murray on the front; and black Vans on his feet. She glanced down at where his shorts stopped and the light coat of black hair on his legs began.

"Yeah, we did. And apparently, every time he saw one of us, he'd told Rita too. So it didn't seem like our information was incriminating when we went to her with it. He was damn good at his game."

Desmond reached for her hand. For a few seconds she only stared at it. Then, slowly, she slid her hand into his, watching with this odd sense of comfort as his fingers entwined with hers. "Then I'd say you did all you could. Stop beating yourself up for something you had no control over."

"But she's my family. She's been like a sister to me whenever I needed her." It had pained her to even think about Rita repeatedly being hurt by Nate.

"And it sounds like you've been the same in return."

She nodded at that. "We both have. Me and Jemel. We were all so happy this morning in Rita's kitchen cooking all that food. How did it come to this?"

Releasing her hand as if he'd decided that wasn't what he really wanted to do, Desmond turned to pull her into his arms. He held her tight, rubbing a hand down the back of her head while the other stayed firmly on her back. "It's going to be all right," he said. "You and Rita will work all this out. You're family," he said. "That's what families do."

Sharae had heard something similar to that before from the Aunts. But they'd never been in a situation like this. What if Rita never forgave her for not speaking up about Nate again? What if she was only doomed to heartache where the people she loved most were concerned?

She couldn't think, could barely breathe, and on instinct jumped up from the couch. Folding her arms around her, she began to pace. So many scenes played over in her mind, and just as many emotions warred through her soul.

"Why are you even here? Why didn't you just go home so I could think about all this without having to answer your questions too?" Her tone was abrasive, but so were her feelings. She loved Rita, but she was pissed at her right now. Why hadn't she listened to her and Jemel all those years ago? Why'd she have to be so good and forgiving while her husband was such an ass?

"I'm here because I care about you, Sharae." His response sounded so normal and sincere, it only irritated her more.

"But don't you see, that doesn't even make sense. You're not supposed to care about me." She walked toward the tiny dining table near the window, then turned back to head toward the couch again. "I was only supposed to be your client. You came to me and said sign these papers and sell these houses, get your father's estate in order. And I did that."

She'd spoken to the Realtor last week and had an appointment to go and visit the two houses in the city next week and the one in Ocean City two weeks from now. Both would be on the market by the end of the month, and once they were sold, she could move on from this estate mess.

"You did." He didn't have to be so agreeable.

She huffed. "I'm just sayin', none of this makes sense. I'm used to handling my feelings and my grief and all my baggage on my own."

"Even though you've had family who were more than willing to help you through it in any way they could."

When she glanced at him this time, he had sat forward, his elbows resting on his knees. The look he gave her was one of understanding and empathy. She hated it.

"I don't want you to feel sorry for me," she said quietly. "I don't need pity."

He waited a beat before standing and walking slowly toward her. It was so slow that she had more than enough time to move out of his path. To go into her room and slam the door shut in his face. Yet she stood there, waiting.

"I don't feel sorry for you," he said, and then his hands were on her shoulders. Holding her firmly as he gave her a gentle shake. "I feel like you may be the most obstinate and disillusioned woman I've ever met."

She opened her mouth to speak, but he shook his head. "No. Let me finish because you need to hear this whether you want to or not."

Now he was getting out of hand. His tone and the way he was handling her left a lot to be desired. And who was he to tell her what she needed to hear?

"People mess up. Men, women, husbands, wives, even children— young and old," he said. "They do things, and then realize that what they've done was a mistake. Sometimes they apologize, sometimes they don't get the chance. But what's really important is that you recognize that it was their mistake and not yours."

His gaze was so intent, his tone so adamant, his touch too real and too perfect, she had to look away.

"No," he said and moved a hand from her shoulder to touch a finger to her chin. With the gentlest motion, he turned her face back to him. "Don't run from this. You've done that for far too long."

"You don't know me," she said in a tone so soft she barely realized she'd said it aloud.

"I know that you hate your father for messing up your family."

"I hate him for killing my mother."

He nodded. "And thus messing up your family."

She sighed.

"He spoiled any hope you ever had of falling and staying in love. Then here comes Nate, showing his ass by not only hurting your cousin, but embarrassing the entire family with who he chose to get pregnant."

"You're making this about us, and it's not." She shook her head. "I'm worried about Rita and how we're ever going to get back to what we were after this. It has nothing to do with what's going on between us."

"It has everything to do with what's happening between us." He cupped her cheek. "Because that's what you're so afraid of. That's why you want to be alone to sulk about a situation that you know will resolve itself in time. You told me how close you and your cousins are and how smart Rita is. There's no way she's going to continue to hold this against you."

Too much of what he was saying sounded right, and she couldn't stand it anymore. She pulled out of his grasp and turned away.

"Like I said, you don't want to be alone. You want to run and keep running, just like you've always done."

"It's what works for me."

"Is it?" She didn't have a moment to answer, because in a flash, one of his hands was on her waist. He'd come to stand in front of her again, and his other hand was at the nape of her neck. Her lips parted on a gasp, but he must've taken that as permission, because his lips met hers and his tongue slipped inside to stroke.

There were words in her head. Some of denial, some of admission, and some of confusion. Being alone had worked for her, but right now, at this very moment, reaching her arms around his waist, pulling him closer so she could bury herself in the feel of him and this brutally erotic kiss, was more important than the past.

It shouldn't be, or should it? She was too confused and too aroused to worry about it at the moment.

When he dragged his mouth away from hers, she wasn't ready. She leaned in, nipping his bottom lip to tell him so. But he only pulled back again. "See, that's the easy part," he said. "I need you to know that I'm the kind of guy who sticks around for the hard stuff too."

She let her hands fall to her sides. What he'd just said had never been an option before. Not one that she offered, or one that had ever been thrown out to her.

"You've had a crappy night, and I'm tired from your cousin harassing me at the card table, to that pregnant woman screaming that she was pressing charges against all of us. I'd like nothing more than to climb into bed and get some sleep."

Was he serious? Did he really think he could kiss her like that and then talk about going to sleep? What the entire hell was going on tonight?

Then he chuckled. "I can see the words working in your mind. But it's late, and all I really want to do right now is hold you. So, c'mon, let's go to bed."

This time, instead of coming close to her again, Desmond simply extended his hand to her. Sharae let her gaze fall from the accepting and at the same time imploring look on his face, to the parts of his arm left bare by the short sleeves of his shirt, to the long fingers of his hand. A strong hand that she'd enjoyed feeling against her cheek moments ago, down her back as he'd comforted her on the couch, cupping her ass just last night when he'd pumped unmercifully into her.

Stop being afraid. If you like him, let him like you back.

Rita had told her that earlier today, before the shit had hit the fan. And Sharae had promised herself she'd take that chance. She'd introduced Desmond to her family—first Jemel and Rita and then to the Aunts. They were the most important people in her life, and she'd watched as they talked to and laughed with Desmond, seamlessly letting him into the Johnson family fold. And for a few hours today, it'd felt good observing him with the people she held dear, hearing him laugh at Ivan's corny jokes and watching as he stood his ground with Tariq. He'd danced with her, gotten her a drink from Uncle Jimmy, and promised Uncle Hale he'd visit NVB soon. It'd felt so right.

"Do you want my arm to fall off?" The deep timbre of his voice asking a question that was vaguely familiar snapped her out of her reverie.

When she responded with a questioning look, he laughed again. "I know you've seen *Lady Sings the Blues*."

She couldn't help the smile that came before her response. "You're no Billy Dee Williams." Then she closed the distance between them and put her hand in his. "But I guess I'll keep you around anyway."

Chapter 27

The newness.

On Wednesday evening, Rita walked into Jemel's house. The text message she'd received yesterday, inviting her to dinner, had said six thirty. It was barely six o'clock, but Rita knew Jemel couldn't cook. She suspected their meal would consist of something Jemel had ordered, and she was there early to help get the meal warmed up and properly plated. Not that Jemel couldn't do that part at least, but because it was habit.

The front door had been ajar, so she'd walked right in and followed the old Motown tunes she heard blaring from the kitchen. It'd been three days since Rita had last seen Jemel. She'd spoken to her over the phone and via text, but aside from her girls, nobody had been to Rita's house since the cookout. And Rita hadn't gone to anyone else's house. She hadn't talked to anyone besides Necole and Taryn either, so seeing the Aunts when she stepped into the kitchen was a bit of a shock.

Aunt Rose had just poured a bowl full of thinly sliced bell peppers and onions into a frying pan. They sizzled as they hit what Rita knew were a couple of teaspoons of hot olive oil. Across the stove on another burner was a cast-iron skillet with a quarter stick of butter melting inside. Her mother stood at the counter closest to that burner, lightly rolling pork chops in flour. Aunt Ceil closed the refrigerator, a bowl of scalloped potatoes in her hand.

"Could make me tell a lie to my guy, my guy," the sisters harmonized along with Mary Wells's soprano voice.

They each had an apron tied around their waists, plain-colored ones that they probably brought with them, because the one Jemel wore as she approached Rita was a ridiculous mess. Anyone who bought a faux-silk cotton-candy-pink apron with *Glam-Cook* in white script across the top wasn't a real cook. At least that was what Rita had told Jemel when she'd first bought the thing.

"Girl, they been rockin' Motown since they got here an hour ago. Lucky for us, I already started pouring the wine." Jemel leaned in to kiss Rita on the cheek and then offered her a glass.

It was pink Moscato, Jemel's personal favorite, and it was chilled the way Rita preferred her wine. So she took a sip before looking around the kitchen again.

"Ain't no time for sippin'," her mother shouted over the music. "Salad needs to be put together, rolls gotta go in the oven, and those brownies should be cut and put on a tray."

Meeting Vi's gaze, Rita swallowed and replied, "Yes, ma'am."

"Still don't stop them from being bossy, though," Jemel whispered before dancing her way to the other side of the kitchen, where she reached into a cabinet to take down drinking glasses.

Rita made her way farther into the kitchen, going to the sink to wash her hands. Aunt Ceil came over and kissed her on the cheek. When Rita only stared at her aunt's smiling face, another song came on, and Aunt Ceil bopped away to the Smokey Robinson tune. In no time, Rita was humming along with the music as she sliced tomatoes and cucumbers, tossing them into a huge bowl with the lettuce she'd already broken apart and washed.

Aunt Rose had glanced at her from the stove, offering a dimpled smile, and Rita had smiled back. It wasn't until Rita was finished with the salad and had gone over to the drawer to get the plastic wrap to cover the bowl that she'd bumped into her mother. The two stared at each other for a couple of wordless seconds before Vi said, "You look nice in that butter-yellow color. It softens your eyes."

Knowing that this, what they were doing in this kitchen, was the "I'm sorry and let's move on" that her family was used to, and feeling that it was all exactly enough, she smiled in return. "Thanks, Mama."

Rita moved easily throughout Jemel's kitchen because she'd used it more than her cousin ever had. She glanced up at the two weird-looking bamboo-covered pendant lights overhead. Jemel had been thrilled to find them on some website and had paid a ridiculous amount of money for them because that was what Jemel did. Shaking her head, Rita moved back to the refrigerator to see if there was something made for them to drink, other than the wine, because the Aunts probably weren't going to drink that. Aunt Ceil loved herself some beer with her crabs, but otherwise didn't drink much. Meanwhile, Aunt Rose preferred the same V.O. Vi had been saying she'd drunk since they were young. As for Vi, she'd have a glass of red wine or two, but that was her limit, and she didn't partake often.

"We're here with the drinks, Aunt Jemel," Necole said as she came into the kitchen.

Rita closed the refrigerator and looked over to see her daughters. "What are you two doing here?"

Necole came over to hug her mother, passing her the plastic bags holding three two-liter sodas afterward. "Aunt Jemel invited us to dinner."

Taryn came over next to hug Rita. "Yeah, but she didn't say it'd be a full house."

Rita knew her daughters hadn't talked to the Aunts since the cookout because they'd told her so on one of the days they'd stopped by the house to see her. Taryn hadn't thought she'd done or said anything wrong, so she wasn't up to offering any apologies, and Rita hadn't told her she needed to. Although there'd been moments in the past few days when Rita started to call her mother—because they'd never gone days without talking at least once before—she'd refrained. What she'd said that night at the cookout had been necessary for her. If others had been offended or irritated by it, then she was going to pray that they could come to terms with it, but she wasn't going to apologize for venting. Had she raised her voice to her mother and the Aunts? Probably. She'd yelled quite a lot that night. So for that she could've offered an "I'm sorry," but they'd covered that already, and she felt they were good now. As for the girls . . .

"Come on over here and give me my hug," she heard Vi saying to Necole.

Aunt Rose had walked over to where Rita and Taryn now stood and swatted Taryn on the butt. "I remember when I could wear little shorts like that. You've definitely got my legs."

To that Taryn had grinned. "You used to wear booty shorts, Aunt Rose?"

Aunt Rose struck a pose. "Girl, you ain't nevah seen a booty like the one I used to have."

"*Used to* are the operative words," Aunt Ceil added.

Rita was shaking her head and grinning at the women in her family when it occurred to her what Jemel had done. She'd gathered them all together to make amends for what had happened this weekend. And they were doing so by preparing a delicious meal to share. It was no wonder Rita loved her family.

"Hey, y'all."

Sharae's voice had Rita's smile slipping and her gaze turning to the doorway, where her cousin now stood.

Jemel came in from the deck at that moment, almost as if she'd been hiding out until this particular guest arrived. "Oh yay, gang's all here," she said and hastily made her way over to Rita.

She grabbed Rita's hand and pulled her toward Sharae. Then she took Sharae's hand and hustled them both into the living room.

"Well," Rita said when the three of them were standing in the center of Jemel's all-white living room. "I guess subtlety is out the window now."

Sharae moved to set her purse on the chair. "That was never her strong point."

"Hush it, both of you," Jemel said. "Now, I've been left to deal with the Aunts, the concerned text messages from Tariq, Ivan, and Benny, and the plans for the event by myself these past few days."

Because Jemel was standing between them with her hands on her hips like she was their elder sent to scold them, Rita raised her hand. When Jemel rolled her eyes in response, Sharae shook her head.

"If it's okay to speak . . . ," Rita started and put her hand down. "I've been emailing you about the event, and you and I spoke on the phone day before yesterday."

Jemel gave an exasperated sigh. "We always talk every day. Since we were old enough to talk, that's been the case."

She wasn't lying about that. Their mothers had always lived close, and the Johnson sisters were always at each other's house, for one reason or another. So the three of them had talked just about every day, until this week.

"We're not kids anymore, Jem," Sharae said.

Rita glanced in her direction. Sharae looked good in distressed denim shorts that came to her knee and a simple white T-shirt. It was her face that seemed to have a sort of glow that Rita hadn't seen before. She figured that could be attributed to a handsome lawyer who just might be exactly what Sharae needed.

"Then the two of you should stop acting like teenage girls who've had a fight," Jemel countered. "Look, I don't have time to stand here and play referee. Aunt Rose wanted to eat out on the deck, so I gotta finish getting the table set out there." She pointed at Rita and then turned to aim the same finger at Sharae. "But there'd better not be a piece of furniture out of place or a smudge of anything in here if you two can't keep this discussion civil."

"My invitation didn't say anything about a discussion," Sharae said and then looked over to Rita. "Did yours?"

Rita shrugged. "Nope."

Jemel rolled her eyes. "Just get it together and fast! I'm not having dinner with the Aunts by myself, and Necole and Taryn are no help because they'll just sit at the table scrolling through their phones."

Jemel continued to mumble as she walked out of the room, and Rita and Sharae chuckled.

"I wonder if we should tell her she still whines like she did when she was a teenager," Rita said.

"Nah, that'll spoil the fun of watching her mini tirades," Sharae replied.

Then silence fell like a boulder between them.

Sharae stood closer to the fireplace, and she reached up to straighten a heart-shaped sterling-silver frame with a picture of Marc and Jemel in its center. The frame wasn't crooked, and Jemel was definitely going to pitch a fit when she saw it'd been moved. Which was precisely why Sharae had moved it. Rita looked away, trying to hold back a smile, but finally shook her head.

She took a deep breath and released it slowly. "I know why you didn't tell me about Nate."

Dropping her hand to her side, Sharae looked at her. "And I know why you were so angry that I didn't tell you about seeing him and Amy last year."

Tucking her hair back behind her ear, Rita sighed. "I was an idiot. All these years I thought that if I just kept praying, kept focusing on building and taking care of my family—" She paused and then gave a wry chuckle. "I thought that if I pretended everything was fine, that it would be. After all, my life had turned out to be everything I'd imagined as a little girl. So why couldn't I just imagine happiness?"

"Because fairy tales aren't the real world." Sharae pushed her hands into the front pockets of her shorts. "And the real world doesn't have to stay as dark as some of the things that happen in it."

With a tilt of her head, Rita said, "You're right. We can choose how we react to things and how those things will affect us."

"And we don't have to blame anyone for them to move on. We can choose to do that as well," Sharae added.

A lightness filled her chest as Rita looked at the girl who'd once shared a bedroom with her. That girl was all grown up now. She was a stunningly beautiful and professional woman who meant the world to Rita.

"I'm sorry," Rita said. While the Aunts hadn't said those words to Rita, nor had Rita thought she needed to say them to the Aunts, they were needed here, between her and Sharae. Despite how the Aunts were used to dealing with disagreements and making amends, Rita felt the clear communication between two adults was necessary for healing. "I shouldn't have lashed out at you when you were only doing what I'd compelled you to do all those years ago."

Sharae dropped her head and let her shoulders hang for an instant. Then she was staring at Rita again, inhaling deeply before releasing that breath and saying, "I'm sorry too. I wanted to respect your wishes and your marriage. I wanted to stand by your side and be the friend, the cousin, the sister, that we'd always proclaimed to be. And I did those things. But in doing them I hurt you, and that was never my intention."

Tears stung Rita's eyes, and her instinct was to wave them away, to tell herself they weren't necessary, that she didn't need to show this emotion at this time. But that was a lie, and she'd told herself these past few days that she was going to stop lying to herself. It was the only way to face things head-on. She had to be honest about her wants and needs, her feelings, and her future. The first tear fell, and relief washed over her.

"We should stay in here longer so she'll have to finish helping the Aunts with dinner," Sharae said.

A burst of laughter came from Rita just as another tear fell. "She'd have a full tantrum then, and we'd never hear the end of it."

Sharae laughed. "I know."

Rita went to her then, pulling her into a tight hug. "I love you, Sharae."

Sharae wrapped her arms around Rita and said, "I love you too, Margaritaville."

"I'd like to make a good-night toast," Rita said a couple of hours later, when three generations of Johnson women sat around the table.

The sun had gone down, and the lights along the railing of the deck provided illumination to their little dinner party. Standing, Rita looked around the table, emotion clogging her throat.

It wasn't the first time tonight she'd felt overwhelmed with love and adoration for these women. After talking with Sharae, they'd both returned to the kitchen. Rita had paused a moment to take in the scene. Her mother had still been at the stove, this time giving Taryn instructions on how to shake the excess flour off the pork chops before placing them into the hot skillet. She told her how long they should cook on each side, the light-brown coating they should have when she turned them, and eventually took them out of the pan to rest on the plate.

Aunt Ceil and Aunt Rose had been discussing the best brands of flour to use for the different types of baking while supervising Necole as she brushed butter over the yeast rolls that would be put into the oven. Jemel had been still rambling as she ran back into the kitchen and grabbed more items to put outside on the table, and Sharae had huffed as she decided to help her.

The scene had held her still for she didn't know how long as she marveled at each woman. Each one of her relatives who filled their own intricate spot in her life. It was because of these women that Rita was who she was today and that she could look toward the future with such determination and excitement. The Aunts who had instilled great values and strength in her, the cousins who'd held her down even when she'd been too blind to see that they were doing so, and the daughters who were her legacy in this world.

Her heart was so full, happiness brimming in every part of her soul.

"Wait a minute," Jemel was saying. "I gotta refill my glass."

They were on the second bottle of Moscato.

"Don't you think you've had enough for one night?" Vi asked.

"Well, at least she ain't gotta drive home," Aunt Rose said as she lifted her glass for Jemel to refill as well. Earlier she'd proclaimed that the wine wasn't as good as her V.O., but it would do.

Taryn and Necole sent each other a knowing glance before giggling at their great-aunt.

When everyone had a glass, Rita cleared her throat and continued. "We're blessed to have this moment in time together as a family." Those first words were so very true. Without her family, Rita didn't know where she'd be.

"Once again we've weathered some storms," she said, glancing at Sharae and then letting her gaze rest on her daughters. "But through it all the Lord has kept us. This family has stood together one more time." She took a shaky breath, feeling the tears spring to her eyes. "We may not have agreed every step of the way, or even said nice things all the time, but there was never any doubt that our loyalty to one another was always there. We are stronger together. Remember Grandma Patty tellin' us that when we were little girls?"

Sharae and Jemel nodded.

"That and 'The next cuss word I hear, you're all gettin' your mouths washed out with soap,'" Jemel said and then laughed.

Sharae shook her head. "And she was always the first one to cuss again."

Aunt Ceil chuckled. "That's my headstrong and spirited girl."

Rita smiled, letting the joy of seeing her family together mix with the pain that had plagued her so much these past weeks.

"To us," she said and held up her glass. Everyone lifted their glasses. "To family, forgiveness . . ."

"And don't forget good food. You put your foot in that gravy you made for the pork chops tonight, Rita," Vi said with a wink to her daughter.

Accepting her mother's compliment, Rita added, "To family, forgiveness, food, and our future. May we continue to live well, praise the Lord, and have each other's back."

"Hear! Hear!" Sharae said, standing to come closer to Rita so she could tap her wineglass to hers.

Jemel stood and moved closer to Sharae and Rita to tap her glass against theirs. The Aunts, who were sitting closest to each other—as always—tapped their glasses together. Necole and Taryn tapped theirs and then turned to do the same with the Aunts.

"Now," Vi said after everyone had taken a sip, "we've got to get started planning this fundraiser and figuring out this catering business. Who's gonna do what and all that." She looked at her sisters, who nodded in agreement.

Sharae and Jemel sent Rita a baleful look, but Rita chuckled anyway—this was just how her family was. The Aunts would always be pushy and opinionated and give them advice they thought was good but Rita, Sharae, and Jemel knew was unrealistic and outdated. Sharae would continue to focus on her job, but now with a little bit of Desmond thrown in. And Rita, she would keep moving forward like she always did.

This was their life, and Rita was grateful for every minute of it, whether those minutes were always filled with happiness or not.

ABOUT THE AUTHOR

Photo © 2012 Lisa Fleet Photography

A. C. Arthur has worked as a paralegal in every field of law since high school, but her first love is and always will be writing romance. A multiple-award-winning author, A. C. has written more than eighty novels, including *The After Party* most recently and those under her *USA Today* bestselling pen name, Lacey Baker. After years of hosting reader-appreciation events, A. C. created the One Love Reunion, designed to bring together readers, authors, and other members of the literary industry to celebrate their love of books. A. C. resides in Maryland with her family, where she's currently working on her next book or watching *Criminal Minds*. For more information, please visit www.acarthur.com.